M000284552

RIBOFUNK

PAUL DI FILIPPO

AVON · EOS

My sincere thanks to Andy Watson, for years of computorial and editorial expertise!

"Little Worker" © 1989 *The Magazine of Fantasy and Science Fiction*
"One Night in Television City" © 1990 *Universe*
"The Boot" © 1990 *The Magazine of Fantasy and Science Fiction*
"Cockfight" © 1990 *Journal Wired*
"Brain Wars" © 1992 *New Worlds*
"Afterschool Special" © 1993 *Amazing Stories*
"Up the Lazy River" © 1993 *Science Fiction Age*
"Streetlife" © 1993 *New Worlds*
"McGregor" © 1994 *Universe*
"Distributed Mind" © 1995 *Interzone*
"Big Eater" © 1995 *Interzone*

AVON BOOKS, INC.
1350 Avenue of the Americas
New York, New York 10019

Copyright © 1996 by Paul Di Filippo
Published by arrangement with Four Walls Eight Windows
Visit our website at **http://www.AvonBooks.com/Eos**
Library of Congress Catalog Card Number: 96-6902
ISBN: 0-380-73076-6

First Avon Eos Printing: October 1998

AVON EOS TRADEMARK REG. U.S. PAT. OFF. AND IN OTHER COUNTRIES, MARCA REGISTRADA, HECHO EN U.S.A.

Printed in the U.S.A.

WCD 10 9 8 7 6 5 4 3 2 1

To all the contributors to and sharers of my gene-pool, both ancient and contemporary, direct and collateral, known and unknown; and to Deborah, my fellow experimenter in all matters biological.

Biology is an extraordinarily digestive science. It throws out a number of broad experimental generalizations, and then sets out to bring into harmony or relation with these an infinitely multifarious collection of phenomena. The little streaks upon the germinating area of an egg, the nervous movements of an impatient horse, the trick of a calculating boy, the senses of a fish, the fungus at the root of a garden flower, and the slime upon a seawet rock—ten thousand such things bear their witness and are illuminated. And not only did these tentacular generalizations gather together all the facts of natural history and comparative anatomy together, but they seemed always stretching out further and further into a world of interests that lay altogether outside their legitimate bounds.

—H. G. Wells, *Ann Veronica*

Biology is the natural domain of diversity as physics is the domain of unity.

—Freeman Dyson, *Infinite In All Directions*

Physics is a special case of biology.

—John Casti, *Complexification*

Contents

Contents

⚡ One Night in Television City

I'M FRICTIONLESS, MOLARS, SO DON'T POINT THOSE flashlights at me. I ain't going nowhere, you can see that clear as hubble. Just like superwire, I got no resistance, so why doncha all just gimme some slack?

What'd you say, molar? Your lifter's got a noisy fan— it's interfering with your signal. How'd I get up here? That's an easy one. I just climbed. But I got a better one for you.

Now that I ain't no Dudley Dendrite anymore, how the fuck am I gonna get down?

Just a few short hours ago it was six o'clock on a Saturday night like any other, and I was sitting in a metamilk bar called the Slak Shak, feeling sorry for myself for a number of good and sufficient reasons. I was down so low there wasn't an angstrom's worth of difference between me and a microbe. You see, I had no sleeve, I had no set, I had no eft. Chances were I wasn't gonna get any of 'em anytime soon, either. The prospect was enough to make me wanna float away on whatever latest toxic corewipe the Shak was offering.

I asked the table for the barlist. It was all the usual bugjuice and horsesweat, except for a new item called

Needlestrength-Nine. I ordered a dose, and it came in a cup of cold frothy milk sprinkled with cinnamon. I downed it all in two gulps, the whole nasty mess of transporter proteins and neurotropins, a stew of long-chain molecules that were some konky biobrujo's idea of blister-packed heaven.

All it did was make me feel like I had a cavity behind my eyes filled with shuttle-fuel. My personal sitspecs still looked as lousy as a rat's shaved ass.

That's the trouble with the tropes and strobers you can buy in the metamilk bars: they're all kid's stuff, G-rated holobytes. If you want a real slick kick, some black meds, then you got to belong to a set, preferably one with a smash watson boasting a clean labkit. A Fermenta, or Wellcome, or Cetus rig, say. Even an Ortho'll do.

But as I said, I had no set, nor any prospect of being invited into one. Not that I'd leap at an invite to just any old one, you latch. Some of the sets were too toxic for me.

So there I sat with a skull full of liquid oxygen, feeling just like the Challenger before liftoff, more bummed than before I had zero-balanced my eft on the useless drink. I was licking the cinammon off the rim of the glass when who should slope in but my one buddy, Casio.

Casio was a little younger 'n me, about fifteen. He was skinny and white and had more acne than a worker in a dioxin factory. He coulda had skin as clear as anyone else's, but he was always forgetting to use his epicream. He wore a few strands of grafted fiberoptics in his brown hair, an imipolex vest that bubbled constantly like some kinda slime mold, a pair of parchment pants, and a dozen jelly-bracelets on his left forearm.

"Hey, Dez," said Casio, rapping knuckles with me, "how's it climbing?"

Casio didn't have no set neither, but it didn't seem to bother him like it bothered me. He was always up, always smiling and happy. Maybe it had to do with his music,

which was his whole life. It seemed to give him something he could always fall back on. I had never seen him
really down. Sometimes it made me wanna choke the shit
outa him.

"Not so good, molar. Life looks emptier'n the belly
of a Taiwanese baby with the z-virus craps."

Casio pulled up a seat. "Ain't things working out with
Chuckie?"

I groaned. Why I had ever fantasized aloud to Casio
about Chuckie and me, I couldn't now say. I musta really
been in microgravity that day. "Just forget about Charlotte and me, will you do me that large fave? There's
nothing between us, nothing, you latch?"

Casio looked puzzled. "Nothing? Whadda ya mean?
The way you talked, I thought she was your best sleeve."

"No, you got it all wrong, molar, we was both wasted,
remember? . . ."

Casio's vest extruded a long wavy stalk that bulged
into a ball at its tip before being resorbed. "Gee, Dez, I
wish I had known all this before. I been talking you two
up as a hot item all around TeeVeeCee."

My heart swelled up big as the bicep on a metasteroid
freak and whooshed up into my throat. "No, molar, say
it ain't so. . . ."

"Gee, Dez, I'm sorry. . . ."

I was in deep gurry now all right. I could see it clear
as M31 in the hubblescope. Fish entrails up to the nose.

Chuckie was Turbo's sleeve. Turbo was headman of
the Body Artists. The Body Artists were the prime set in
Televison City. I was as the dirt between their perpetually
bare toes.

I pushed back my seat. The Slak Shak was too hot
now. Everbody knew I floated there.

"Casio, I feel like a walk. Wanna come?"

"Yeah, sure."

T Street—the big north-south boulevard wide as old
Park Ave that was Television City's main crawl (it ran

from 59th all the way to 72nd)—was packed with citizens and greenies, morphs and gullas, all looking for the heart of Saturday night, just like the old song by that growly chigger has it. The sparkle and glitter was all turned up to eleven, but TeeVeeCee looked kinda old to me that night, underneath its amber-red-green-blue neo-neon maquillage. The whole mini-city on the banks of the Hudson was thirty years old now, after all, and though that was nothing compared to the rest of Nuevo York, it was starting to get on. I tried to imagine being nearly twice as old as I was now and figured I'd be kinda creaky myself by then.

All the scrawls laid down by the sets on any and every blank surface didn't help the city's looks any either. Fast as the cleanup crews sprayed the paint-eating bugs on the graffiti, the sets nozzled more. These were just a few that Casio and I passed:

> PUT A CRICK IN YOUR DICK.
> STROBE YOUR LOBES.
> BOOT IT OR SHOOT IT.
> HOLLOW? SWALLOW. FOLLOW.
> SIN, ASP! SAID THE SYNAPSE.
> MATCH IT, BATCH IT, LATCH IT.
> BEAT THE BARRIER!
> SNAP THE GAP!
> AXE YOUR AXONS.
> KEEP YOUR RECEPTORS FILLED.

"Where we going, Dez?" asked Casio, snapping off one of his jelly-bracelets for me to munch on.

"Oh, noplace special," I said around a mouthful of sweat-metabolizing symbiote that tasted like strawberries. "We'll just wander around a bit and see what we can see."

All the time I was wondering if I even dared to go home to my scat, if I'd find Turbo and his set waiting there for me, with a word or two to say about me talking so big about his sleeve.

Well, we soon came upon a guy with his car pulled over to the curb with the hood up. He was poking at the ceramic fuel-cell with a screwdriver, like he hoped to fix it that way.

"That's a hundred-thirty-two horsepower Malaysian model, ain't it?" asked Casio.

"Yeah," the guy said morosely.

"I heard they're all worth bugshit."

The guy got mad then and started waving the screwdriver at us. "Get the hell out of here, you nosey punks!"

Casio slid a gold jelly-bracelet off his arm, tossed it at the guy, and said, "Run!"

We ran.

Around a corner, we stopped, panting.

"What was it?" I said.

"Nothing too nasty. Just rotten eggs and superstik."

We fell down laughing.

When we were walking again, we tried following a couple of gullas. We could tell by their government-issue suits that they were fresh out of one of the floating mid-ocean relocation camps, and we were hoping to diddle them for some eft. But they talked so funny that we didn't even know how to scam them.

"We go jeepney now up favela way?"

"No, mon, first me wan' some ramen."

"How fix?"

"We loop."

"And be zeks? Don' vex me, dumgulla. You talkin' like a manga now, mon."

After that we tailed a fattie for a while. We couldn't make up our minds if it was a male or female or what. It was dressed in enough billowing silk to outfit a parachute club and walked with an asexual waddle. It went into the fancy helmsley at 65th, to meet its client no doubt.

"I hate those fatties," said Casio. "Why would anyone want to weigh more than what's healthy, if they don't have to?"

"Why would anyone keep his stupid zits if he didn't have to?"

Casio looked hurt. "That's different, Dez. You know I just forget my cream. It's not like I wanna."

I felt bad for hurtin' Casio then. Here he was, my only proxy, keeping me company while I tried to straighten out in my head how I was gonna get trump with Turbo and his set, and I had to go and insult him.

I put an arm around his shoulders. "Sorry, molar. Listen, just wipe it like I never said it, and let's have us a good time. You got any eft?"

"A little . . ."

"Well, let's spend it! The fluid eft gathers no taxes, es verdad? Should we hit Club GaAs?"

Casio brightened. "Yeah! The Nerveless are playing tonight. Maybe Ginko'll let me sit in."

"Sounds trump. Let's go."

Overhead the wetworkers—both private and government dirty-harrys—cruised by on their lifters, the jetfans blowing hot on our necks, even from their high altitude. Standing in the center of their flying cages, gloved mitts gripping their joystix, with their owleyes on, they roved TeeVeeCee, alert for signs of rumble, bumble, or stumble, whereupon they would swoop down and chill the heat with tingly shockers or even flashlights, should the sitspecs dictate.

Club GaAs occupied a fraction of the million square feet of empty building that had once housed one of the old television networks that had given TeeVeeCee its name. Ever since the free networks had been absorbed into the metamedium, the building had gone begging for tenants. Technically speaking, it was still tenantless, since Club GaAs was squatting there illegally.

At the door we paid the cover to a surly anabolic hulkster and went inside.

Club GaAs had imipolex walls that writhed just like Casio's vest, dancing in random biomorphic ripples and tendrils. On the stage the Nerveless were just setting up, it being still early, only around eight. I had only met Ginko once, but I recognized him from his green skin and leafy hair. Casio went onstage to talk to him, and I sat down at a table near one wall and ordered a cheer-beer.

Casio rejoined me. "Ginko says I can handle the megabops."

The cheer-beer had me relaxing so I had almost forgotten my problems. "That's trump, proxy. Listen, have a cheer-beer—it's your eft."

Casio sat and we talked a while about the good old days, when we were still kids in highschool, taking our daily rations of mnemotropins like good little drudges.

"You remember at graduation, when somebody spiked the refreshments with funky-monkey?"

"Yeah. I never seen so many adults acting like apes before or since. Miz Spencer up on the girders—!"

"Boy, we were so young then."

"I was even younger than you, Dez. I was eleven and you were already twelve, remember?"

"Yeah, but them days are wiped now, Casio. We're adults ourselves now, with big adult probs." All my troubles flooded back to me like ocean waves on the Big-One-revised California shoreline as I said this konky bit of wisdom.

Casio was sympathetic, I could fax that much, but he didn't have the answers to my probs any more than I did. So he just stood and said, "Well, Dez, I got to go play now." He took a few steps away from the table and then was snapped back to his seat like he had a rubber band strung to his ass.

"Hold on a millie," I said. "The wall has fused with

your vest." I took out my little utility flashlight and lasered the wall pseudopod that had mated with Casio's clothing.

"Thanks, proxy," he said, and then was off.

I sat there nursing the dregs of my cheer-beer while the Nerveless tuned up. When the rickracks were spinning fast and the megabops were humming and everyone had their percussion suits on, they jumped into an original comp, "Efferent Ellie."

Forty-five minutes later, after two more cheer-beers thoughtfully provided by the management to the grateful friend of the band, I was really on the downlink with Casio and the Nerveless. I felt their music surging through me like some sonic trope. Tapping my foot, wangle-dangling my head like some myelin-stripped spaz, I was so totally downloading that I didn't even see Turbo and his set slope on into Club GaAs and surround me.

When the current song ended and I looked up, there they all were: Turbo and his main sleeve, Chuckie, who had her arm around his waist; Jeeter, Hake, Pablo, Mona, Val, Ziggy, Pepper, Gates, Zane, and a bunch of others I didn't know.

"Hah-hah-hah-how's it climbing, molars?" I said.

They were all as quiet and stone-faced as the holo of a cheap Turing Level One AI with its mimesis-circuits out of whack. As for me, I could do nothing but stare.

The Body Artists were all naked save for spandex thongs, he's and she's alike, the better to insure proper extero- and interoceptor input. Their skins were maculated with a blotchy tan giraffe pattern. The definition of every muscle on their trim bods was like *Gray's Anatomy* come to life.

Now, to me, there were no two ways about it: the Body Artists were simply the most trump set in TeeVeeCee. The swiftest, nastiest, downloadingest pack of lobe-strobers ever to walk a wire or scale a pole. Who else were you gonna compare 'em to? The Vectors? A bunch of wussies dreaming their days away in mathspace. (I didn't buy their propaganda about being able to disappear along the fourth dimension either.) The Hardz 'n' Wetz? Nothing but crazy meat-grinders, the negative image of their rivals, the Eunuchs. The Less Than Zeroes? I don't call pissing your pants satori, like they do. The Thumbsuckers? Who wants to be a baby forever? The Boardmen? I can't see cutting yourself up and headbanging just to prove you feel no pain. The Annies? A horde of walking skeletons. The Naked Apes? After seeing our whole faculty under the influence of funky-monkey that day, I had never latched onto that trip. The Young Jungs? Who wants to spend his whole life diving into the racemind?

No, the only ones who might just give the Body Artists a run for their eft were the Adonises or the Sapphos, but they had some obvious kinks that blocked my receptors.

So you'll understand how I could feel—even as the center of their threatening stares—a kind of thrill at being in the presence of the assembled Body Artists. If only they had come to ask me to join them, instead of, as was so apparent, being here with the clear intention of wanting to cut my nuts off—

The Nerveless started another song. Casio was too busy to see what was happening with me. Not that he coulda done much anyhow. Turbo sat liquidly down across from me, pulling Chuckie down onto his lap.

"So, Dez," he said, cool as superwire, "I hear you are Chuckie's secret mojoman now."

"No, no way, Turbo, the parity bits got switched on that message all right. There ain't not truth to it, no sir, no way."

"Oh, I see, molar," said Turbo, deliberately twisting things around tighter'n a double-helix. "My sleeve Chuckie ain't trump enough for a molar who's as needlestrength as you."

I raised my eyes and caught Chuckie sizing me up with

high indifference. Her looks made me feel like I was trying to swallow an avocado pit.

Charlotte Thach was a supertrump Cambodian-Hawaiian chica whose folks had emigrated to TeeVeeCee when the Japs kicked everyone outa the ex-state in the process of forming the Asian-Pacific Economic Cooperative. Her eyes were green as diskdrive lights, her sweet little tits had nipples the color of strong tea.

After she was done sizing me up, she held out one beautiful hand as if to admire her nails or something. Then, without moving a single muscle that I could see, she audibly popped each joint in her fingers in sequence. I could hear it clear above the music.

I gulped down that slimy pit and spoke. "No, Turbo, she's trump enough for anyone."

Turbo leaned closer across Chuckie. "Ah, but that's the prob, molar, Chuckie don't do it with just anyone. In fact, none of the Artists do. Why, if you were to try to ride her, she'd likely snap your cock off. It's Body to Body only, you latch?"

"Yeah, sure, I latch."

Turbo straightened up. "Now, the question is, what we gonna do with someone whose head got so big he thought he could tell everyone he was bumpin' pubes with a Body Artist?"

"No disinfo, Turbo, I didn't mean nothin' by it."

"Shut up, I got to think."

While he was thinking, Turbo made all the muscles in his torso move around like snakes under his skin.

After letting me sweat toxins for a while, Turbo said, "I suppose it would satisfy the set's honor if we were to bring you up to the top of the George Washington Bridge and toss you off—"

"Oh, holy radwaste, Turbo, my molar, my proxy, I really don't think that's necessary—"

Turbo held up his hand. "But the ecoharrys might arrest us for dumping shit in the river!"

All the Body Artists had a good laugh at that. I tried to join in, but all that came out was a sound like "ekk-ekk-ekk."

"On the other hand," said Turbo, rotating his upraised hand and forearm around a full two-seventy degrees, "if you were to become a Body Artist, then we could let it be known that you were under consideration all along, even when you were making your konky boasts."

"Oh, Turbo, yeah, yeah, you don't know how much—"

Turbo shot to his feet then, launching Chuckie into a series of spontaneous cartwheels all the way across the club.

"Jeeter, Hake! You're in charge of escorting the pledge. Everyone! Back to nets!"

We blew out of Club GaAs like atmosphere out of a split-open o'neill. My head was spinning around like a Polish space station. I was running with the Body Artists! It was something I could hardly believe. Even though I had no hint of where they were taking me; even though they might be setting me up for something that would wipe me out flatter than my eft-balance—I felt totally frictionless. The whole city looked like a place out of a fantasy or stiffener holo to me, Middle Earth or *Debbie Does Mars*. The air was cool as an AI's paraneurons on my bare arms.

We headed west, toward the riverside park. After a while I started to lag behind the rest. Without a word, Jeeter and Hake picked me up under my arms and continued running with me.

We entered among the trees and continued down empty paths, under dirty sodium lights. I could smell the Hudson off to my right. A dirty-harry buzzed by overhead but didn't stop to bother us.

Under a busted light we halted in darkness. Nobody was breathing heavy but me, and I had been carried the last half mile. Hake and Jeeter placed me down on my own feet.

Someone bent down and tugged open a metal hatch with a snapped hasp set into the walk. The Body Artists descended one by one. Nervous as a kid taking his first trope, I went down too, sandwiched between Hake and Jeeter.

Televison City occupied a hundred acres of land which had originally sloped down to the Hudson. The eastern half of TeeVeeCee was built on solid ground; the western half stood on a huge platform elevated above the Conrail maglev trains.

Fifteen rungs down, I was staring up at the underside of TeeVeeCee by the light of a few caged safety bulbs, a rusty constellation of rivets in a flaky steel sky.

The ladder terminated at an I-beam wide as my palm. I stepped gingerly off, but still held onto the ladder. I looked down.

A hundred feet below, a lit-up train shot silently by at a hundred-and-eighty mph.

I started back up the ladder.

"Where to, molar?" asked Hake above me.

"Uh, straight ahead, I guess."

I stepped back onto the girder, took two wobbly Thumbsucker steps, then carefully lowered myself until I could wrap my arms and legs around the beam.

Hake and Jeeter unpeeled me. Since they had to go single file, they trotted along carrying me like a trussed pig. I kept my eyes closed and prayed.

I felt them stop. Then they were swinging me like a sack. At the extreme of one swing, they let me go.

Hurtling through the musty air, I wondered how long it would take me to hit the ground or a passing train and what it would feel like. I wouldn'ta minded so much being a Boardman just then.

It was only a few feet to the net. When I hit, it shot

me up a bit. I oscillated a few times until my recoil was absorbed. Only then did I open my eyes.

The Body Artists were standing or lounging around on the woven mesh of graphite cables with perfect balance. Turbo had this radwaste-eating grin on his handsome face.

"Welcome to the nets, Mister Pledge. You didn't do so bad. I seen molars who fainted and fell off the ladder when they first come out below. Maybe you'll make it through tonight after all. C'mon now, follow us."

The Body Artists set off along the nets. Somehow they managed to coordinate and compensate for all the dozens of different impulses traveling along the mesh so that they knew just how to step and not lose their balance. They rode the wavefronts of each other's motions like some kinda aerial surfers.

Me? I managed to crawl along, mostly on all fours.

We reached a platform scabbed onto one of the immense pillars that upheld the city. There the Body Artists had their lab, for batching their black meds.

I hadn't known that Ziggy was the Artists' watson. But once I saw him moving among the chromo-cookers and amino-linkers like a fish in soup, if you know what I mean, it was clear as hubble that he was the biobrujo responsible for stoking the Artists' neural fires.

While Ziggy worked I had to watch Turbo and Chuckie making out. I knew they were doing it just to blow grit through my scramjets, so I tried not to let it bother me. Even when Chuckie—Well, never mind exactly what she did, except to say I never realized it was humanly possible to get into that position.

Ziggy finally came over with a cup full of uncut bugjuice.

"Latch onto this, my molar," he said with crickly craftsmanly pride, "and you'll know a little more about what it means to call yourself a B-Artist."

I knew I didn't want to taste the undiluted juice, so I

chugged it as fast as I could. Even the aftertaste nearly made me retch.

Half an hour later, I could feel the change.

I stood up and walked out onto the net. Turbo and the others started yanking it up and down.

I didn't lose my balance. Even when I went to one foot. Then I did a handstand.

"Okay, molar," said Turbo sarcastically, "don't think you're so trump. All we gave you is heightened 'ception, extero, intero, and proprio. Plus a little myofibril booster and something to damp your fatigue poisons. And it's all as temporary as a whore's kisses. So, let's get down to it."

Turbo set off back along the nets, and I followed.

"No one else?" I asked.

"No, Dez, just us two good proxies."

We retraced our way to the surface. Walking along the I-beam under my own power, I felt like king of the world.

Once again we raced through the streets of Televison City. This time I easily kept pace with Turbo. But maybe, I thought, he was letting me, trying to lull me into a false sense of security. I made up my mind to go a little slower in all this—if I could.

At last we stood at the southern border of T-City. Before us reared the tallest building in all of old Nuevo York, what used to be old man Trump's very HQ, before he was elected president and got sliced and diced like he did. One hundred and fifty stories worth of glass and ferrocrete, full of setbacks, crenellations, and ledges.

"Now we're going for a little climb," Turbo said.

"You got to be yanking my rods, molar. It's too smooth."

"Nope, it's not. That's the good thing about these old postmodern buildings. They got the flash and filigree that make for decent handholds."

Then he shimmied up a drainpipe that led to the second floor faster than I could follow.

But follow I did, my molars, believe me. I kicked off my shoes and zipped right after him. No disinfo, I was scared, but I was also mad and ecstatic and floating in my own microgravity.

The first fifty stories were frictionless. I kept up with Turbo, matching him hold for hold. When he smiled, I even smiled back.

Little did I know that he was teasing me.

A third of the way up we stopped to rest on a wide ledge. I didn't look down, since I knew that even with my new perfect balance the sight of where I was would be sure to put grit in my jets.

We peered in through the lighted window behind us and saw a cleaning robot busy vacuuming the rugs. We banged on the glass, but couldn't get it to notice us. Then we started up again.

At the halfway mark Turbo started showing off. While I was slowing down, he seemed to have more energy than ever. In the time I took to ascend one story, he squirreled all around me, making faces, and busting my chops.

"You're gonna fall now, Dez. I got you up here right where I want you. You ain't never gonna get to lay a finger on Chuckie, you latch? When you hit, there ain't gonna be anything left of you bigger'n a molecule."

And suchlike. I succeeded in ignoring it until he said, "Gee, that Ziggy's getting kinda forgetful lately. Ain't been taking his mnemos. I wonder if he remembered to make sure your dose had the right duration? Be a shame if you maxxed out right now."

"You wouldn't do that—" I said and instinctively looked over my shoulder to confront Turbo.

He was beneath me, hanging by his toes from a ledge, head directed at the ground.

I saw the ground.

Televison City was all spread out, looking like a one-

to-one-hundred-scale model in some holo studio somewhere.

I froze. I heard one of my fingernails crack right in
half.

"Whatsamatter, Dez? You lost it yet, or what?"

It was the konky tone of Turbo's voice that unfroze
me. I wasn't gonna fall and hear his toxic laugh all the
long stories down.

"Race you the rest of the way," I said.

He changed a little then. "No need, proxy, just take it
one hold at a time."

So I did.

For seventy-five more stories.

The top of the building boasted a spire surrounded on
four sides by a little railed off platform whose total area
was 'bout as big as a bathroom carpet.

I climbed unsteadily over the railing and sat down,
dangling my legs over the side. I could already feel the
changes inside me, so I wasn't surprised when Turbo
said, "It's worn off for real now, Dez. I wouldn't try
going down the way we came up, if I was you. Anyway,
the harrys should be here soon. The stretch for something
like this is only a year with good behavior. Look us up
when you get out."

Then he went down, headfirst, waggling his butt at me.

So, like I asked you before.

Now that I ain't no Dudley Dendrite anymore, how the
fuck am I gonna get down?

⚡ Little Worker

LITTLE WORKER CAME AWAKE INSTANTLY. LYING curled on the red-and-black-figured carpet before Mister Michael's bedroom door, she stretched her limbs beneath her plain beige sleeveless shift, then stood on bare feet. Mister Michael, she could sense, was still asleep. Mister Michael deserved to sleep, for Mister Michael worked hard. Little Worker worked hard too, but she never slept late in the mornings, for there was too much to be done. (If Mister Michael stayed put in his office today, Little Worker would nap at his feet.) But in the mornings, Little Worker always awoke before Mister Michael. She always would. It was her way.

Little Worker appeared unwontedly reluctant to leave her nightly station. Something, this morning, did not smell right. She sniffed the air intently, nostrils twitching. The troublesome odor was nothing she could identify. It was new. This was not necessarily bad, but might be. The new smell emanated from behind Mister Michael's door. It was not a dangerous smell, so Little Worker could not bring herself to knock or otherwise disturb Mister Michael. He would be up and about soon enough, for Mister Michael had a busy schedule. Perhaps then the source of the new smell would be revealed. Perhaps not.

In either case, Mister Michael would instruct her about anything she needed to know.

Little Worker tucked strands of her moderate-length, stiff brown hair behind her ears. She brushed the wrinkles out of her shift. They disappeared swiftly from the dull utilitarian fabric. She curried the short fur on her face and licked beneath her arms. Her morning grooming completed, she set out for the kitchen.

First Little Worker had to go down a long hall. The long hall had a veined marble floor, down the center of which ran the red and black carpet with its oriental design. The long hall had large mullioned windows in its stone walls. Some of these windows had panes of stained glass. Through the eastern windows came bright winter sunlight. When it passed through the colored panes, it made lozenges of various hues on the carpet. Little Worker admired these dapples, for they reminded her of dabs of jelly on toast. Little Worker liked jelly on toast. She would have some this morning. She usually had some every morning, except when she took an egg to add glossiness to her coat. Little Worker, with the aid of the food-center, could cook whatever she wanted for herself. This was one of her privileges. Mister Michael himself had said, when first she came to live here, "Little Worker, you may order the food-center to prepare whatever you want for yourself." This had made her proud. In the Training School, she had had to eat whatever the trainers set out for her. But Mister Michael trusted her.

The next door down the long hall from Mister Michael's belonged to the bedroom of Mister Michael's wife. Little Worker lifted her nose as she came abreast of the door, intent on passing without stopping. However, noises from beyond the door made her stop. The noises were thrashings and moanings and grunts. Little Worker suspected what the noises were, but curiosity impelled her to look anyway.

The handle of the door was shaped like a thick curled

gold leaf. Above the handle was a security keypad. Below was an old-fashioned keyhole. Little Worker put one big hazel eye to the hole.

It was as Little Worker had suspected. Mister Michael's naked wife was draped bellydown over a green plush hassock, being covered by her latest andromorph, a scion of the Bull line. Little Worker could smell mixed male and female sweat and a sexual musk.

The sight disturbed Little Worker. Mister Michael's wife was not the kind of wife he deserved. Little Worker ceased her spying and continued on toward the kitchen.

At the end of the long hall was a curving flight of wide marble stairs. Here the runner ended. The marble was cold beneath Little Worker's feet. She went down the stairs quickly.

On the ground floor, Little Worker first crossed a broad reception hall along the walls of which were ranged busts on plinths, potted plants, and gold-framed paintings. She passed through a huge salon used for formal affairs, then through Mister Michael's study, with its big walnut desk and shelves of books and wall-sized plasma screen. Several more chambers intervened before the kitchen, but finally Little Worker reached that chrome and tile room.

Most mornings, as now, the large kitchen was empty. On the mornings of those days when there were to be state dinners, the kitchen was bustling early with hired chefs, who prepared the more complex dishes the food-center could not handle. Little Worker disliked such interruptions of her normal schedule. However, this was not such a morning. The kitchen was empty.

Little Worker advanced to the food-center.

"Food-center, prepare me toast with jelly," she said.

"There is no more bread," replied the food-center.

No more bread. Little Worker was disconcerted. She had had her heart set on toast and jelly. What could have happened to the supply of bread? Yesterday there had been plenty.

"What has happened to the bread?" asked Little Worker.

"Last night Mister Michael's wife fed it all to the Bull andromorph. He ate three loaves. There were only three loaves. Thus there are no more."

Mister Michael's wife had fed all of Little Worker's toast to her Bull. It was the fault of Mister Michael's wife that there was no toast this morning for Little Worker.

"The bakery delivery occurs at ten o'clock this morning," offered the food-center helpfully.

"I will be gone with Mister Michael by then. I will not be home at ten o'clock. I must eat something different." Little Worker paused to reflect. "I will have hot cereal with a spoon of jelly on it."

"There is no jelly. The Bull ate that also. With peanut butter."

Little Worker tensed her fingers reflexively. Her morning, disturbed already by the new odor coming from Mister Michael's bedroom, was not getting better. The change in routine upset her. It felt like a morning when chefs came. But no chefs were here.

"I will have an egg then," said Little Worker.

"There are eggs," said the food-center.

"There is no jelly for an egg?" hopefully asked Little Worker one last time.

"There is no jelly even for an egg."

"Then I will have an egg alone."

Little Worker sat at a table with metal legs and white tile top. When her egg came she ate it, licking the plate to get all the yolk. It would serve to make her fur glossy. But it did not taste as good as jelly.

When she was done, Little Worker ordered the food-center to prepare and serve breakfast for Mister Michael and his wife in the south dining room. Then she walked through halls and storage rooms until she arrived at the south dining room.

Mister Michael was already there, seated at one end of a long polished table, reading a newspaper and sipping coffee.

"Good morning, Mister Michael," said Little Worker.

"Morning," said Mister Michael somewhat gruffly.

Little Worker quivered inside. Mister Michael did not seem himself this morning. He worked too hard, thought Little Worker. He had too much on his mind. The state demanded too much of him. He should be better to himself.

Little Worker coiled up at Mister Michael's feet beside the table, where she could watch everything that happened.

Breakfast was served. Mister Michael's wife did not arrive on time. Mister Michael began to eat anyway. Only when the fine Canadian ham and scrambled eggs and poached fish were cold did she come through the door.

Mister Michael's wife was dressed for shopping. She wore an ivory jacket short in front but with long tails that hung to her knees in back, over a pale blue silk blouse and tulip-hemmed ivory skirt. She wore blue metallic stockings and creamy high heels. She smelled heavily of expensive perfume, which failed to conceal entirely from Little Worker's keen nose the aromas of her recent mating.

Sitting gingerly, as if sore, Mister Michael's wife picked idly at the food set before her. Neither she nor Mister Michael spoke for some time. Finally, though, setting down his paper, which rustled loudly to Little Worker's ears, Mister Michael said, "There are some important people coming up today from Washington. They'll want to meet you."

"How very tedious. And what time would that be?"

Mister Michael seemed to be restraining his anger. "Around two."

"I'll try to be there."

Mister Michael's anger escaped. "Try! You'd damn

well better be there. As my wife, you have certain official responsibilities, just as I do.''

''No one elected me to be the prime minister's wife.''

''You elected yourself when you married me. You can't pretend you didn't. You knew quite well that I might end up as prime minister someday. I told you so from the outset. God, what do I ask of you, other than to show up for a few ceremonial occasions? Do you imagine I've got it any easier? It's not a part-time job, governing a whole bloody continent!''

''You wanted the job. I didn't.''

Mister Michael folded his hands, as if afraid of what they might do. Little Worker's hands clenched in sympathy.

''Let's not argue, shall we? Please make every effort to be at the Ministry by two.''

''I'll simply rush through the stores then.''

''Good. I appreciate it.'' Mister Michael looked down at Little Worker. ''It's time to go. Would you please get my briefcase? I left it by the bed.''

Little Worker quickly gained her feet, eager to please. ''I will get your briefcase. Where will you be?''

''Just inside the front door. Oh, have the car pull around also.''

''I will have the car pull around,'' agreed Little Worker.

On the way to the garage, Little Worker considered the argument she had overheard. She reached the same conclusion she had arrived at while standing before Mister Michael's wife's bedroom door: Mister Michael's wife was not a good one for him.

In the garage, Little Worker confronted the sleek, low-slung car. ''Mister Michael wishes you to idle at the front entrance.''

''I will exit the garage, after opening the door. I will proceed down the drive, through the gate, after opening that also, and around to the front entrance. There I will await further orders."

"Good."

The car started its ceramic engine and opened the garage door. Little Worker left it. She took the back stairs to the second floor and approached Mister Michael's bedroom from a direction different than that by which she had gone earlier.

The door was ajar. Little Worker entered.

The room was not empty.

Lying languidly on the bed among the rumpled sheets was a naked gynomorph. When she heard Little Worker enter, she opened her eyes.

"Hello," said the gynomorph. "I am a hetaera, of the Lyrical line. Do you wish to hear me sing?"

Little Worker was stunned. "No. I do not wish to hear you sing. What are you doing here?"

"I am now owned by Mister Michael. He brought me here. Do you wish to know my pedigree?"

"No."

"I will recite it anyway. I am comprised of five species, with three percent being human. My skeletal structure is avian, insuring a lightness and appealing fragility. I weigh only forty kilos. My musculature is feline, my skin a derivative of chamois. My brain is based on that of a mink. I have a vaginal contractile index of ninety. My pheromones are tailored specifically to arouse Mister Michael."

The gynomorph moved her legs and arms luxuriously and arched her back slightly, elevating her pubis. Little Worker stared furiously, her mind in turmoil.

"I am comprised of twelve species, with a full ten percent being human," she finally countered.

"My measurements, in centimeters, are one hundred, forty, eighty. What are yours?"

Little Worker looked down at her stocky, compact, and

muscled form beneath her shift. "I do not know my measurements," she said.

The gynomorph smiled, revealing delicate pointed
teeth. She ran a tongue over her lips. Little Worker could
hear it rasp.

"Well," said the hetaera, "I guess you don't know
much, do you?"

"It seems not," said Little Worker.

Now they were at the office. The office was different
from home: different noises, different smells. There were
no windows in Mister Michael's office, no blots of jelly-
light on the tan carpet, into which Little Worker's gar-
ment nearly blended. At home, Little Worker could do
pretty much as she pleased, as long as she was there
should Mister Michael need her. At the office—and in
other public places—she had to be more circumspect and
diligent. Little Worker was on duty here, in a way that
was more intense than behind the electrified fence and
active sensors of the estate. Little Worker normally
prided herself on her diligence. (Once, one of the men at
the Training School had said: "Little Worker, you are
the most diligent companion I've ever trained." The men
of the school had been nice, in their stern way. But no
one was like Mister Michael.)

Today, however, Little Worker's mind was not on her
work.

Mister Michael's first afternoon appointment had been
shown in. Little Worker lay quietly behind Mister Michael's big brown leather chair with the brass studs. Mister Michael was meeting with the people from
Washington. Little Worker paid scant attention to them.
They had been cleared by Security and smelled harmless.
Little Worker couldn't even see the visitors from her van-
tage. They were just a collection of mildly annoying
voices, which interfered with her contemplation of the
new and disturbing events at home.

When Little Worker and Mister Michael had gotten into the car, Little Worker had circumspectly sniffed Mister Michael to see if any of the hetaera's odors still clung to him. She was relieved to find that none did. Mister Michael must have washed. For a moment she felt heartened. But as the car accelerated down the front drive, picking up its entourage of armored outriders on cycles at the security station on the periphery of the estate, Little Worker realized that her relief was wrong. Mister Michael might smell normal, but his attitude was disturbed. He was not his usual self.

Little Worker wished she could somehow make everything right for poor Mister Michael, who worked so hard and whose wife was so bad that he had to seek relief in the arms of that disturbing gynomorph.

Little Worker would do anything to make Mister Michael happy.

The visitors continued to talk. Little Worker was hungry. Mister Michael had worked straight through their regular lunch hour. She would have toast with jelly for her belated midday meal, the first chance she got. Surely the Ministry's kitchens would be able to supply some. Perhaps she could convince the home food-center— which was rather stupid—not to dispense any more bread or jelly to the Bull andromorph. It would be worth a try.

Little Worker was suddenly bored with her own problems, since no easy solutions presented themselves. She decided to listen to the conversation.

"—tell you that you can't ignore them," said a visitor. "The Sons of Dixie may seem like just another fringe group to you up here in Toronto, but back home, they command a lot of sympathy—some of it from powerful folks."

The man had a funny way of speaking. He sounded emotional. Mister Michael, to the contrary, spoke calmly and in the proper way.

"I'm not proposing that we ignore them. All I said

was that we cannot afford to cater to extremist elements in the Union. The whole political structure is still too fragile, too new. Naturally, for the first decade or so, there's bound to be a bit of confusion and uneasy integration, as people settle down to a new way of being governed. But we've had quite a bit of experience with our own separatist element over in Quebec, and the major lesson we've learned is that one must be firm. In fact, I intended to sound out you gentlemen on how your constituency would react to a ban on such groups as the Sons of Dixie.''

There was shocked silence for a moment. Then one of the visitors spoke. ''Why, that's outrageous. It's—it's unconstitutional!''

''I'll have to remind you that the Union no longer functions under that document. New times call for new measures. Unless you can convince me there would be outright revolt, I believe I'm going to propose such a measure to Parliament. No group which advocates the overthrow of the Union—by violent or peaceful means— will be permitted to function.''

Confused grumbles and mutters and chopped-off phrases issued from the visitors. Mister Michael let them babble for a moment, before cutting through their objections.

''Gentlemen, I'm afraid you'll have to consider it done. Let's turn to more important matters. The Brazilians are pushing us on the boundary negotiations. Do we want to let them north of Chiapas, or don't we?''

Little Worker tuned out the unimportant talk. She was more concerned with her delayed meal.

At last Mister Michael, consulting his watch, said, ''Well, enough of work. We have a few more days during your stay to discuss such things. I believe you expressed a desire to meet my charming wife. She should be here any moment.''

Everyone waited. Little Worker shifted positions to

ease a cramp in her right haunch. Mister Michael's wife never arrived.

When the vistors had been shown out with many apologies, Mister Michael returned to his seat. He was silent for a time. Then he banged his fist on the desk. "Something has to be done about that woman," he said. "Something has to be done."

Little Worker silently agreed.

One day not long after this time, Little Worker found herself home alone.

This was highly unusual, for she was seldom separated from Mister Michael. In public or private, Little Worker was always by his side. Even when he traveled abroad, Little Worker went with him. (Little Worker had been to a lot of places with odd names, mostly other cities; aside from a few curious smells here and there, they all seemed alike.) But today Mister Michael was at the doctor's, getting his anti-aging treatment. He had just started the treatments six months ago, when they became available. The location of the doctor's clinic was secret, even from Little Worker. Mister Michael had explained to her that it was for her own protection, so that no one could capture her and force her to reveal where the clinic was. Little Worker had to smile at the thought of anyone capturing her. For one thing, no one ever paid any attention to her. Who would think she knew anything worth knowing? Little Worker felt it would have been all right for her to go with Mister Michael, but he wouldn't hear of it. It was just him and the car, and the car would have its short-term memory wiped clean after the trip.

As for Mister Michael's wife—Little Worker didn't know where she was and didn't really wonder. After the trouble she had caused, Little Worker couldn't have cared what happened to her.

All that mattered was that for the first time in six months—and only the second time since she had become

Mister Michael's companion—she was without him.

It made Little Worker very uneasy.

So Little Worker wandered through the big empty house, searching for something to occupy her until Mister Michael should return.

Upstairs, a fleeting impression made her pause outside the door of the bedroom of Mister Michael's wife. Aromas of Bull seeped out to her. Impulsively, Little Worker tried the golden handle of the door. It turned without resistance, and the door opened. Little Worker entered.

The Bull was lying on a couch. He wore nothing but a spandex thong that held his large genitals as in a pouch. He was flipping the pages of a colored picture book. When he heard Little Worker enter, he laid the book on his hard muscled stomach, pictures up. Little Worker could see that the pictures were of matings, illustrating various positions.

"Hello," said Bull. "Do you wish to have sex?"

"No, I do not wish to have sex. I am Little Worker. I do not have sex with anyone. I wish to talk."

"I can talk."

"Very good. Would you like something to eat while we talk?"

"Peanut butter is good."

Little Worker went to an intercom. "Food-center?"

"Yes?"

"Please send a jar of peanut butter to the bedroom of Mister Michael's wife."

"With a spoon?"

Bull looked guilty, as if doing something wrong. "No spoon."

"No spoon," repeated Little Worker into the intercom.

When the peanut butter arrived, Bull greedily unscrewed the cap and, dipping blunt fingers in, began to eat. Little Worker watched with approval. She knew very well how nice it was to feast on one's favorite food.

"Do you enjoy making sex with Mister Michael's wife?"

Bull looked confused. "What do you mean? It is what I do. Sex is sex. Peanut butter is what I enjoy. Am I supposed to enjoy sex also?"

"I do not know. Perhaps you would enjoy it more with someone else."

"Someone else? I don't understand. You said you did not wish to have sex with me—"

Little Worker was suddenly inspired. "I am not the only one home."

"There is another in the house who desires sex?"

"Yes. Would you go to her?"

"I am not supposed to leave this room—"

"You are supposed to provide sex when asked."

"That is true. You have stated a fact which contradicts the order not to leave the room. What am I to do?"

"I tell you that you may leave this room."

"Who are you again?"

"Little Worker, Mister Michael's companion."

"Then I suppose I must listen to you."

"Very good. Please come with me."

"Let me finish this peanut butter first—there. Show me to the one who desires to have sex."

Little Worker led Bull out into the corridor and up to Mister Michael's bedroom door, which was locked. However, Little Worker knew that code.

Inside, the Lyrical gynomorph was found taking a bath. Amid the welter of sudsy bubbles in the large sunken tub, only her delicate face and one knee were visible.

When the gynomorph saw Bull, her eyes widened and her nostrils flared. Bull developed an immediate erection.

"You are the one who wishes to have sex," said Bull.

"It is my nature."

"Mine also. Is it convenient to have sex in the bath?"

"Yes, it is."

Bull tore off his thong.

Little Worker left the pair of morphs together.

Mister Michael's wife was the first to return home, five hours after Little Worker had arranged the illicit introduction. Soon, she discovered Bull's absence and his current whereabouts. Little Worker watched from the corridor as Mister Michael's wife attempted in vain to separate the two morphs, who had ended up on the floor beside the bed, soaking the carpet with bathwater. Even striking at the pair with the sharp heel of her removed shoe failed to end the coupling. Eventually, special handlers had to be summoned. They too failed to halt the couple's pistoning.

"It's no use, miz, they've developed a destructive feedback loop. We'll have to take them in to be put down."

"Just do it, then!" shouted Mister Michael's wife. "It's disgusting!"

"Yes, miz."

The morphs were loaded still interlocked and bucking into the back of a truck and driven off.

Little Worker was secretly happy.

But within days, Mister Michael's wife had procured a Stallion, while Mister Michael solaced himself with a Moon Moth.

Little Worker came awake instantly. She had not been sleeping well lately anyway. Her life had not been right since that long-ago morning of no toast and jelly. (One good thing about the Stallion was that he preferred oatmeal.) Mister Michael was always preoccupied and distant. At times Little Worker almost resented having to be in constant attendance on him. When she had such feelings, she became violently sick, for the bad thoughts conflicted with her lessons from the Training School. Then she had to remind herself that Mister Michael and his welfare were all her reasons for being.

And now there was noise from downstairs.

There should have been no noise from downstairs. It was the middle of the night. Oh, yes, once there had been noise in the middle of the night from downstairs. Guards from the security booth had come in to check on a possible breach of the perimeter. But it had been only a sensor failure. Perhaps there had been another sensor failure tonight. Little Worker would go see.

She got as far as the head of the marble stairs.

There she confronted four men. The men wore optical-distorting garments and infrared goggles. They carried light-rifles and had other weapons slung from their hips. They were not security men.

"Well, well," said one intruder. "Lookee here. It's one o' them fuckin' cultivars. I'm gonna blow its head off."

"Don't get cocky, son," said a man who appeared to be their leader. "Just cuz we took out the local boys, don't mean we can make all the noise we want. No shooting unless I say so. Anyway, maybe this thing can save us some time. You there—where's the Pee Em sleep?"

Little Worker was not afraid. She carefully considered the terrorists before replying.

"I will show you. But you must collect his wife too, or she might summon help."

One terrorist whistled softly. Another said, "Shee-it, these vars ain't got no loyalty at-tall!"

"Okay, Beautiful, lead on."

Little Worker conducted the men to the bedroom door behind which slept Mister Michael's wife. They slapped an illegal unscrambler to the lock. The device ran through all the possible combinations in three seconds, and they were in.

Mister Michael's wife lay sleeping in the arms of the Stallion. The men made various apparently honest grunts of shock, which awoke Mister Michael's wife and her bedmate.

Soon, she and the Stallion had been herded into Mister Michael's room, where the Prime Minister was found in a similar situation with his new gynomorph.

One of the terrorists flicked on the lights, which seemed unnaturally bright at this forlorn hour. The men removed their goggles and shut off their suits, which had begun to hurt Little Worker's eyes. She was grateful.

The two human captives and their morphs stood shivering in the center of the room, the morphs naked and Mister Michael and his wife in robes. Three of the terrorists seemed calm, but one swiveled his gun nervously from side to side.

Little Worker curled unconcernedly at Mister Michael's feet. She knew that Mister Michael was trying to catch her eye, but she ignored him.

"Who—who are you from?" at last demanded Mister Michael.

"Sons of Dixie, folks. We felt our point of view wasn't reaching the proper ears. So we're aimin' to change things. Ain't that right, boys?"

"You're—you're all wired on something."

"Mebbe so, boss. But that don't prevent us from shooting straight. 'Zact opposite, in fact. So let's just follow orders, if you don't want to get hurt."

"What do you intend?" asked Mister Michael's wife.

"We're taking you 'n' the Pee Em on a little vacation. You'll go free when the gummint listens to us and does somethin'."

A second terrorist spoke. "What about these friggin' vars?"

"Slag those sex toys," said the boss. "Make it quiet though. But save the one that helped us—it might come in handy again."

One of the men unholstered a pistol. Before anyone could react, it spat twice.

Gelatin capsules hit the morphs and burst, releasing lysis catalysts. In under a minute, the two morphs were a single mingled puddle of thick slime, atop which for a minute floated the Moon Moth's tougher gemmed wings.

"Okay, folks—" began the leader.

Unnoticed, Little Worker had slyly extended an arm toward the bare ankle of Mister Michael's wife. Now, she pricked it deeply with a newly unsheathed razored claw.

Mister Michael's wife screamed.

The terrorist with unsteady nerves shot her through the eye.

Before the man's trigger-finger could relax, or any of the others could tighten theirs, Little Worker moved.

The part of her inheritance that was 30 percent wolverine took over.

The four intruders soon lay dead with their throats torn out, soaking the carpet with their blood where once the Bull and Lyrical had coupled.

Little Worker calmly licked the blood from her lips. She really preferred the taste of jelly. Wetting her palms repeatedly with her tongue, she meticulously cleaned the fur on her face. When she was done, she turned toward Mister Michael.

He had collapsed across the body of his wife and lay sobbing.

Little Worker gently approached. She touched him tenderly. He jumped.

"Mister Michael," said Little Worker, "everything is all right now.

"You and I are alone."

⚡ Cockfight

I WILL ALLOW AS HOW BEIN' A WASTE GIPSY IS not the most settled way of life, nor the easiest on the nerves. And it's surely no career for a married man—as Geraldine never tires of remindin' me.

But I ain't married. And I never listen to Geraldine.

Anyway, what's so rough about the life? First off, there's the constant travel. You got to learn to keep as little in your kit as a blind Bhopal beggar and generally stay as loose as a Bull's balls. Your in-demand ass is always bein' faxed around the globe, from one hotspot to another, whenever some muni or fabrik or werke or abe gets to feelin' a tad guilty and decides they're gonna clean up a little piece of the big, big mess they've all made durin' the last filthy century.

Some of these places ain't so bad, in terms of relaxin' when the job's over for the day. When we were in Milan, Italy, for instance, reamin' out their toxic sewers where some asshole way back in '86 dumped twenty tons of assorted pollutants and contaminated the whole city's water supply, I was able to do all kinds of cultural things, like visitin' churches, and seein' *The Last Supper* (considerably improved, in my opinion, since they sprayed the restorative bugs on it, despite all the juicer critics sayin' it looked digitally enhanced), and checkin' out the architecture of the Eye-tie chickenhouses. (One was in a real palace, and some of the girls was supposed to be real princesses. It was just possible, too, cuz I remember that when Monaco was forbsed-over and trumped-up, there was a whole generation that had to latch onto jobs real quick.)

Other times, you're gonna find yourself in the ass-end of nowhere, some god-forsaken place that makes Robert Lee, Texas (my birthplace), look like New Orleans at Mardi Gras. I have shivered at fifty below with no audience but dumb greasy penguins, cleanin' up an Antarctic oil spill, and baked my sandy britches at one hundred plus, decommissioning a Mideast CBW plant. And both times there was nothin' to do after your shift except play flashcards, get wiped on needlestrength-one tropes, and spill atmosphere with your fellow gipsies. (Maybe summa the talk might lead to bumpin' uglies with one of your fellow gips, if that's what fills your receptors, but I try to stay away from the gals that work in the same line as me, they all bein' as familiar and excitin' as your elderly mustache-wearin' aunt or some old-maid grade-school trope doser.)

It's times like these that you tell spine-tinglin' kings and barkers about all the shit you have seen. Times when the rems was sleetin' around you thicker than fleas on a junkyard dog, knockin' your chromos loopier than those of a two-headed snake, and you were wrasslin' a hot core. Times when you were standin' waist-deep in some stinkin' swamp full of PCB's and dirty antique motor-oil and industrial solvents and God knows what-all, and you seen the snout of a mutant Amazonian 'gator barrelin' toward you faster'n the Orient Express, and you barely had time to raise up your force-multiplier for a single blow before the 'gator was on you.

But surprisin'ly enough, the net effect of all these after-hours horror stories is not to discourage us gips, but rather to make us feel special and important. After all, who else has such a vital job as us? Cleanin' up this poor abused planet is—or should be—society's number-one priority, after all, and they ain't invented a robot yet that's smart enough or tough enough to do what we do, or take the shit we endure. Imagine some hunk of heuristics pokin' its sensors into the hells we gotta enter, without fryin' its CCD's and crispin' its boards. As for the splices, the union keeps them out. And as long as we get our regular search-and-repair silicrobe shots, we ain't gonna suffer any more weird diseases or terry-tomas than your average New Yorker or Nevadan.

Not that I do it mainly for glory or outa some sense of duty to humanity. Shit, no. I don't think you'll find one greenpeacer out of every thousand gipsies you talk to. I do it cuz the eft's damn good, and so are the bennies, and you can retire after fifteen years. (My company, Dallas Detox, Inc., was one of the first to pioneer that particular policy, and that's one of the reasons I'm purely proud to work for them. Another's that they are one hunnerd percent American, and there's not many companies left that can make such a claim, 'specially since they fully phased the Union in ten years ago. Now, I don't hold with them Sons of Dixie, or any of the other constitutionalist groups, legal or underground, but there is something about being ruled by Canucks that just goes up my craw a mile. And if I got to be ruled by them, leastwise I don't have to work for them. Yet.)

Anyway, it's a decent life, and sometimes an excitin' one, even if, as I said, it's no career for a married man—as Geraldine never tires of remindin' me.

But I ain't married. And I never listen to Geraldine.

When Stack came into the dorm, wavin' the metamedium printout that bore the DDI logo in its upper corner (a pair of tweezers nippin' a double helix) and smilin', we all knew we had gotten a good postin'. But we couldn'ta guessed how good till the crewboss spoke.

"Parliament has voted, boys and girls. The Slikslak is deadmeat, and DDI's gonna pick the corpse."

Well, the roar of excitement that greeted this announcement rattled the biopolymer panels of the big Komfykwik Kottage we were livin' in, there on the shores of Lake Baikal in Greater Free Mongolia, which stagnant pisshole we had finally finished de-acidifyin' and ecobalancin' and revivifyin' and such-like. We were goin' home, stateside, back to the good old U.S. of A. (and I'll continue to call it that till my dyin' day, despite all laws to the contrary). To actually get an assignment back in civilization—it was too good to be true. No more funny food or dark-skinned women or comic jabber which you couldn't understand without takin' a pill. It was hog heaven for a poor gipsy.

I was emptyin' my locker and packin' my kit on my bunk when Geraldine sidled up to me all innocent-like. I pretended not to notice her.

"Lew," she said, in a voice as sweet as corn syrup on candied yams, "Stack is making up the room-roster for Waxahachie. We are going to put up at a local motel, and all the rooms're doubles. I don't suppose . . ."

I looked up at Geraldine then. She was wearin' earrings shaped like biohazard signs, her brown hair was cropped shorter'n mine, with a lopsided swatch across her brow, her face was naked of makeup, save for sili-crobe tattoo butterflies at the corners of her lips, and she barely filled out her size small DDI-issue coverall. She reminded me of the kid sister I'd never had.

"Geraldine, I do appreciate the offer or suggestion or proposition or whatever you wanna call it. But if I have told you once, I've told you a million times. The chemistry is just not there. My probe don't match your target. Look, I like my women big, busty, and dumb, and you are neither."

The tattoos a milli beneath Geraldine's skin fluttered

their wings in agitation as the tears leaked like Israeli root-drips from her eyes.

"I—I could be dumb for you, Lew, if that was what you really wanted. There's new tropes for that, I heard. Dumbdown, MoreOn . . . As for the other stuff, well, it'd cost me plenty, but I'd do it for you. Honest, I would—"

I slapped my own forehead. "Holy shit, Geraldine, I ain't askin' you to change, get that into your head right now. I was only outlinin', like, the kind of woman that jumps my gaps. Listen." I put an arm real uncle-like around her shoulder. "You're a helluva gipsy. I never seen anyone better at dredgin' a bay or sprayin' a forest full of pear-thrips than you. I am proud to be your partner on any job Stack gives us. But that's where it ends, you latch? Strictly a professional relationship."

Geraldine had turned the taps off by the time I finished my speechifyin'. She knuckled her eyes, then extended one hand. We shook.

"Okay," she said, sadder'n a preacher who's seen the collection come up empty, "if that's the way you want it. It's better than nothing, I guess."

We loosed our shake. "See you on the plane, Lew."

I went back to my packin'. What a mixed-up gal. I wondered why people had to lose it when it came to their emotions. Thank the Lord we at least had tropes and strobers nowadays to help. It was hard to imagine how it had been just a few decades ago, before the bioboys understood all there was to know about the brain. Not that you should come to rely too much on such aids, I believed. There was something to be said for a natural life. Why, look at me, for instance. Once I had taken all the mnemotropins prescribed in school and learned what I had to, did I keep on takin' 'em? Nope, not me. As my daddy always said, "Son, if we was meant to get our experience outa a pill, the Good Lord woulda made 'em easier to swallow."

Before that day was over, we were boardin' a DDI

suborb, all laughin' and jokin' at the thought of hittin'
the streets of Dallas once again. We had barely settled
into the flight, however, when we were told to buckle up
once more for the landin' and take our circadian-
adjusters. That's the problem with these hour-long jumps:
they don't give you no time to feel like you really been
travelin'. One minute your ass is in Mongolia, the next
minute you're home. It does require some mental gym-
nastics.

We got hung up in Customs for a couple of hours—
longer'n the flight itself. Turned out a couple of our gips
had tried to make a little extracurricular eft for themselves by attemptin' to smuggle back Mongolian bugs in
their blood. Probably some kind of ethnic-specific high
that they figured would sell well among the Dallas community of ex-pat Hong Kongers. The Customs probes
had unzipped the nongenotype codes faster'n spit dryin'
on a griddle, and Stack had some fancy dancin' to do to
get off with just a bloodwash, by claimin' our innocent
liddle boys was infected without their knowledge.

In the terminal we were crossin' the atrium when a
squad of IMF crick-cops bulled through, carryin' their
chromo-cookers and packin' splat-pistols, lookin' mean
as eighty-year-old virgins with libido-locks, headin'
doubtlessly for some Fourth-World infection or infestation of some sort. We gave 'em a wide berth outa respect,
as they are about the only ones with a dirtier job than us
gips. We got it relatively easy, dealin' with old well-
known hazards, while they get all the new and superdan-
gerous shit.

Outside DDI had a couple of Energenetix cowbellies
with drivers waitin' for us. Most of the folks clambered
right into the minivans (I made a point of gettin' in a
different one from Geraldine), but Tino and Drifter—the
boys who had gotten pinched by Customs—had to take
a piss real bad. Side effect of the bloodwash. They'd be

leakier'n a sharecropper's cabin in a hurricane for the next day.

Stack called out, "Don't waste the biomass, boys."

Tino and Drifter grumbled, but they each opened up a fuel intake cap, unvelcroed their flies, butted their groins up to the vans, and did their best to top off the tanks.

Refastenin' their coveralls, the two climbed in rather sheepishly. Tamarind, a bantam-weight black gal sittin' next to me, who always managed to get off a great zinger with perfect timin', said, "A lot different than the last sockets I seen you boys plugging."

Everyone cut loose with all the laughter we'd been holdin' in, roarin', and howlin' fit to burst. Even Drifter and Tino eventually joined in the gipsy camaraderie. Hell, we knew it could've been any of us that'd got caught, and we couldn't hold the wasted time against them. Come what may, us gips hang tighter'n the plies of steelwood laminated with barnacle-grip.

Thus enjoyin' ourselves in our loose gipsy way, we motored south out of the mass of gleamin', glassy Dallas towers, headin' toward our latest assignment.

Waxahachie was about twenty-five miles south of the city, so we had roughly a forty-minute drive. (You can't push a cowbelly much faster'n sixty kph, especially when fully loaded.) Some gips settled in for a nap, which helps the circadian-adjusters kick in, but I was too excited to be back home to sleep, so I levered open a window and let the familiar dusty scents of a Texas summer waft in while I watched the scenery laze by.

We passed a small orchard of peachtrees at one point. The trees were full of splices harvesting the force-grown fruit. The human overseer lay in the shade, collar-box by his side, within easy reach. To me the splices looked about 50 percent chimp, 40 percent lemur, and 10 percent human. But I coulda been off by a few percent either way.

"I sure do dislike those splices," said Tamarind.

"Thank heavens we got laws keeping them down."

"Not to mention the collars and diet-leashes," I added. Then I got a funny notion which I had to share. "Hey, Tam, you ever feel weird about the splices and your heritage and all? I mean, like maybe they hold the same position now that your folks did, a couple of centuries ago?"

"Shit no. They aren't human, after all, are they? And that makes all the difference."

I could see her point. "Well, I guess in a way the splices make it possible for an old redneck like me to be buddies with a gal of color like yourself and mostways not think twice about it."

Tam punched me in the shoulder. "You got it, Lew."

Shortly after that, we pulled into the parking lot of the motel Geraldine had mentioned to me back at Lake Baikal. There were a lot of other DDI vehicles there, all with the tweezered helix on their sides, and, as I later found out, some other gipsies were even bunkin' in the quarters that used to house the Slikslak staff. I figured this for one of the biggest deconstruction jobs I had ever taken part in. With any luck, it'd last a good long time, so I could continue to enjoy the comforts of a real bed, good American food, and sweet Texas poontang, a juicy sample of which I was gonna make haste to lay my hands and stiff probe on as soon as possible.

In the motel lobby, Stack called our names off a roster. "Shooter, you're bunking with Benzene Bill in three-sixteen."

I swore. Benzene Bill—so called for the tattoon of a spinning snake-in-mouth Kekule ring he sported on his massive right bicep—was a mean-natured sumbitch I had never gotten along with. Maybe I woulda been better off with Geraldine, even if I had hadda fend off her constant feminine advances.

I found Bill in the crowd, and we headed for our room together in tense silence.

Inside, Bill said, "Lissen, Sludgehead, if I want to bring some nookie back here, you'd better clear out on my say-so, whether it's for the whole night or not."

I put my kit down and calmly faced him. "Bill, the facts is, you are as ugly as an ape 'n' hornytoad splice, and no sleeve is gonna look twice at you, lessen she's paid some big eft, or she's maybe been dosed with a combo of uglybuster and lubricine."

Bill grabbed the front of my coverall. "Why, you cocksucker—"

"Bill," I said all calm and gentle-like, "do you remember Marseilles?"

He snorted then, but he let me go right fast. Retreating to his bed, he began unpacking his kit, and there was no more said about me clearin' out for his improbable ruttin'.

It's good to get the terms straight in any relationship right from the start.

Well, the day was pretty shot by then, but we still had time for a tour of the Slikslak itself, to get acquainted with the place we were gonna be demolishin'.

Everyone was kinda disappointed when we arrived at the old Superconductin' Supercollider, which had had such a checkered, on-again, off-again history. Wasn't much of the SCSC aboveground. It was all buried beneath the prairie, a ring of deep-cooled magnets and beam-bouncers and particle-chambers some fifty miles in diameter, all contaminated by decades of experimentation in a nice mild way that promised low rems. (I understand the lunar facility that replaced the Slikslak is twice as big, and cost half as much to build, what with the free vacuum and new superwire.)

When we got down below, though, everyone's enthusiasm picked up. This job was gonna be easy—hardly any exotics aside from liquid hydrogen—and the sheer size of the place meant it would take practically forever. What a sugartit assignment!

Back at the motel, with dusk comin' down like silk sheets in a Paris helmsley, we found that DDI had laid on a humongous Tex-Mex barbecue for our first night. As I've said a hundred times—and not just when Stack was around to overhear—they are swell employers with a lot of class. Smellin' the beefaloes and leanpigs turnin' on their spits, holding a cold cheer-beer in my hand, watchin' the stars poppin' out one by one like random pixels on God's antique monochrome display, listenin' to the joyful chatter of my fellow gips, contemplatin' the easy job ahead of me, I was as near to heaven as I have ever been on this mostly sad ol' earth.

And that peaceful feelin', so pure and unnatural, I reckon now, is what should have alerted me to my comin' troubles.

It was the first weekend after we had started the Slikslak job, and we gips were ready to party. Several days of bone-breakin' labor, with nothin' to do after hours except raster whatever gaudy gore 'n' garters plasma-com the flatscreen was offerin' or play a hand of flashcards or metabolize some samogon at the dingy Waxahachie road-house known as Mustang Sally's (the lady owner wore a palomino's tail), had left us achin' for some release.

So a bunch of us—me, Geraldine, Tam, Tino, Spud, Geneva, IgE, even Benzene Bill and some others—signed out a van and made the trip into Dallas, lookin' for some Big Fun.

I was drivin' and all my actions felt effortless. We had all had a thorough tonin'-up performed on us by the company cell-scrubber, so all my workweek aches and pains were gone. My skin was as tingly as that of a playpet from Hedonics Plus. Beyond the ultrapure single-crystal windshield, the speedy nighttime scenery looked partic-ularly hi-rez, with all the shadows dithered to fractal depths. I was confident tonight would rack up some me-gadigits on the Fun Readouts.

Once in Dallas, we headed straight for Deep Ellum, the prime pleasure district of the city. Parking the van and setting its defenses, we hit the crowded sidewalks, walkin' with our kickass gipsy style, guys as if we had a barrel between our legs, gals like they were slidin' along on a greased pole right at crotch height.

I tell you, it made me proud as the ten-year-old who knocked up the neighborhood widow to be stridin' through the city with my fellow gips, confident in our solidarity and fully aware of our so-ci-et-al importance.

Deep Ellum was thronged with folks of every stripe and pedigree enjoyin' the false halogen day. There were splices runnin' errands for their owners. There were pre-teeny peptide-poppers four or five cohorts down the genetic line from my own, streamin' free 'n' wild with the members of their sets and posses, sportin' their fancy Action Potential clothes. There were gerrys and gullas. There were NU cops carryin' flashlights and shockers to keep the peace amongst the various factions, not to mention the local dirty-harrys. All in all, it was a highly stochastic and organic scene.

Well, we began hittin' the bars around eight, exposin' our receptors to various bands rangin' across the noise spectrum, from multipolar music to old-fashioned country-western picked out on a lone synthesizer, and meanwhile not neglectin' to ingest all manner of delightful deliriants and insidious intoxicants.

Around midnight I seemed to come back to myself as if my consciousness was a balloon on a tether light-years-long, which I had to oh-so-slowly reel in.

''Where are we?'' I said to Tino.

''In Parts Unknown.''

I gathered that was the name of the bar where we sat. It was a smoky, noisy, jam-packed troglo kind of place. On its raw stone walls hung neo-neon signs that said stuff like REDRAW YOUR MAP2 and WHAT'S YOUR *AMP*-ERAGE? The bartender was a simian splice which hung by its tail from an aerial rail and mixed drinks with four human hands.

All of a sudden, like storm waters through an arroyo, or the opening of petcocks on the feedline of a breeder-tank, I remembered my urges of a few days ago, to bury my face in some down-home Texas target. In an instant I was hornier'n a kid's pet unicorn. I scoped out the dance floor, spottin' Geraldine shakin' her skinny little butt with some local dude. Then my eyes passed over her to alight on my dream girl.

She stood a good six feet tall, thanks to her hi-heels. Five-inch ivory spikes that grew out of the calcaneum of her tarsus bones, they were tipped with gold caps. The rest of her feet were bare, with special hi-impact soles that I could see when she kicked toward the ceiling. She wore some Wind Skin neoprene tights, but nothin' above the waist. Her tits were enormous, and thanks to the implanted cantilever lifts, projected out as firm and confident as a CEO's handshake. She had had the refractive index of her aureoles altered so that they were mirrors. On her cheeks were little patches of iridescent fish-scales. I was willin' to bet a week's eft that her tongue was cat-raspy. In short, she was just what the cell-scrubber ordered.

I pranced out onto the dance floor, cocky as a dirty-harry carrying heavy metal and a journal full of wires.

Her partner was a little south-of-the-border dude that I pegged right from the start as a Brazilian. The Brazzes was heavy into Texas lately, ever since The Doctor's Plot to assassinate the PM had caused such chaos in the upper echelons of the NU.

I tapped the Brazz on the shoulder. "Hey, meninio, how's about lettin' me cut in?"

The little sludgehead just ignored me. His sleeve, though, seemed to like the idea. She stropped her lower lip with her tongue, and I swore I could hear the sand-paper sound of it above the music. The Brazz's cockiness and his sleeve's allure got me so damn inflamed that I did something rash. I spun the Brazz around and cold-cocked him with a right to the jaw. Then I grabbed his sleeve and tugged her toward the door. She didn't resist for more'n a milli.

Outside in some shadows I backed her up against a wall and stuck my tongue halfway down her throat. Then I took a handful of her crotch.

I was like to die when I encountered a basket full of male equipment. I disengaged quickly from the kiss, but was too shocked to withdraw my hand.

"What's the matter, honey?" she said. "Looking for this?"

I felt everything squirm and writhe beneath my palm like a hooked crawfish, resultin' in a slow and stealthy envagination and labiation.

Holy radwaste! I'd picked up a maff!

Last time I was stateside, maffs had hung out in their own clubs, and a feller was mostly safe from accidentally hittin' on one. I guessed things had changed since then.

I backed off and trod on someone's foot.

It was the little Brazz. I fell into an offensive posture, then stopped.

He was holding something out to me. His card. I felt sorta dumb, still makin' deadly-like with my hands, so I relaxed and took it.

"Senhor," said the Brazz, "you will have the honor of meeting me, Flaviano Diaz, in the local cockpit, *daiqui a oito dias*, or your carcass will grace the window of the local *emporio*."

He bowed and left. That was when I looked at his card.

It said: Flaviano Diaz, Capoeira Instructor, Redbelt, First Degree.

I stood barefoot and barechested in the dusty yard behind the motel, sweatin' under a Saturday noontime sun hot as an episode of *Siouxie Sexcrime*. What a hell of a way to be spendin' my free time, practicin' for an engagement that was like as not gonna result in my own bloody death by evisceration. But I had no one to blame except my own fool self, and as my daddy always said, ''Son, there is no point in beatin' up on yourself if you can beat on someone else.'' And that was what I fully intended to do, or die tryin'.

I lifted another five-pound bag of flour from the crateful I had borryed from the commissary. I walked somewhat awkwardly over to the shade cast by the scrawny pin oak that was the motel's sole foliage. Hangin' over a branch from a rope was a sling of plastic netting, just at head-height. I took out the empty slashed flour bag that was inside the ripped net and substituted the full one. When I walked off a few paces, I left a trail of white footprints leadin' from the pile of flour on the ground.

Facin' the suspended flour sack, I went all cat-like, tryin' to will the tension and doubt from my body and mind. I moved in on the enemy, fakin' and feintin', dippin' and glidin'. When I felt I had that dumb ol' flour sack completely befuddled, I pivoted and launched a high arcin' perfect kick at it.

Sunlight flashed off a crescent of glass as it razored through the bag and nettin', spillin' flour like a cloud of construction silicrobes.

Someone whistled behind me. I turned. It was Benzene Bill.

''I'm glad you wasn't wearing those when we tangled before,'' he said.

Bill's words flashed me back to Marseilles, when we had been involved in the big Mediterranean cleanup. He was new to the team then and seemed to have taken an instant dislikin' to me, probably cuz I was the only one his size. I got sick of his endless hasslin' of me and decided to settle things once and for all. In the city, I found an academy that taught savate, or ''ler box fransay,'' as they call it otherwise. With appropriate trope

conditionin', I was soon qualified to kick the wings off
a fly in flight. Shortly thereafter, I put Bill down once
and for all. Bill, being a lazy bully, never upped the
stakes by goin' in for his own conditionin'.

Later, when we were stationed on the Thai-
Kampuchean border doin' jungle-biome restoration at the
site of some old refugee camps, I took the chance to
study a little at a monastery, under the monks what taught
Thai kick-boxin'.

I had thought I possessed some pretty slick moves. But
that was before I had seen the tapes of various capoeira
masters.

Capoeira was Brazz hand-and kick-boxin'. The moves
had an African basis, salted with Bahian tropico-funk.
Sometimes it looked almost like innocent dancin'. Until
the capoerista rocketed his opponent with a heel upside
the jaw.

Me 'n' Flaviano Diaz in the cockpit was gonna be an
interestin' match. I hoped I would survive to appreciate
it in my old age.

Now I looked down at my moddies that Bill was ras-
terin'.

My spurs.

I had visited the bodyshop the mornin' after the mess
at Parts Unknown, reckonin' I had no time to waste. The
proprietor was a gerry who musta been born a good hundred years ago. I listened close when he spoke, figurin'
to benefit from his experience.

"Believe me, I know these Brazilians. They share the
Argentinian fascination with the knife. Your man will
chose a superalloy steel pair of spurs, most likely the
Wilkinson or Gilette. Those are fine spurs, but too heavy.
They invariably slow one down. Now these"—he took
down a slim case, opened it, and revealed two transparent
scimitars nestled on black velvet—"are superior in every
way. Bioglass by Corning. They hold just as sharp an
edge as superalloy, but are featherlight. Hard to focus on,

too. Moreover, they provide superior bonding at the bone-interface. We will grow the glass right into your tibia.''

The old man paused. ''Oh, by the way, the law requires me to remind you that these are sold strictly for decorative purposes. Now, if you agree to that condition, shall I begin the installation?''

What could I say? I took 'em. I also let the guy talk me into a pair of musky scent-glands, located right at my wrist pulse-points. He said it would make me feel more macho and attract more women. I didn't have the heart to tell him that was how I had gotten into this jam in the first place.

Archin' my soles, I jerked the spurs up and down a hair, showin' off for Bill.

''Yeah, pretty neat,'' Bill agreed. ''However, the outlaw line still has Diaz favored over you at three-to-two. I plan to make some hefty eft off your loss, sucker.'' Bill started laughing. ''See you in the pit tonight.''

He left before I could contradict him. But I wasn't sure if he wasn't right.

I was gettin' another flour bag set when Geraldine came into the yard. I pretended not to see her.

''Lew,'' she said, ''please, don't do it. You know DDI will protect you from Diaz. There's no need to risk your life with something illegal like this.''

''You say somethin', Geraldine?''

''Yes, I said something, you damn stubborn pig's asshole. I said don't throw your life away for your stupid pride.''

''Sorry, Geraldine, I can't rightly hear what you're sayin', for some reason or other.''

''Oh, go to hell, you ignorant shitkicker!''

Flour filled the air as my foot thumped back to the earth.

''When you see me whippin' that spic's butt, Geraldine, you will feel different about things.''

She just glared at me, then stormed away. At the door of the motel, she stopped and yelled out, "And those scent-glands make you smell like a wet ox!"

I quit practicin' after that. With supporters like Bill and Geraldine, the spirit had gone plumb out of me. Standin' one-footed and lifting my ankle to my knee, I used a bandana to wipe off first my left spur, then my right.

At suppertime I stoked up by eatin' a big steak, a pound of pasta, and a whole apple pie, chased with a dose of Digestaid. By fight time my stomach would be empty, and my body would have all that protein and carbs to burn. Then I turned in for a little nap, sleepin' surprisin'ly easy, considerin' what I faced. When the alarm woke me, I got up and showered. I put on my ostrich-skin boots, which I had had to slit up the back to accommodate the spurs. With my jeans tugged down over 'em, they didn't look so bad. Then, without sayin' goodbye to anyone, I took a one-man fuel-cell utility vehicle into the city to keep my appointment. I didn't feel like travelin' with the others. Let them show up on their own, if they were comin' at all, I figured, after all the crap they had given me.

The cockpit was located in an old warehouse in the Camspanic barrio. The abandoned look of the place was somewhat belied by the quantity of cars parked in the neighborhood. I added mine to the ranks and went inside.

There were rickety bleachers up to the shadowy rafters, and they were all packed with a restive crowd jacked up on Sensalert. At their focus was an ankle-high wooden ring about as big as a backyard swimmin' pool. It was filled with sand. Two guys were rakin' some blood under, so I figured a match had just ended.

I found the referee, a blonde with pinfeathers where her eyebrows should have been and told her who I was. In a minute she had rounded up Diaz from out of the crowd and brought him over to me. Sure enough, I could see he had gone for the Wilkinson blades.

"I am gratified to find you are a man of honor, Senhor."

"Honor, my pecker, I'm just here for the satisfaction of thrashin' the ass of a perverted little foreign maff lover."

"Whatever the anatomical peculiarities of the lady, Senhor, she was an excellent dancer, and I will be happy to defend her character by leaving you expiring in the dirt from which you arose."

After this exchange of front-porch pleasantries we both stripped down on the sidelines, while the ref fetched the Bloodhound.

Diaz had a midriff that coulda been carved outa chocolate-colored granite. Despite his bein' three-quarters my size, his upper-body musculature nearly matched mine. I prayed my longer reach would count for somethin'.

We peeled down to just our Kevlar crotchguards. I made Benzene Bill—who had moved up to the front row to gloat—hold on to my clothes and boots. Not that I was gonna survive to wear 'em. My balls felt 'bout as big as a Hamster's.

The ref brought the Bloodhound round. It came up to me first, licked some of my sweat, then nipped the flesh between my thumb and forefinger to draw blood.

"Nuffin," growled the augie-doggie, after rolling the juices around on its palate. Then it did the same for Diaz, who came up clean too.

"Okay, gents, you're both operating under correct physionorms, without enhancements. Let's get this show on the road."

We entered the ring, and the crowd cut loose with a barbaric roar that musta resembled what the spectators at the Coliseum sounded like.

The ref spoke into her lapel mike. "Okay, citizens and otherwise, we have a grudge match here. On my left is a visitor to Greater Dallas, Senhor Flaviano Diaz from south-of-the-border way.''

Diaz got a big round of applause, which was only natural considerin' the ties here to his region.

''And on my right is a homeboy, originally from Robert Lee, Texas—Mister Lew Shooter.''

My applause matched Diaz's—more or less. I scanned the audience and thought I spotted Geraldine and some other gips. Then I yanked my concentration back to the cockpit.

''All right, roosters, you both know the rules—there are none. Except of course that the winner gets to decide if the loser receives medical treatment or not. Go to it, and may the best cock win.''

The ref backed out in a hurry.

When her foot left the ring, Diaz moved.

He tried a *galopante* first, a blow of the hand to my ear to knock my balance out. I deflected it so that it glanced off my temple with stingin' force. Then I drove two stiffened fingers into his sternum. It was like pokin' a plank. But I've pierced a few plys of steelwood before, and I knew he felt it, though he barely showed it.

The crowd was screamin' for blood. As if to oblige, Diaz launched a *bencao*, a forward kick. I watched as his foot seemed to travel in slow-mo, its slice of sharpened steel headin' straight for my throat. At what seemed like the last possible moment, I dropped below the blow. Restin' on one hand, I kicked his single supportin' foot out from under him.

But instead of hittin' the sand, Diaz converted his motion into an *aus*, or cartwheel, finishin' up on his feet across the ring.

I closed with him, figurin' to soften him up with a few punches. We traded blows to the torso and head for a few dizzy seconds, and I won't say who took the worse punishment. We clinched, then pushed apart.

Somehow Diaz had ended up with his back to me. This

was it, I thought, your first and last mistake, you little bastard. I got lined up to slice him open when he turned.

But he didn't turn. Instead, arching his back, he flew into a *macao*, or monkey, shootin' halfway across the ring.

Now I had my back to him.

I spun around.

Too late.

Before I knew it, I felt two slices across my upper thighs.

The fucker had opened up both my femoral arteries.

I wavered, then collapsed onto my stomach, feelin' strength drain out with my blood.

"Now," said Diaz, "I will keep my promise."

His voice told me where he stood. With the last of my energy, I pulled a mule.

Goin' into what amounted to a handstand, I hooked both my spurs into his gut. And ripped down, draggin' Diaz to the sand and spillin' his innards onto the bloody sand.

"Any farmboy knows not to fuck with a mule, ass-hole," I managed to say, then blacked out, wonderin' as I did what kind of medical attention two losers would get.

I musta been out only thirty seconds or so when the dirty-harrys showed up.

(I later learned that Diaz had diplomatic immunity, and the authorities were worried about him comin' up zero-sign and causin' a scandal. That was the only reason they'd crashed the usual Saturday night frolics, admittedly a little late.)

Well, they blew down the doors and dispersed a cover of Fear-o-Moan and Whammer Jammer to handle any resistance. The folks in the crowd who wasn't pukin' were shriekin' and clamorin' like a buncha Girl Scouts who had wandered into a nudist camp, while me 'n' Diaz lay bleedin' to death. (Flat on the floor, I escaped most of the aerosols.)

Then I blacked out again.

Next time I came to, my head was in Geraldine's lap.

Geraldine was cryin'. Musta been the cop-gas, I guess. Through her tears, she said, "Don't worry, don't worry, don't worry, Lew, I had a medikit, I brought it with me just for you, I patched you up."

I tried to lift my hand up to feel my thighs, but couldn't. Geraldine grabbed my paw and brought it up to her face. Then, unconsciously or not, she started rubbin' my scented wrist up and down the side of her neck.

"You'll be all right, Lew, I'll post your bail and visit you in the hospital. You'll see."

I found my voice deep down in some lonesome cavern of myself. "I—I ain't listenin' to you, Geraldine," I croaked like a bullfrog flattened by a semi.

"Yes you are, Lew. Oh yes you are."

⚡ Big Eater

THIS IS THE STORY OF HOW I SAVED CHICAGO from a Second Flood, stopped my sister from going totally Buggy, and earned a promotion right out of the liteservo class to alpha-symbland, all in the same day.

With a little help from Big Eater, of course.

That fateful morning started like any other.

The wordbird woke me at seven out of my heaven. Not at all synthetic, just the old deltawave-syncretic. Rem-memories hazed my gaze. Just like a screamcurse, I seemed stuck in my dreamverse. Though it wasn't so bad, maybe even triple-gonad. Something about drifting forever down a river of feathers. On my back, I was catching up on my slack. Coasting along just humming a song. Mighty nice change from my strife-life braindrain. Which the nerdbird was still harp-harp-hopping on.

"Time to get up, time to get up! Now seven-oh-one-oh-three! You'll be late for work, Corby! Time to get up!"

The sweet dream had fled, so shaking my head, I climbed out of bed. It reverted to a couch almost before I could uncrouch.

"Okay, okay! Shut your trap, I'm done with my nap."

The wordbird closed its beak right in midsqueak.

I could tell from the rhymes that ran through my skull that it was way past time for me to get well. So the first bore-chore I attended to was to rip-strip my old Kabi-Pharm latch-patch off and slap a fresh one on behind my ear. The sensitive sensor, so as not to offend, changed to rich cocoa brown, my own skin-blend.

As the tropes perfused, I asked for the news.

The TogaiMagic endoplants in the wordbird reacted to my voice-choice. The big bright parrot on its perch, interrupted in midpreen, began to recite the CNN audio feed coming through the multiplex tether that also fixed it to its perch.

"Yesterday Mayor Jordan launched a week-long celebration of his eightieth birthday by officially opening the new Joliet station on the extension of the Chi-Mon DASA magnatrain line. Attending the ceremonies were the North American prime minister, the director of the Great Lakes Bioregion, several World Bank officials, and many of the mayor's old teammates. All were present at an exclusive party later that night, featuring entertainment by a host of the most uptaking stars from Bollywood to Taikong, including the Newsy Floozy, Jonny Kwesti, and Wubbo the Whale.

"A spokesdemon for the Transgenic Oversight Committee has issued a warning that the notorious rogue splice known as Krazy Kat is suspected to have infiltrated the GLB. All franches are asked to report any suspicious sightings to their commensal buzzworms or to patrolling TAC-TOCs.

"An Anti-Em demonstration in front of the Board of Trade erupted in violence late in the afternoon. The familiar chant of 'No mods, no mixes!' soon changed to shouts of 'Burn the miscegenators!' Authorities declared an emergency risk-bubble of ninety naders intensity covering three square blocks for a duration of thirty minutes plus-minus and dispersed clouds of Riotnip and Inconti-barf.

"On financial fronts, the Hang Seng Index registered a day of heavy trading, reflecting the turmoil on the Prague exchange. Dalal Street responded by . . ."

"Softer," I ordered the bird, and the parrot voice of the Central Nerve Net dipped in audibility to a low reassuring murmur.

A wordbird is a primitive, limited way to interface with CNN, I know, but it was all I was permitted by my altered bioparms. The same incident that had left my neurocircuits a bit scrambled and prone to rhyme-times made it impossible for me to experience virtuality or even plain three-dee anymore.

You see, I was one of the Hiphop Heads.

Not many people remembered the incident. I mean, so much happened nowadays, and things changed so fast. What with the Temp-Trop War and the Grey Goo Booboo intervening—Well, it's not surprising lots of lesser scandals and yocto-minute-wonders were forgotten. After all, the whole affair happened over ten years ago. Though it did affect three million plus-minus people. But scattered across the whole North American Union, the victims were only about 4 percent of the population. Anyway, what happened was this.

Some three million percipients were tuned into Virtual Music Transmission's half-hour show known as "Rap Klassix" when VMT experienced an act of sabotage. (As I recall, the individual or group responsible was never positively identified; suspects ranged from the Sons of Dixie to the Limbo Cannons.) In an instant, before any of the perks knew what was happening or could disengage, VMT's baud rate was tripled, safety overrides were disabled, and new templates were laid over the standard transmission.

The add-on routines consisted of an illegal copy of Microprose's Hardcore Reform, which was normally licensed only to government and gembaitch penal institutions.

The intruder master software did its job. Locking out the volition centers of the perks, taking as its text the innocent raps, Hardcore Reform reamed new neural pathways in three million brains, establishing the fifty-year-old raps as dominant behavior paradigms.

By the time the authorities shut VMT down, three million people had had their brains rewired.

At age thirteen, innocent cheb still living with his mom and sis in the gecekondu projex, I was one of them.

Well, to make a hairy narry less scary, the trope dosers and mccoys eventually fixed most of the neural damage the terrorists had wrought. Except for one minor tic.

> *All us perks who got our brains skew-fried*
> *Would carry inside till the day we true-died*
> *A distributed web of spurting nerve gaps*
> *That made us want to rhyme out our urb raps.*

The best that the big labs like Novo Nordisk and Cantab and NeosePharm could do was batch up a trope that alleviated the symptoms. A daily dose of poemasomes kept the Tourette-like syndrome mostly in check. Except during times of stress, or often just upon waking, or if I ingested any other really radical tropes, I was pretty much normal in my speech and thought patterns.

Naturally there were lawsuits and, eventually, damages awarded. Each victim got ten thousand NU-dollars.

I gave half to my mom. I'm sorry to say that she nulled the whole balance on a single trip to the tribal casinos at Second Mesa, without even enough left for the side excursion to the Grand Canyon by LED-zep that she had always wanted to take. I gave a thousand to my sister, Charmaine, and we all know how she spent hers. As for me, I was determined not to waste my share.

Although before the incident I hadn't really devoted much thought to getting out of the projex, afterwards I was really determined to make a life for myself, having seen the trouble that could come from lying around all day on the prole-dole just inhabiting virtuality. So I daleyed a minor city official and got my name illegally posted to the list of lottery-chosen prospects for CivServ jobs. With the remainder of the eft, I latched the black meds that allowed me to pass the aptitude test with a low grade. (I would have scored higher, but under the stress my essay came out rhymed, and they took off points.) Combined with my official disability status, the score got me my first-ever and still current job: humble Eater Feeder under the boss of our corps, Cengiz Ozturk.

Who was going to be mighty pissed this morning if I was late again.

So I poured Pioneer plantmilk over a bowl of Stressgen Supercereal and slurped it down. I slipped into my blue and gold CivServ Windskin uniform and was almost out the door of my fission-cee when a personal message with a high-priority code got past my filters and loudly interrupted the barely audible CNN feed.

"Corby," squawked the parrot, "this is your mother! I'm calling from home! Get over here right away, it's your sister!"

Before I could argue back that I'd be late for work if I did what she wanted and couldn't she handle things herself, Mom had cut the connection, leaving me with no choice except to jump my rump to her bawl-call.

I kicked a chair and started to swear, then I bolted down the stairs.

On the intrametro train I cudgled my brain. What could have gone amiss with Sis?

Before you could count from two to six, there I was at the gecekondu projex.

The projex had been old when I was a tad; now they looked ancienter than Adam's NAD. Unsmart buildings lined dingy streets; hustling nonfranches littered the plazas of grocrete. Each had a scam or a story to tell; a tale of woe or something to sell. Mutawins and hojats were on stroll-patrol, encountering vexy derision from baby-dolls with sexy sincisions. The scene was total jhuggi jopri, and all my troubled past flooded back on me. But I held my head high and walked on by. In blue and gold, now adult-old, I strode past the various hawkers proud and tall, showing them I didn't belong here at all.

Hoping I could control my rhymes if only I thought about neutral times, I remembered the history of the projex.

Way back in the teens, during the Last Jihad, just after the Fall of Istanbul, the IMF began allotting refugees to various countries, cities, and bioregions. Chicago had gotten mostly Turks and a smattering of Crobanians, who had all been forcibly funnelled into the hastily constructed projex.

One of these flee-gees had been my dad.

Dad had fallen in love with a local girl named Chita Garvey—my mom, of course—who happened then to be a very xinggan Cubaitian some sixteen years old. Dad's relatives weren't too uptaking about the eventual multicult marriage, which was soon followed by the birth of a son, then a daughter.

One day when I was eight and Sis was just born, Dad and a hardline cousin named Zeki got into a serious argument about how Dad had betrayed his heritage. Zeki claimed Dad had been verraten und verkauft. Words escalated into blows, and that's when cruel cuz put the boot in.

Out of his pocket, Zeki whipped a military model neural shunt (Snowy surplus from Operation Rock the Casbah) and slapped it on Dad's neck. Quickly burrowing spineward, the boot grabbed control of Dad's motor impulses and literally forced Dad to choke himself to true-death.

Ever since I had kind of been the man of the house.

Which was why Mom was turning to me now, even though I no longer lived with her and Sis.

As I climbed the worn steps of familiar old Building Nine (referred to croak-jokingly by its residents as the Golden Horn), the slow shadow of a laser-entrained dirigible passed over me, and I sadly recalled Mom's long-unsatisfied moonbeam-dream of visiting the Grand Canyon in person. It seemed like everyday strife-life just had a way of mind-grinding a person right down. Look how much eft and trouble I had gone through just to land this cysting lite-servo job, and how events like today's kept conspiring to put me in danger of losing it.

If only, I thought as I rode the smelly elevator upwards (the car was liberally bespotted with the glandular signatures of rival tribes and zokus), if only I could do something really uptaking to show everyone what I was capable of. Maybe then I could get some real security in my life. . . .

Little did I know then the fate-date the near future had in store for me.

On the forty-fourth floor I came to the family door. I could hear Mom and Charmaine yelling right through the macromolecule walls, so I didn't bother knocking but just palmed the sweat-vetter gene-screener and stepped right in.

A burst of overdue deja vu hit me. Nothing had changed in the year since I had moved on, and that meant nothing had changed since time began. My childhood Build-a-Cell kit still sat on a shelf. The aging Philips virtuality rig still sported spots of dumbpaint from an attempt at redecoration three years ago. The forever-dying orchidenia plant still clung to life.

Mom had her back to me, blocking sight of Charmaine. When Mom turned and stepped aside, I could see what had made her roughride and chide so snide.

Charmaine had added feelers to go along with her old familiar antennae. And a row of itchy, twitchy buglegs running down each side of her torso. Her clothing had been grommetted to accommodate the new members.

"Oh, no, Charm," I said. "I thought you had given up on the Roaches? . . ."

My sister had a perez-pretty face, despite the wispy, feathery, living proteoglycan antenna-rods projecting out a good meter from her forehead, iridescent black. But now, messed up with grief, anger, fear, and tears, her face looked really bug-ugly.

"I'll never give up on the Roaches! I was just waiting to add more mods until I got enough eft!"

Mom burst in. "Tell your brother how you got two thousand NU-dollars! Go ahead, tell him!"

Charmaine straightened up defiantly. "Just like you, Ma. I won it at the cats."

Mom glared at me for support. "You heard her. She stole her own mother's stake for the track—my one little luxury—and bet it all on one race. She, jeune fille estupida, who couldn't tell a cheetah from an ocelot!"

"I won, didn't I? And I paid you back double."

"But look how you spent the rest! Mutilating your beautiful body like that!"

"It's my thorax, and I'll do what I want with it! Besides, you're one to talk! You ain't hardly no Miss Baseline Betty yourself!"

I realized that there was something different about Mom that hadn't registered in the confusion till now. She had had her chocolate complexion spotted-dotted like one of the racing cats she loved. And translucent feline whiskers bristled around her kisser.

"Pah! My little vanity is like my memere's old-fashioned eyeshadow compared to your craziness. And besides, the belle gato is a mammal like us. But roaches—"

That was the match to Charmaine's fuse.

"Go ahead!" she exploded. "Say it! Roaches are bugs! Well, you're not insulting me by saying that. Bugs are glorious! They're not our inferiors, they're our superiors! Bugs were here long before mammals, and they'll be here long after we kill ourselves off! I'm proud to be a Roach! And as soon as I get some more money, I'm gonna get a full carapace! Neurocrine and Berlex are in a price war, and shells're getting cheap as prostaglandins! Weevil has one, and it's beautiful!''

Mom wailed. ''Ai-yi-yi! Damballah, Erzulie, and Jesus save me from this disrespectful girl!''

All of a sudden, my legs felt like puddin'. I had heard this whole argument a hundred times before. Their life was on replay, mine was on delay. How long was I going to be trapped while these two yapped? Didn't they see I had my own probs that made my head throb? I was trying to make something of myself after a bad start, but these two fighting were ripping out my heart.

I sat down all dreary-weary in a chair, and my eyes fell on a fishbowl tabletopped near there. In it swam four flaking trilobites. The sight of the watery wigglers reminded me of my job, and I shot to my feet.

''Listen, you're not going to solve anything by yelling at each other. That's no way to act for a daughter and mother. Ma, you and Charmaine both need to get your fingers off the hot buttons. What's done is done and should be forgotten.'' I had a sudden inspiration. ''I'm going to take Charmaine to work with me. We can talk about things and see what we see. I'll bring her back tonight, and we'll all have a meal together.''

Mom smiled. ''You were always such a good boy, Corby. I knew I could count on you to talk some sense into la cucaracha here.''

Charmaine stiffened. ''Ma, I'm warning you—''

I grabbed Charmaine by the elbow, brushing one of her new abdominal legs, which jerked reflexively. I hustled her out the door.

''I'll make your favorite, Corby,'' Mom called out down the hall. ''Grilled mammoth steaks!''

We were on the train heading crosstown before Charmaine would talk to me.

"Mammoth steaks!" she huffed. "I'm lucky if she nukes me a lupinovine chop!"

I felt myself relax a little, the annoying rhymes retreating into some unprobed lobe. At least Charmaine wasn't going to stick to her sullen silence. Maybe there was a chance to straighten things out.

"You've got to let up on Ma, Charm. You know she's not exactly the domestic type. And life's been hard for her since Dad died. You shouldn't block her receptors about her gambling, for instance. It's really the one pleasure she's got these days."

Charmaine stiffened, and her new abdominal additions began to wave like the legs of a stepped-on roach. It seemed she didn't quite have full control of them yet.

"What about me? Ain't I nothing to give her some pleasure? Why can't she take some interest in me and my life, huh? She's always praising you to the skies. But me—all I get is her gleet and pus."

"Charm, there's no need to get nasty. Look, Ma likes me better because somehow, I think, I remind her of Dad. And she's proud of me because I got out of the projex. Not that this job is anything much, believe me. As for why she keeps catalyzing your leukotrines, it's—"

"I know, I know, it's the Roaches. Well, I got news for you and Ma. I am not a larva any more, I'm an adult. And my mind is made up. The Roaches are the best thing that ever happened to me. Once a Roach, always a Roach. And pretty soon, I'm gonna be a Roach all the way! And it won't be any too soon. Because big things are gonna happen any day now, and the Roaches—"

Charmaine stopped herself.

"What? What kind of sneaky-freaky things are the Roaches up to?"

Folding all eight of her arms—two baseline and six add-ons—across her body, Charmaine clammed up, and nothing I said would get her to reveal anything further.

When the train pulled into our stop, we got in line to

get off and found ourselves behind a Visible Man. The fright-sight of all his working viscera through his transparent gut-bucket made me want to hurl my cereal.

What a mayday payday this was turning out to be!

Aboveground, we stood for a zepto on the tree-green lakeshore. A tart breeze flustered our hair. Sunlight played on the clean waters of Lake Mitch. Not far from the transit stop loomed the headquarters of the Eater Corps, a subdivision of the GLB Authority. Toward this, Charm and I made our way down paulownia-shady ped-paths.

EC HQ used to be the Shedd Aquarium, back in the last century. But like all old-time zoos and such, with the advent of splices the Shedd had quickly gone out of business. With transgenics of all types—many of them more exotic than anything nature had ever produced—visible and touchable (even, in the case of a Hedonics Plus product, beddable), to be found in street, home, and store, public interest in seeing dull caged specimens had nulled out. All the retro exhibitors had quickly sold their stock as raw lab material and folded. And as far as a zoo's utility as a repository of endangered species went—well, the Great Restockings had ended that use.

But this old-time tourist diz still retained some connection to animals, which I frequently had cause to think on.

At the door I met up with one of my proxies and fellow Eater Feeders, Sharpy, who seemed in a bit of a flushed rush.

''How's Ozzie this worn morn?'' I asked a bit nervously.

Sharpy's face was a mass of long drooping folds and corrugated wrinkles, like his doggie namesake. Even when happy, he looked doomy-gloomy. And as now, when actually preoccuplexed, he could make a technogoth resemble a gameshow vannawhite on Pollyannamide.

''The Khan has me scared. He's just not his old apop-tositic self. He's given all of us the day off to attend an official blyfest over in the Loop. Some kind of sensitivity training in how to deal with Anti-Em demonstrators. Now I ask you, would the Khan we know and detest shed a yocto-tear about the feelings of some friggin' rifkins?''

Inexplicable as Ozzie's actions were, they seemed good news for a change. At last on this crazy day, some-thing was finally going my way, and I felt zetta-okay. Until Sharpy's next words.

''Except you. He's been asking everyone if they've seen you yet. Seems he has a special chore just for Cadet Corby.''

''Mighty Ogun! Now my ass is grass, no sass!''

''Not necessarily. Remember, I told you, he's not act-ing like the old Khan. Maybe he'll go easy on you. But you'd better get in there soon.''

''Right. Thanks for the warning, Sharp.''

''No skin off my dewlaps. Hey, who's the Love Bug? Want to spend the day with me, Cricket?''

During our conversation, Charmaine had stood in bored silence, wiggling her new legs in a programmed sequence to gain greater control over them. (I hoped she was remembering to take her cecropins.) But now she bristled at Sharpy's remarks.

''Eat pyrethrum, chordate!''

''Charmaine, please. She's my little sister, Sharp, and she's not in a good mood today. I apologize for her.''

''No mammal has to apologize for a Roach!''

''Put it in a vacuole, Charm. Listen, Sharpy—I'll see you later. I'd better go take my bitter meds from the head.''

I hauled Charmaine along to the office of Cengiz Oz-turk.

In the anteroom, I pushed Charmaine down onto the Biospherics slouch-couch. ''Stay here. We haven't finished talking about the probs of our little germline yet. I'll only be a zepto—I hope.''

"What am I gonna do while I wait?''

"I don't care if you count your hairs. Raster some vid, you selfish kid. Can't you tell I'm gonna catch hell?''

This rough talk—which her loving brother never used toward her—seemed to waken Charmaine to the variety of my anxiety, and she sulkily picked up a pair of retinal painters provided for waiters.

"Olivetti Eye Blasters,'' she sarcastically intoned. "These are shit.''

The expression on my face caused Charmaine to shut up and don the glasses.

I entered the zig-zaggy light-trap to Ozturk's inner sanctum.

Cengiz Ozturk was a veteran of the Last Jihad. An officer of the secular Turkish government, he had been among the last evacuees from Istanbul during its seige by the Jihad's shahada-sicarios and consequently had caught the worst of their assault, taking a hit from a bizarre new weapon.

There used to be a basal disease called xeroderma pigmentosum. Those who had it were so sensitive to sunlight that an average day in the pre-ozone-hole sun would give them cancers and other cyto-malfunctions.

Ozturk had been hit with a designer infective agent based on this retro disease. Now it lurked ineradicable in his soma.

A few photons at the frequency of visible light impinging on his skin today would be enough to trip a cascade of death-agonists throughout his body, resulting in a yotta-painful death.

He had been med-evacked in a light-tight homeopod and installed in a null-photon underground facility, where bonestretchers and cellsmelters could investigate his condition. But in the end all that could be done for

him was to adapt his vision to infrared and find him an
alpha-symbland desk job.

Which had turned out to be director of the Eater Corps,
my boss. And needless to say, this whole experience had
left him a less-than-cheerful sort.

As I felt my way down the last zag, I braced myself
for the Dow-Hughes shrink-wrap that was the final safety
barrier between Ozturk and the world.

I met the bedsheet of pliable film face on and pressed
ahead. I really hated this. The semiorganic film wrapped
itself around me from head to toe, sealing shut, pinching
off behind, more drawn from the dispenser and ready for
the next entrant. Mouth-and nose-holes opened of their
own accord. My useless eyes remained hooded.

Now I was no danger. Had I been carrying a weapon,
I couldn't have reached it beneath the wrap. Even if I
had a flashlight in hand, ready to fire, the film would
have frustrated it by invading the mechanism or reflexively immobilizing my twitchy trigger finger. Sure, there
were sophisto ways around the wrap, but who really
wanted to smoke an old soldier like Ozturk anyhow? The
extra security was just paranoia and status-flash on his
part.

I stopped just inside the door. "Uh, Captain Ozturk?
It's me, Cadet Corby. . . ."

The room was flooded with low-freak illuminating
rads, and I could almost feel Ozturk sizing me up with
his altered eyes as I stood here blind. What I put up with
for this job! But it was still better than the projex—or so
I told myself.

At last Ozturk spoke. His voice sounded funny, mechanical almost, and I could see what Sharpy had meant
about his not being his old self.

"Cadet, I need you to help conduct a small experiment. You are aware that the terrorist splice known as
Krazy Kat has been reported in the vicinity?"

"Yes, sir."

"Well, I'm very concerned that he not subvert our Eaters. Accordingly, I've redesigned their dietary leash. I'd like to run a field trial before switching over entirely, however. Make sure the NOAEL is as simulated. Please take this sample and feed it to the Rivermouth Colony."

I extended my hand slowly, so as not to trip the wrap's freeze-reaction. Into my outstretched palm was placed a packet.

"Do you wish to dataglove the leash's new molecular structure?" Ozturk asked.

"I'm sorry, sir, I can't use datagloves. It's my disability—"

A strange satisfied tone crept in Ozturk's voice. "Oh, of course, I should have remembered. Very well, Cadet, that will be all."

I held my breath, waiting for some reprimand about being late. But it never came. I had the impression, in fact, that I now stood alone, Ozturk having disappeared into his attached living quarters. I didn't wait to get kissed or dissed, but figured I was dismissed.

Midway through the light-trap, I was freed by a mist from the shrink-wrap. Gathering up Charmaine—who of course had to complain I was interrupting her S&M vid of "Hot Purple Pain"—I signed out a Skoda Skooter and a Taligent poqetpal and got ready to carry out my assignment.

Riding north through city streets, Charmaine behind me on the saddle-seat, her pinchy insectlegs digging into my ribs as she hugged me, I pondered why Captain Ozturk had chosen me for this mission—it bugged me. Was it a prelude to promotion, a mark of my devotion? Or just sheer chance, no cause for flights of romance?

When no answer came clear, I pushed the question to the rear and motored on.

Soon we arrived at the point on the shore opposite the Rivermouth Colony, roughly six blocks south of Oak Street Beach, where lucky franches basked in the heat.

Charmaine and I stood on the low grocrete jetty painted with the EC insignia and reserved for official use—vehicle moorings and Eater feedings and such—and I pointed out the Eater habitat to her, some half-klick offshore.

Shading her eyes against the lake-sparkle, Charmaine said, "Wow, that's big! You know, I never bothered to come look at this before. Kinda like a New Yorker never visiting Television City. Is it made out of—rocks?"

"Stones, mud, trees, driftwood, old car parts—whatever the Eaters can scavenge from the lake. They're master builders."

There was a note of pride in my voice that was there by choice. After all these years of working with the Eaters, I had become one of their virtue-repeaters. The splices were honest, humble, and dutiful. And despite naysayers, I even believed they were beautiful.

And to think that without a terrorist act, the Eaters would be fiction, not fact!

Twenty years ago, the first designer-waterweed invasion of the GLB had occurred. The initial invader had been a modified Canadian pondweed, *Elodea canadensis*, introduced into the St. Lawrence Seaway. Its repro-rate was low-mag compared to what followed: *Elodea* took a whole week to double its initial biomass. Well, the GLB eradicated by lo-tech smart-chem means the infestation of pondweed, only to find itself attacked by an even fiercer milfoil-alligator-weed cultivar. They zapped that too, but it was just the edge of the wedge.

For next came the infamous water-hyacinth/kariba-weed splice.

Within days the entire GLB was declared a disaster zone of plus-minus one kilonader.

Now, a youngster like Sis, who hadn't even been born at the time of the disaster, might wonder just how much trouble a little nontoxic flowering aquatic plant could cause. Based on the training materials I'd seen, and my own toddler-memory of being taken to look at the enormous floating mats of vegetation, I'd say the trouble was yotta-nasty.

The hykariba (as it came to be called) doubled its numbers every two days, individual plants breaking off from their clonal parents and drifting off to colonize virgin territory. Coalescing in enormous floating rafts two meters thick in some places, the hykariba soon blanketed the entire GLB. The plants impeded shipping, clogged the intake pipes of industrial and drinking-water plants, and contributed to flooding by displacing watermass. As the oldest of the shortlife plants began to decay, they used up available oxygen, axphyxiating fish and phytoplankton. The stench from the big finny kills was incredible. As a last insult-result, the mats were excellent breeding grounds for mosquitoes.

It took bioremediation forces from across the whole Union to null the invader. Before they succeeded, the genetically identical mass of plants grew to form the largest single organism in the history of the world.

One of the weapons in the fight had been the Eaters.

Hastily but deftly morrowed out of nutria, manatee, and, of course, human germlines (which is what always got the rifkins so upset), the hykariba-hungry Eaters—otherwise known as mantrias, nutratees, or coypu-cows—were introduced into the devastated ecosystem as fast as they could be turned out by Invitrogen and Prizm, Biocine and Catalytica.

Once the crisis was over the Eaters remained, first line in the GLB's defense against future intruders. They patrolled and roamed in the waters they called home. Restrained by diet leashes, they always returned to their beaches. Where they were met by a Feeder such as yours truly, who pampered his charges with applause unduly.

"How do you get them to come?" Charmaine asked with what I hoped was unfeigned interest.

"Like this."

I took the poqetpal out and tapped in my private code. Then I stuck the unit underwater, where it began to broadcast its ultrasonic call.

Within minutes, the first Eater arrived.

Big Eater.

Head of the colony, Big Eater was larger by half than any other nutratee and twice as smart. Befitting his leader's rank, the head bull was the only one in the colony who had the speech feach.

Gushing up out of the water like a furry brown torpedo, Big Eater sprayed us in his usual greeting, and Charmaine squealed. Gripping the jetty with his crafty paws, he left the bulk of his body still underwater. Rivulets ran from his coypu-cow muzzle, off ears and jowls that were part of his special gene-puzzle.

Big Eater smiled. "Cor-by. How are you?"

I tousled the sleek oily fur. "Doing okay, Big Guy. How's the missus and all the little calves?"

"The she is good. The lit-tle ones are good. We eat. We watch for bad things. We sleep. We build. Life is full."

"Great, great, I'm glad to hear it."

Charmaine squatted down beside me. "Can—can I pet him too?"

"Sure. Big Guy, this is my sister, Charmaine."

"Char-maine, hel-lo."

I watched Sis instinctively scratch Big Eater's favorite spot, right behind his ears. She seemed to have reverted to her innocent chrono-years. "Oooo, he's a real teddy-weddy, yes he is. . . ."

Unable to resist a prod, I said, "I thought you Roaches weren't keen on mammals. . . ."

Charmaine instantly got all hard. "Humans are what we hate, the privileged ones. These poor splices—they don't bear any responsibility for what they are. We show solidarity with all downtrodden species. And someday—"

"Someday what?" Charmaine didn't answer. "You know, you're almost talking Krazy Kat-style trash. You might even get arrested for it if the wrong people heard."

Standing, Charmaine said, "I don't care. We're willing to fight for what we believe in."

Before we could argue anymore, Big Eater interrupted. "Why did you call me, Cor-by?"

"Oh, right. It's time to try a new pill." I opened the packet Captain Ozturk had handed me.

Big Eater seemed puzzled. "It has not been e-nough days for more pills."

"I know. But this is a special pill. Protection."

"Pro-tec-tion?" Big Eater looked fierce. "Who wants to harm the pod?"

"A bad splice," I said, ignoring Charmaine's impolite snort.

Big Eater pondered. "I will get the o-thers."

He was gone with a splash, we hung in like a rash, soon they came en masse.

Now, most Eater Feeders, lazy CivServs that they are, just broadcast the pills on the waters and assume every coypu-cow will snatch one. They don't really care if an individual misses out and dies a nasty programmed deficiency death shortly thereafter, all hemorrhages and tachycardia. After all, they're just splices, right? You can always breed more.

I didn't buy it. I always fed my charges individually. It was my job.

So now, as Big Eater watched proudly from the sidelines—he was always the last to get his dose, insuring that all his pod were provided for first—I doled out the new pills one by one to the mantrias as they surfaced, gulped, and disappeared, a never-ending stream of whiskered snouts.

About halfway through—twenty minutes and fifty mantrias—I noticed out of the corner of one eye that a young nutratee had approached Big Eater and was chittering something at him. Big Eater swam up to the jetty.

Before I knew what was happening, Big Eater had knocked the remaining pills from my grasp and into the water.

"Bad pills!" Big Eater said. "Make cows swim mad."

"What? What do you mean?"

"Cows don't go home. Go to Sta-tion Eight."

Station Eight was one of the artificial islands erected in Lake Mitch to help prosecute the hykariba war. Abandoned for many years, it was nothing more than a graffiti-sprayed trysting spot, or a place for a picnic when the weather got hot.

"I don't know what to say. It wasn't supposed to work out this way—"

"Big Eater must go. Must help the sick ones."

"No, wait! We'll come with you."

I hopped onto an EC jetski. Charmaine dropped down behind me.

"Charm—"

"Forget it! You wanted me along. You're not gonna leave me behind just when things get interesting!"

Big Eater was already gone. I didn't have time to argue.

I gave the ski its codes and powered up the flownodes. We shot off across the water like Neptune and his daughter, outpacing the remaining Eaters.

Once we were beyond the Eater construction, Station Eight appeared, a small isle dotted with some crumbling structures overgrown with vines and weeds from wind-sown seeds.

As we drew nearer, things became clearer. From a few meters offshore, this is what we saw: nutratrees lay on an old launch ramp, while around them stood figures fussing with straps and clamps.

Charmaine recognized them before I did.

"It's—they're Roaches!"

I didn't like the scene and I tried to swerve, but there

came a volley of shots and I lost my nerve.

"Beach it! Now!" yelled a gun-toting Roach.

I ran the jetski aground and climbed down.

Charmaine rashly approached the hot-tempered Roach. "Weevil—?"

The Roach eyed us meanly with Orthoptera optics. Resplendent in his winged shell, he had us pinned like bugs with his gun barrel.

"I don't know what you're doing here, Charmaine— how you found us, or whether you're here to help or hinder us—but you can't be allowed to delay our plans. These vars won't stay responsive forever."

"What are you doing to them?" I demanded.

Weevil focused now on my uniform. "A CivServ boy, huh? This must be your brother, Charmaine. It seems we were right not to trust you enough to let you in on the scheme."

"What scheme?"

"These transgenics have been suborned by Krazy Kat himself. A new trope. They're running on a carefully timed set of instructions now. Each one is going to carry an explosive pack up the Chicago River. We're going to breach all the underground utility tunnels beneath the river and flood the whole Loop. All kibernetic maintenance will be brought to a standstill."

"But the poor Eaters . . ." said Charmaine.

"A few expendables in the cause of freeing their kind."

"No!" I shouted.

Charmaine tried to reason with Weevil. "It's okay to hurt the humans. They deserve it. But can't you spare the splices?"

"Too late. The plan won't tolerate changes. We have to detonate the explosives as soon as they're in place, or risk detection. And that just doesn't give the cows time to escape. And who really cares? So long as we win. Both of you now—over there, behind that wall."

Under the gun's threat it looked like our sunset. We turned to march off.

And then they came.

A coypu-cow is hardly a dolphin, but they can swim awfully fast and flow like a fountain. Out of the water the remaining loyal Eaters launched themselves up the slippery slope, each one a hundred kilos of wet flesh, that's dope. They bowled over the Roaches like a living wave, coming their human Feeder to save. Knocked the Bugs off their feet, pinning them to the wet grocrete.

I rushed that evil Weevil then, cracking his carapace with a kick and a grin. Gun in hand, I was now topman.

Down to the waterside I sped, looking for one familiar head.

"Cor-by," said Big Eater. "This is what we need pro-tec-tion from?"

"Not any more, Big Guy. More like the other way 'round."

Well, of course it was Krazy Kat himself whom I had talked to in the dark of Captain Ozturk's office. Poor Ozzie—or his corpse anyhow—had been at the interview too. The bad splice had picked me on purpose. You see:

> He knew I couldn't handle a glove,
> Thought I'd be sloppy when push came to
> shove.
> Didn't know I took pride in my work—
> Made that Kat look like a yotta-jerk!

Not many humans can claim they've been in a room with the notorious Kat and walked away, and for a while I was the metamedium darling of the hour. It seemed only natural for the EC to reward me with the Khan's job.

And as for Charmaine—well, she was naturally pretty soured on the Roaches, and the Eater Corps was now one Cadet short, and I was head of the Corps—

And you know what kind of town Chicago is.

🗲 The Boot

I WAS SITTING IN MY OFFICE, FEELING AS BORED as the caretaker of a New Mexico solar farm on a cloudy day and wishing for a client. After two months of inactivity, I didn't much care what kind. Any client would do. A socket looking for her runaway plug. A gerry wanting a line to the hottest new semi-illegal, demi-sanctioned golden-age dreamscene. (This year, the hundredth anniversary of Woodstock made that particular nostalgiaware top of the bops, especially for the original attendees who still survived.) A ten-year-old hoping to siliconeslide his way through the legal thicket that blocked the path to full franchise. (The NU Parliament had just lowered the age to twelve, but even that envelope was being pushed by the newest tropes.) Even a grieved and angry spouse itching to get the burst on the mate she suspected of weekly sex-change flings with maffs. I had had them all before, at one time or another, and would no doubt get them all again someday. And when I did, I would take their eft and do what they wanted, no questions asked. Someone with finances as precarious as mine can't afford the same scruples as your average trumps and forbeses. It's an augie-doggie eat augie-doggie world, after all.

But right now it looked like I wouldn't have to worry too much about exercising my ethics. Already noon, and the day was shaping up as dull as a debate between the Green and Conservative candidates for governor of Cuba. In other words, an instant-replay of the past sixty. Outside my self-cleaning windows (one of the nice features of this new building; but I was starting to wonder how much longer I could afford the rent), sunlight glinted off the Charles River. On the far bank bulked the black silicrobe-built bubble the authorities had hastily erected around MIT ten years ago, during the Grey Goo Booboo. The hemisphere visible above-ground continued below, forming a completely enclosed sphere. It had gone up in less than twenty-four hours, but it had seemed like as many days. I remember watching, from my front-row seat, along with the rest of the world, as divisions of NU militia, guided by the top cricks and watsons, kept the mocklife tendrils and feelers at bay with water-cannons pumping enzymatic lysing fluid, until the silicrobes could complete the container. No one knew what, if anything, was now going on inside the shell. There hadn't been time to engineer any sensors in. The dome was still patrolled around the clock, by guards in liftcages. It was just another thing you lived with.

I was thinking about popping open a cheer-beer and rastering some thrid-vid (I had become addicted to day-time gameshows, particularly *Your Life's on the Line*), when I heard footsteps in the hall outside my door. I hastily took my feet down off my desk and tried to project the image that I was busier than a four-armed bartender at happy hour.

The footsteps didn't go past my door, as so many had before. Instead, there came a knock.

I checked the security screen, liked what I saw, and said, "Come in." The door unlatched itself and swung open.

She had on a stylish suit in acidic purple and orange.

The jacket had asymmetrical lapels trimmed with blue vat-grown mink; on the larger one was pinned an orchidenia that I could smell from six feet away. Her skirt hung down to her ankles on the left side, but revealed her whole right leg. She wore chrome chopines that added four inches to her height. Her black curly hair was piled high, with a blonde curl dangling down over her forehead. She had canary-yellow irises and a small tight mouth. On one cheek she wore a small love-cicatrix shaped like the astrological symbol for Venus.

"Please," she said, "could you cover the windows."

"Lady, we're on the fortieth floor—"

"You can't tell what optics are out there. Nanocams are everywhere these days. Please, do it."

I shrugged and spoke. "Shutters."

Sheets of opaque piezoplastic that had been curled up at the top of the windows stiffened down like tongues across the glass, under the impulse of a mild electric current. I boosted the lights.

"Have a seat," I offered. "Can I get you something to drink?"

She sat and crossed bare right leg over left. I saw the tattoo of a panther she wore on her outer upper thigh. Every thirty seconds it opened its mouth in a silent snarl.

"Yes, thank you. I'll have a Foma Froth, if you've got it."

I kicked the splice sleeping at my feet. "Hamster, wake up, we've got a visitor."

Hamster opened its eyes and blinked. It preened its whiskers and said, "Yes, sir, my help is needed now?"

"Damn right, you dumb trans. Get a cheer-beer for me, and a Foma Froth for the lady."

Hamster got up and adjusted its short tunic. It walked to the small magnetic fridge, got the drinks, served them, then asked, "Will that be all that is needful, sir?"

"Yeah, go back to sleep."

Hamster did just that.

"Cheapest transgenic they make," I apologized.

She waved her hand negligently. "No matter. My name is Geneva Hippenstiel-Imhausen. May I see your licenses?"

I passed my ID card over. Showing topmost was my Massachusetts PI license. She repeatedly flexed the card to reveal my North American Union, EuroComm, IMF, Brazilian, and orbital credentials. She flexed it one final time, and a naked pinup of the thrid-vid-star Siouxsie Sexcrime in one of her more notorious poses was revealed. I had to admire Geneva's composure. No expression, just a faint reddening of her cicatrix. She handed the card back. "It seems to reveal everything I need to know about you."

"That puts you a leg up on me," I said, eyeing the leg in question. "Could I ask what you're here for?"

She leaned forward. "I want you to put a boot on someone."

Well. That took me by surprise. I wouldn't have guessed that was what she needed.

"You do do boots, don't you?" she asked, lifting one neatly scribed eyebrow.

"Oh, sure, but they're tricky. It'll cost more than my average rates."

"That's no matter. There's much at stake."

I mentally raised my rates by half. "I'll need to know more before I can definitely take the case. Who are you booting, and what does he have that's not his?"

She sighed. "It's my husband. Jurgen von Bulow. He's made off with the latest trope from the company I own. Perhaps you've heard of Hippenstiel-Imhausen? We're a German firm, specializing in bioactives. Our most recent product is still in the experimental stages. It's an explosive new neurotropin. Even to speak of it now is rather risky. That's why I wanted the shutters down. And I assume your office is recently swept. . . ."

I nodded. She continued, rather reluctantly.

"What my husband took is a trope that allows stochastic reasoning, insight into the dynamics of chaos. We
were hoping to have it perfected before word of it
reached our competitors. But my husband absconded
with some doses of a test-batch and plans to use them,
I'm certain. He'll ruin our secrecy. And, if anyone ever
got to him and unwound the codes from his blood-
stream—there go our patents."

"Why'd your husband steal from his own company?
Doesn't he stand to gain from your eventual profits?"

Geneva looked both disgusted and embarrassed. "My
husband married into the company. I control it. He's
something of a wastrel, and I've had to keep him on a
short leash. Apparently it was too galling, and he's finally
slipped it."

"I don't understand enough about this new trope.
How's he going to use it? What makes you so sure he
won't just sell it to one of your rivals?"

"No, no, that's not his plan. You see, he loves to gamble. And this trope—"

"You're not claiming it'll let him beat the odds—"

She nodded. "Exactly right. Insight into the underly-
ing patterns of apparently random events."

Mother of mutants, this was big. I redoubled my fees.

"The regular authorities—"

"Too many leaks. I need a single man."

I stood up then and walked around to her side. I raised
a hand to her face. She didn't flinch. I lightly dragged
my roughened thumb over her cicatrix. The love-scar was
packed with more pleasure 'ceptors and nervepaths than
a tenth-generation biochip. When she climaxed, her panther reared up on its hind legs.

After she opened her eyes, I said, "I'll bet you do."

I don't talk to anyone on a personal level much anymore
since my wife left me. Mostly it's just hard raps with the
perps and the bad numbers and the dirty-harrys and the

clients and the streetlife I encounter in my investigations. And when I don't have a case going, there's just Hamster to talk to.

I still can't say why I bought the little transgenic. It wasn't a deadly model like some guys packed. The most it could do in that line was give you a bite that might get infected in a week or two if you didn't wash regularly. It wasn't particularly smart. Every command had to be phrased with a minimum of ambiguity, or you'd run the risk of a major quench. Like the time I told it to "fill the car up with methane. . . ." It couldn't play any games more complicated than checkers, and it lost every time. And Lord knows it wasn't a playpet. Sterile, technically female, Hamster had as much sex appeal as a cold mackerel. It was essentially shapeless, and its special diet made it smell like wet hay. Not offensive, but hardly sexy. Now, if I had been able to afford a Golden Colt or a Snakehips, that would have been another story. . . .

Still and all, I was used to the splice. It was sort of like a pair of old slippers, or a chair worn to my shape, except that it could nuke supper and clean the office and nod when I bounced ideas off it.

That's why I was talking to it, now that Geneva had left.

"I guess the first thing we'll have to do is head out to Logan and see if we can pick up von Bulow's trail from there. His flight arrived three days ago, but I've had colder starts."

"Yes, you have, sir. I am certain you have, although I cannot remember exactly when. I am trying to think now. This is hard work, sir, just give me a moment. There was one time, I am sure I will think of it in a minute—"

"Hamster—"

"Yes, sir?"

"Cut the crap and get me my gun."

I don't pack deadly force. No flashlights or splat-pistols or pellet-throwers for me. In most tense situations, I prefer the cool, calm voice of reason, or flight. If I have to take someone out, I do it temporarily, with a shocker. All you need is an inch of bare skin to deliver a patterned jolt of current that overloads the higher neural functions, such as making the decision to kill a harmless PI.

I slapped the gun Hamster passed me to my hip, where its biopoly barrel mated to the holster-patch on my pants. It would be there when I needed it, coming free at the touch of my hand alone, thanks to onboard sweat-vetters. I opened a desk drawer and took out my boot unit and a pad of fluorescent-orange adhesive stickers. I slipped them into an outer pocket on my vest, where I could reach them easily. Then I headed for the airport, Hamster tagging along. In my mind, I was already spending the EC money Geneva was going to pay me.

Once at Logan, I headed straight for the cab stand. I was betting that a plug with von Bulow's tastes wouldn't have taken mass transit.

Sure enough, the third cab I questioned was the one he had ridden in. It was a Turing Level Two and had all the quirks of its kind, including a high redundancy factor.

"I must see authorization first. If you have authorization, I must see it. Please show your authorization."

I fed my credentials into a slot. The cab seemed satisfied and spat them out. "Yes, sir, I picked up the human you describe. Here is his picture."

The cab flashed a view of von Bulow that matched the digitals Geneva had shown me: dirty blonde hair atop a craggy profile and dangerous lilac eyes. Handsome the way a purebred basal dog like a Borzoi is and likely just as neurotic and skittish. Some of those frigging European aristocrats are so inbred, especially now that they can fix up any little congenital trouble like leukemia or hemophilia, that they make the king of England look like a mongrel. This was not going to be an easy boot, I could feel it all the way down to my mitochondria.

"Here is his pedigree, as read by my chromosniffers, sir." Wave after wave of numbers and metagrafix rolled across the screen.

"Okay, give me a hardcopy of both." The pedigree would be handy if von Bulow changed his looks. But I wasn't betting on that, as he seemed a self-satisfied type, too obsessed and complacent to imagine anyone might be after him.

"Where'd you drop him?"

"Drop, sir? I am not allowed to injure humans—"

"What was his destination?"

"The Copley Plaza."

I should have guessed. It figured he'd vector for the biggest casino in town.

I drove so fast back into the city that my car's shell could barely keep up with the aerodynamic changes, shifting shape a dozen times a second. A metro dirty-harry in his fan-lifter buzzed me, but I transmitted a priority code that made him veer off. This case looked like it was going to be wrapped up sooner than I could have hoped.

At the Copley I went straight to the registration console. It was actually being manned by a human, but that's just the Copley's policy: no splices on their staff, and all the ones owned by guests kept discreetly out of sight (except, of course, for bodyguards). I had to check Hamster at the stable.

The clerk was a piebald black man wearing a topknot laced with gold wire. I flashed him my card. "Mass Pee Eye." He blinked twice, without expression. I looked at my own ID. The stupid cab had left Siouxsie Sexcrime uppermost when it had read the card. I flexed the plaz back to the right creds.

"Yes, sir, how may I help you?"

Slipping my left hand into my vest pocket, I palmed the boot. "Do you have a guest named Jurgen von Bulow?"

The clerk ran a mental eidetic. "He just checked out this morning, sir."

Bugshit! "Let me guess. He broke the bank, wired his winnings to Paraguay, and caught a suborb south."

"No sir, not quite. Mister von Bulow lost heavily. In fact, had we not taken the precaution of pre-debiting his proxy—as we do with anyone who intends to play the games—he would not have had enough to pay his bill. As it was, he left here very much down on his luck. As I might phrase it, were I off-duty, 'His lily-white ass was dragging.' "

That didn't make sense. Either the casino games were rigged worse than a Fourth-World election, or the stolen trope was junkbond. Neither alternative seemed likely.

"Did he happen to mention his plans?"

"No, sir, he did not."

Dead end. I turned ruefully away.

Something bumped my ankles.

I looked down.

It was Flipper.

Flipper was a fishboy I knew from around town. He was a Fuser, a member of a sect that sought personally to atone for the extermination of the dolphins. (They claimed humanity's guilt was not diminished by the subsequent restocking of the seas.) Flipper's arms had been melded to his torso, his legs fused shut from toes to crotch. He wore a slick grey suit that handled bodily functions and made him look like a sleek torpedo. He rode a little wheeled dolly that ran on fuel cells.

"Hey, Flip, what's metabolizing?"

"Not much. But I heard what you were asking the clerk just now."

"Why don't we go outside?"

I walked—and Flipper rolled—out the Copley. On the busy sidewalk, no one paid any attention to us.

"So, whatcha know, Flip?"

"I was hanging around the casino all day yesterday,

hoping to hit a big winner up for a donation to the church. I saw the plug you're looking for. He was really off the far-end of the spectrum. After a while, when he began zero-summing worse than ever, he started talking to himself. 'Turbulence,' he said. 'It's all turbulence, noise, and strange attractors. I can't ride the flow.' "

Sounded to me like the tropes hadn't quite kicked in yet, or von Bulow was having a tough time coordinating the new dataflux.

"Yeah, go on."

"When he was wiped out, he came up to me. 'Fishboy, I need some black meds. Who's on top in this town?' "

"And you sent him to—"

"Who else? The Vat Rats."

I nodded. It was a solid lead.

"Thanks, Flip. I'd shake your hand if it were possible."

"Screw that human chauvinism. Just make sure the church gets credited with a good-sized chunk of eft."

"Will do. Catch you later."

"Swim free."

I went back and got Hamster out of the stable, tipping the splice-check girl.

"Thank you, sir, it is good to see you again, sir, I was waiting most patiently, sir."

"Hamster, shut the fuck up."

"Immediately, sir."

We went looking for the Vat Rats.

Over the past half century Boston had been hit by a dozen gang invasions. First it was the Bloods and the Crips, out of LA, back in the eighties and nineties. Then it was the Hong Kong Tongs, when that entrepot went red. They segued into the Cambodians, Hispanics, Camspanics, Colombians, Novascots, Brazzes, Jamaicans. . . . Each had ruled the metro for a brief period that always ended in a bloody dustup, with the victors setting up exclusive shop. Finally, though, the pattern of foreign invasions had been disrupted by two factors: the establishment of the North American Union, and the dominance of tropes and other lab-bioactives over organic drugs. The NU had sewn up its borders tighter than a dose of Lipzip. That kept out the nonlocal competitors. And the slimemold spread of legal neurotropins through schools and socially santioned avenues created the young local biobrujos, who proceeded, with their home amino-linkers and chromo-cookers, to brew up the sublegal tropes and strobers. Various sets fell into particular special niches, turf struggles were minimal, the social order was not disrupted, and the authorities looked the other way at most of it.

Despite such a diffuse network and the impossibility of figuring out a strict hierarchy, there were some sets that had more status than others.

Those generalists, the Vat Rats, were one of the posses at the pinnacle.

The V-Rats lived in the labyrinth of abandoned pipes that had once fed sewerage into the formerly toxic harbor. When the whole city was retrofitted with D-compoz silicrobe sanitation units, there had been no need for the antique system. Every once in a while someone still raised the topic of digging it all out, but the payback wasn't bottom-line enough, and the metro would just drop the matter.

Cold water dripped down my neck. It felt like a zombie's caress. I stood in a pool of sludge up to the ankles of my boots. Hamster was shivering, but it wasn't from the cold.

We were surrounded by Rats, illuminated by my lantern. They all shared the dental moddies that gave them their name. Other than that, they were as motley a lot as your average set.

"Lookin' for some Rat poison, slimjim?"

"No thanks. Let me see Zuma Puma."

"The Puma's a busy slagger. He don't see just any-one."

"He knows me."

The Rat looked dubious. "What's the log-on, then?"

I told him.

"Wait here."

I waited. The Rats watched. One was gnawing what looked like a human femur. Hamster kept shivering.

"Calm down. No one's going to hurt you while I'm around."

"I cannot help it, sir. These are not nice folks."

The Rats tittered.

The spokes-Rat returned. "Puma'll see you."

"Like I said."

We exited the maze of pipes into a big dry bubble-room littered with personal effects: the Rats' nest. A door led to the Puma's private quarters. Hamster and I went through alone.

The Zuma Puma reclined on a pile of cushions. He wore flexible piezoplastic armor, its effectors slaved to his own electro-chemical biosystem. From out the neck, wrists and ankles of the armor protruded tawny fur. His face was bare. A playpet I recognized as a Green Canary model sat beside him, stroking his fur. When we entered, she let out a brief trill of song.

"Haven't seen you in a while, slagger," said the Puma.

"Not since I saved your tail from the Marrow Moth-ers."

The Puma laughed. "That's one version of the story."

"Commonly called 'the truth.' For which I figure you owe me a favor."

"Depends on the magnitude."

"You had a client this morning." I described von Bu-low. "What did he want?"

"Sorry, slagger, can't tell you that. You know all our

transactions are eyes-only. Who'd come to us if they thought we'd, ah, rat on them?''

"You know it won't get any further than this room."

The Puma was feeling mean. "Sorry. Anything else?"

I pulled my shocker off my hip. The Puma laughed.

"What are you gonna do with that toy, knock me out? When I come to, you still won't know anything."

I aimed at his chest and pulled the trigger. The dart embedded its microhooks into his armor.

"Bad shot, slagger. You didn't even connect with the flesh."

"I know." I sent current down the wire. The Puma stiffened boardlike out on his couch, just like a window shutter.

"The fuel cell in this is rated for a month of constant output. When I leave by your bolthole with your Canary, your Rats will try breaking in. I don't imagine they'll succeed, given your security. I understand dying of thirst is particularly nasty."

"I'll sue the cartel that sold me this piece of shit armor!"

"Only if you tell me what I want to know."

The Puma gave an exaggerated sigh. "Okay. The guy wouldn't let us unravel his blood. That made us curious, and we were gonna try for a sample anyway. But he was launch-on-warning and pulled a flashlight on us. Put a quick end to any fiddle and diddle, and we desisted. He proceeded to describe his prob. Sounded like he needed a high-powered math coprocessor and some grafix wetware. We laid them in, and it seemed to satisfy him."

"He say what he intended to do with 'em?"

"Hey, it's getting hard to breathe in this suit—"

"It'll only get harder. C'mon. Where was he going?"

"Well, our fee pretty much wiped him out. He wanted to know where he could get a big stake to gamble with. I told him the casinos in this town were too conservative to loan him anything. It's true, you know, Boston's as far out of things as the Oort Cloud. I sent him to Atlantic City.''

"Right." I reeled the dart back in. The Puma relaxed.

"You make it hard to act friendly," he said.

"Not my biggest worry. See you around, Zee Pee."

Back on the streets, I joined a line at a Bank of Boston machine. Flipper's tip had paid off, and I was going to credit the church's account before I headed for Atlantic City.

The guy in front of me took back his card from the machine. He went to pocket it, then something made him halt. He looked at his card, swore, then drew his gun and fired into the bank machine.

The machine let out an electronic squeal. It shot out of its wall-alcove on four wheels and tried to race off. It knocked down a salesman. The salesman's sample case hit the ground and broke open. Shards of music filled the air. A woman screamed. The guy with the gun fired again. This time he brought the machine down.

A crowd was collecting around the shattered and smoking bank machine. The smell of frying circuits hung thick in the air. The angry customer bulled through the bystanders. He reached into the machine's guts and retrieved his original card. "Fucking mimics," he said. "Last time my card was stolen, I lost fifteen thousand NU-dollars."

"It's a hard world," said someone in the crowd, with incomplete sincerity.

"Bet on it," said the guy, and patted his holstered gun.

The Seraphim trip from Boston to Atlantic City was a good ninety minutes plus. Von Bulow was a few hours ahead of me, and there was no way I was going to catch up with him any faster than this. I was just as glad. It gave me a little time to think.

Hamster sat asleep in the seat beside me. I couldn't say why I was bringing the splice along. It would have been just as happy sitting at home, watching the special transgenic thrid-vid channels, and Papa Legba knows it was absolutely no help on a case. Maybe I needed the company. Maybe I felt Hamster was my good-luck talisman. Maybe my dendrites were tangled. What the hell, though. The little trans rode for half-fare.

I scratched behind Hamster's ears while I considered the case.

Von Bulow must be a certifiable monomaniac. Here he was, carrying some codes in his blood which, if they worked, he could sell to any of a dozen companies for practically a month's GNP from APEC. Instead, he was going to use them to get a few jolts from the casino games. I couldn't decrypt it. Maybe someone had wired his boards this way. For all I knew, he could be creaming in his jox every time the dealer called "vingt-une." I had run into kinkier stim-rep loops.

After half an hour, I gave up pondering the matter. I couldn't be bothered trying to figure out why people acted the crazy way they did. If I had any talents in that area, I would have been able to tell you why I came home one day to find my apartment packed solid with self-replicating Krazy Foam, and my wife gone. All I can handle is what people actually do, not whatever wordless impulses they might be working from. I had my assignment, and that was that. Geneva Hippenstiel-Imhausen wanted back what was hers, and I was being paid to get it for her.

I remembered the feel of her hot love-scar under my thumb and wondered what else she wanted.

The scenery rushed by the single-crystal windows of the train in a blur like fast-forward video. Eventually, under New York, I dozed off for a few minutes too. It had been a long day.

We pulled into AC about eight P.M. Hamster and I debarked and made our way to the Boardwalk.

I hadn't been here since they rebuilt the Boardwalk

behind the new dike that kept the rising Atlantic at bay. They had used Bechtel-Kanematsu-Gosho superwood and elevated the structure four stories in the air, to wind its way past all the casinos. It was spectacular, in Atlantic City's usual tawdry style.

The walk was crowded with citizens and splices. Tourists gawped at the street performers. There was a crowd around a bikini-clad socket who had dosed herself with plenty of Bonemelt. She had put a half-twist in her body before grabbing her feet, turning herself into a human Mobius strip. To prove she was one-sided as she lay on her mat, she had little sucker-footed crawlers walking over her common ventral-dorsal surface. Good trick.

I stopped to grab a spirulina-dog and an orange soda. If von Bulow was here, he would just be settling down, not moving on, and I could take my time.

"Want something?" I asked Hamster.

"Oh, yes, sir, if you please. One of those nice chili-dogs, with extra sauce."

I made Hamster take its special supplement. One a day, or goodbye world. Sold only to registered human owners. That's why there are no runaway transgenics. Or not so many.

When we were finished, I crumpled my napkin and threw it on the Boardwalk. A litter-critter snatched it up.

"Let's go get Mister von Bulow," I said to Hamster.

"If you say so, then that's what we must do, sir."

I found him inside the Time-Warner-Sears casino, at the roulette table. His ID card lay on the betting board, flexed to show his eft balance. He kept sliding the card from one red and black number to another, and his balance kept getting bigger and bigger. I watched him for a while. His lilac eyes were half-glazed over, his face wore a zoned-out expression. The experimental H-I trope, as modified by the Vat Rats, was plainly a success. Von Bulow was rapt up in the nonlinear dynamics of the wheel, seeing chance and aleatory patterns materialized in intelligible forms that guided his play.

He never lost a spin. His balance was rising toward geostat orbit. His winning streak had attracted a crowd of ginza-joes and dolly-dears, house playpets and freelance eft-lifters, not to mention members of the management, who stood around looking like they had swallowed a quart of worms. I doubted if they'd object when I booted von Bulow.

I worked my way to his side. The management had halted play to check the wheel and scan the crowd for remote interference. I used the opportunity.

"Jurgen, I've got a message from your wife."

He jumped. "What? Who are you? How do you know my wife?" He narrowed his eyes, as if to use his new insights to unriddle me. A muscle jerked along his jaw. "That is, if you even do know her."

"Ask not who the panther roars for, slagger, it roars for you."

He pushed back his chair. "All right, all right, not here, for Christ's sake. Let's step outside."

We walked out to a deserted balcony. Overhead the stars glistened like scales on a snake. Von Bulow and I stood about four feet apart. I sensed Hamster by my side.

"Geneva wants her trope back, Jurgen."

He snorted. "Let her come and get it."

"She was busy, so she sent me instead." I had the boot concealed in my palm.

Before I could move, I was facing his flashlight, a Krupp pocket model.

"Don't complicate things, Jurgen—" I said, then went for him.

Laserlight lanced past my side, scorching my vest so I could smell burning ripstop. One shot was all he got off before I slapped the boot on his neck.

The neural shunt burrowed under his skin and fastened

itself to his spinal cord in a millie. Von Bulow collapsed to the floor.

I turned around. Hamster was twitching with a scorched hole through its tunic over its heart. I went over to the splice and picked it up.

"Not nice, not nice, sir—" it said, then died.

I went back to von Bulow. First I kicked him a half dozen times in the gut and balls. He didn't say anything, because he couldn't feel anything below his neck, and couldn't see what I was doing. Then I slapped an orange sticker on him to show he was booted. I got an autochair from the casino, put him in it, and headed for the train station.

As predicted, the management put up no fuss. I left Hamster for them to dispose of. Geneva would find a surcharge on her bill equal to the splice's original cost.

At the station, I copped a dose of Double-up from a public S&M parlor.

The ninety minutes back to Boston was enough to express my displeasure fully to von Bulow.

I was going to have to mention to Geneva to block her ears when she had the boot removed.

🎏 Blankie

THE SECOND-FLOOR NURSERY WINDOW HAD BEEN left open on a temperate summer day.

That was the fatal invitation.

No antique wire screen protected the opening into the sensate house. An intelligent invisible air curtain defeated insects, large particulates, and drifting organic debris such as clothtree leaves and airfish spume. Barnacle-like microjets around the window frame constantly tracked the incoming intruders in jerky chaotic patterns before emitting their dissuasive blasts. Large intruders over five hundred grams would be anticipated and neutralized by the house's alarm net and its entrained armaments.

But a small, alert wren-form bird, like the one alighting now upon the window sill, was anticipated by neither system.

The bird surveyed the nursery interior.

The walls held embedded silicrobe animated pictures: fairytale characters that capered across the constantly shifting backgrounds. The Big Bad Wolf pursued a cloaked Little Red Riding Hood; the young ballerina in her cursed red slippers danced till exhausted.

In the middle of the room stood a white biopolymer crib shaped like an egg halved along its long dimension and resting in a bip support base. The Bayer logo blinked orange from portside. In the crib lay a naked baby boy of several months, tummy up. Above him floated a mobile representing the Earth and some of its myriad orbiting artificial satellites. The large globe revolved and its tiny attendants spun in their intricate, never-intersecting orbital dance supported only by shaped magnetic fields emitted from the crib.

Beneath the baby was a Blankie, its Ixsys brandmark plain in one corner.

The Blankie was approximately as big as a large bath towel. Its glycoprotein-glycolipid paradermal surface was colored a delicate pastel blue and resembled in texture antique eggcrate bedding foam. Except that the individual nubbins of the Blankie were much more closely spaced, and in the shallow dimples of the Blankie gleamed a subtle organic sheen like a piece of raw liver.

The bird flew from its perch on the sill and landed on the crib's edge, its claws clutching the material of the Bayer halfshell.

At that point two things happened.

All of the flat silicrobe characters on the wall stiffened and stopped. The Woodsman, who had just emerged to rescue the swallowed Little Red Riding Hood, was the one exception. He dropped his one-dimensional axe and began to yell.

"Intruder! Intruder! All security kibes to the nursery!"

Simultaneous with the alert, the baby began to pee. A fountain of yellow shot up a few centimeters from it.

When the first drops of pee hit the Blankie, it responded in its trophic instinctive way. The portion of the Blankie between the boy's legs elongated like a pseudopod or flap and reached up to cap and drink the urine for its own metabolic purposes, simultaneously cleaning and drying the infant's wet skin.

The bird dropped down into the crib while the Blankie was preoccupied. It jabbed its beak into the Blankie.

Then, in one spastic implosive moment it pumped the contents of its nonbasal nasal sacs into the Blankie.

In a flash, its load of venom delivered, the bird darted to the rim of the crib and launched itself toward the window.

Now alert, the window caught it instantly in a flash-extruded web of Ivax Stickum.

The bird self-destructively exploded, charring the windowframe.

In the crib the Blankie was writhing and churning like a wounded octopus. Fractal blooms whipped up from it, then fell across the baby, who began to cry.

Within a second or two, the blooms coalesced into a blue webwork. When a strand fell across the baby's mouth, its cries ceased.

The door to the nursery flew open and assorted kibernetics appeared.

But it was too late.

The Blankie tightened its embrace like a basal anaconda.

The sounds of snapping bones were registered by the confused and helpless kibes.

I popped the silver datapins from the player, abruptly terminating the sounds of little Harry Day-Lewis's death, collected less than a day ago. Although I had watched the tragedy unfold a dozen times since then, I hadn't quite yet gotten used to that fatal, snapping-sticks sound. I doubted I ever would.

I was sitting in my office in the building that housed the Boston branch of the North American Union's Internal Recon and Security division. Although I had occupied this fiftieth-floor corner room for sixteen months, since my last promotion, it still felt alien to me. All those years operating my own private investigating firm out of increasingly cheaper quarters had left me unused to luxuries such as Organogenesis self-cleaning carpets and Zeneca squirmonomic chairs. Not to mention the steady posting to my eft-account.

But I had had to get out of the PI biz after the job I had done for Geneva Hippenstiel-Imhausen. That had been my last case before my crackup.

While booting her husband, I had lost my sidekick, a useless low-end splice named Hamster. If you had asked me prior to the murder of the cut-rate transgenic what the little shag meant to me, I would have said zepto-nothing. But there was a lot I hadn't known about myself back then, and my fatherly affection for the splice had been one such secret.

I had purchased Hamster right after my wife left me and apparently had transferred a lot of unresolved feelings to it. Anyway, that's what Doctor Varela, the expert in Behavioral Pragmatics, had told me during my analysis. But the beep analysis hadn't happened until I hit planck-bottom, winding up in a clinic for mel-heads. In illegal doses, the melatonin-an-alogue-based trope I became addicted to let me sleep all day except for an hour or two, lost in pleasant dreams inspired by a second trope, TraumWerks (produced, ironically enough, by the H-I gembaitch owned by my ex-client).

I had wasted away to a muscleless ninety pounds before a routine sweep of streetlife picked me up and deposited me in Varela's rehab joint.

When I got out, officially a functioning member of society again, I had opted to continue in law-enforcement, rather than be regrooved for a different job. Accepted by the IRS, I had started as a simple walkabout operating out of my Kenmore Square koban, eventually reaching my current status, a detective in the Unit for Polypeptide Classification and Monitoring, better known as the Protein Police. (Our motto: "We collect strings.")

Now, rolling the datapins reflectively between my fingers, as if hoping to feel the intangible nanoscratches that encoded Harry Day-Lewis's death, I wondered if maybe

I was getting too old for this job. I had thought I was used to nasty. But this was a new magnitude of evil.

My office door said, "Kasimzhomart Saunders wishes to enter."

"Let him in."

K-mart was my current human partner. His parents had emigrated to the NU from Kazakhstan during the tumult of the Last Jihad. As NUish as me, he looked more exotic, affecting a dark complexion, Mongolian topknot and long drooping mustachios. Today he wore a sleeveless shirt (at our rank, uniforms were not mandatory) that bore the demand of the Selfless Viridians: "Give me euthanasia or give me death!" My partner was big into irony.

Waggling his poqetpal significantly in the air, K-mart said, "Finally got the burst on the Day-Lewis family. Their respective peltsies took their time cleaning up the data. Ran it through a dozen intelligent filters before they'd release it. No proprietary secrets left. But there's still everything we need. Want a squirt?"

"Sure. Pipe it over."

The file showed up on my desk screen a second later. I picked up the flimsy and flung it at the wall like a floppy pizza. The flexistik screen clung upside down, sensed its new orientation, and flipped its display. Now both K-mart and I could read it.

After letting me have a quick scan, K-mart summarized. "Standard plutes. Politics just what you'd expect from members of the tekhnari. Semideviationist nouveau peronistas. Marshall, the plug, works for Xytronyx, field-testing mosaics. The socket, Melisma, heads a crada sired by Cima Labs out of Phenix Biocomposites. No major kinks—except for occasional separate visits to Hedonics Plus. She favors the Paris Percheron lines, while he goes in for the Moon Moth."

I made an admonishing mudra as deftly as I could, lacking hyperflexion. "Unless this is strictly necessary—"

K-mart smiled at the notion of having official access to the peccadillos of others. He was still young. "Just thought you should know all the angles. Anyway, they decided to put the prodge together last year, when their combined eft topped two hundred kay. Set themselves up as prime candidates for a kidnapping and ransom demand from any posse of wackos. Sons of Dixie, League of Country Gentlemen, Radical Optimists, Plus Fourierists, you name 'em—they'd all like a crack at such a scion."

"But there was nothing overt, right? No warning posts, no anonymous messenger splices, no letter bombs?"

"Right. The attack on the Blankie was the first sign of any trouble."

"No chance they're behind it themselves? Some insurance scam? Post-vitrio depression?"

"Nope. If you want to drop the pins on the interrogation, you'll see how authentically quenched they were."

"I didn't really think so. But you have to trace all the pathways."

K-mart twirled his mustachios like some reductionist-paradigm villain. "You know what I figure?"

"What?"

"The Blankie itself was supposed to do the kidnapping. Crawl away with the prodge out the window, after it got its subversion-shot from the bird. But the ganglia-mappings were screwy—bad engineering—and the heist went sour."

I thought about K-mart's theory for a moment. It just didn't ring true to me. How would the combined mass of the Blankie and its human burden have gotten past the sensate alarm? Surely any kidnappers sophisticated enough to gimmick a bird like that would have considered such a crucial detail. Maybe the Blankie could have bypassed the house's circuits somehow after its alteration. But then where would the pickup have occured? I couldn't picture the Blankie inch-worming its way through town unnoticed. And there had been no suspicious intruders located in the immediate neighborhood. No, the whole kidnapping angle, although it was the obvious answer, seemed wrong somehow.

"These Blankies—I've never heard of them before this. Are they new?"

K-mart chased down a few hyperlinks and found the information. "Ixsys submitted all the documentation and beta-test results on them six months ago. The NUdies approved the Blankies for the domestic market a month after that. Global licensing from the WTO still pending."

"What's their market-share?"

"Only ten percent. The Blankies don't have a lot of the higher functions of other childminders. Most parents still favor Carebears and Mother Gooses when the prodge gets a little older. But the Blankies are cheap and easy for round-the-clock sanitary functions and monitoring. They never sleep, for one thing. Helps explain how they went from a zero to ten share in just under half a year. . . ."

I got up from my imipolex seat, which flattened out into its default shape, awaiting the next occupant. "Sign a lie-detector out of the stables." I didn't work with the IRS splices directly anymore, leaving that part of the job to K-mart. "We're going to pay the swellheads and trumps at Ixsys a little visit."

"You smell corprotage?"

"Does the Goddess's Daughter on Earth wear Affymax tits?"

Like many peltsies and beeves, Ixsys had no centralized headquarters *per se*, being a distributed organization. The local node was just a few minutes away from central Boston, in the edge city of Newton.

I met K-mart down on the street. He had signed out both a cruiser and a lie-detector. The vehicle was a standard Daewoo Euglenia, the hydrogen source for its ceramic engine plain water continuously and smoothly broken down by a bioreactor full of cytofabbed algae with photon input piped from roof solar traps. The lie-detector was an Athena Neurosci Viper model. With a combination of infrared, vomeronasal and lateral-line sensory input, the transgenic creature could read epidermal and subdermal blood-flow, as well as ambient pheromone and respiratory data, right off a suspect to make its judgment on veracity. With basal humans, its accuracy rate approached unity; highly modified subjects introduced varying degrees of uncertainty. But most innocent citizens didn't sport the kind of moddies necessary to defeat a Viper, and the presence of such blocks was in itself evidence of a sort. In my book, if not a court of law.

"I'll drive," said K-mart, and we all got in, the Viper sinuously slithering into the backseat without saying anything.

The bawab at the Ixsys node was one of their massive Ottoman Eunuch models, 15 percent human pedigree, the rest a mix of simian and water buffalo. I saw the same kind as doorman at my apartment complex every night. He towered over us, his shaggy head level with the door's lintel. The scimitar by his side was, I knew, really a quick-lysing device: liquid protease compressed in the handle could be released as a spray from micropores in the blade, melting flesh in picoseconds.

The Eunuch growled wordlessly when he saw our lack of Ixsys tags. But a flash of our UPCM idents triggered a hardwired servility response, and he let us in.

We hadn't called ahead, not wishing to precipitate any kind of cover-your-ass reaction. (Although news of the Day-Lewis murder had already been culled from the net and disseminated by millions of newsie demons throughout the metamedium, and any half-smart executive with damage suits glimmering in his brain would have already gotten ready for our visit.) So we had to wait while the receptionist arranged for one of the Ixsys trumps to meet us. I spent my time admiring the colorful, throbbing, hot-blooded plants in their terrariums and trying to decipher the circuit diagrams of signaling pathways that hung decoratively on the walls.

The company rep finally emerged: a broadly smiling young plug with a modest crest of small bronze-colored dragon-like spines running from his brow over his head and down his back, his suit slit to accommodate them. Pride in a recent degree in biobiz administration was written all over his face. Sacrificial lamb, an expendable toe dipped into possibly shark-infested waters. Achieve maximal deniability at all costs. It made me sick.

He stuck out his hand. "Pleased to meet you, Officers. I'm Tuck Kitchener, in charge of community relations and risk bubble analysis. How can I help you?"

"You're aware of yesterday's Blankie murder, I take it?"

Kitchener tsk-tsked. "Most unfortunate and deplorable. A clear case of warranty violation. The Blankie should never have been exposed to exo-avian secretagogues under any circumstances. The owners of the Blankie were clearly at fault. I hope you agree. There's no question of corporate responsibility, is there?"

"I don't know yet. That's why we're here. I'd like a look at your design facilities. Talk to the team members responsible for the Blankie."

"Why, certainly! Nothing could be easier. If you'll just accompany me to the sterilization lock—"

Before long, K-mart, the Viper and I were sluiced, dusted, and wrapped. The exit procedure would be even stricter, involving internal search-and-destroy, to insure we didn't try to smuggle any proprietary secrets out.

Once through the lock, we made our way past breeding vats and reactors, paragenesis chambers and creches, wunderkammers and think-tanks, all staffed by efficiently bustling Ixsys staff.

"As you can see," Kitchener said boastfully, "we run a tight ship here. All by the regs. No spills, no chills, that's our byword—"

K-mart interrupted. "We're not inspectors from NU-SHA, Peej Kitchener. We're the Protein Police. And we're trying to solve a murder. A murder involving one of your products."

It still amazes me that anyone falls for good-cop-bad-cop, but they do. Uncertain of who was senior, Kitchener looked imploringly at me. But I just raised my eyebrows. The young trump began nervously to stroke his cranial comb, which bent like stiff rubber. "Ah, yes, of course. Why don't we proceed directly with your interview of the Blankie team?"

"Why don't we?"

So Kitchener took us to the swellheads.

Although I had dealt with doublebrains in the line of duty before, the sight of their naked bulging encephaloceles always made me somewhat queasy. Cradled in their special neckbrace support chairs, surrounded by their digitools and virtuality hookups, their basal metabolisms necessarily supplemented with various nutritional and trope exofeeds, they seemed to regard us visitors with a cold Martian scrutiny.

K-mart appeared unaffected by the massed clammy gaze of the eight Cerebrally Enhanced—or at least capable of putting up a better front than I—and plunged right into querying the swells.

"Okay—how many backdoors did you jokers install in the Blankie ganglia?"

The team members exchanged significant glances among themselves, then one spoke. "I am Simon, the leader of the octad. I shall answer your questions. There are no hidden entrypoints. All is as the published specs declare."

"For the moment, I'll assume that's true." K-mart glanced meaningfully at our Viper, who had not objected yet. But I wondered how good its skills would be against the swells. "Who did you steal from to build it? Come on, I know you seebens are always plundering each other's finds. Who's got a mindworm against Ixsys and wants you to look bad?"

Simon actually betrayed a tiny measure of affronted dignity. "We derive all our insights and findings direct from the numinous sempiternal sheldrakean ideosphere. Our labors are unremitting and harsh, as we prospect among uncharted territories of ideospace. To accuse us of theft is to demean our very existence!"

The rest of the interrogation went just as awkwardly, yielding nothing. Finally even the tenacity of K-mart wilted.

As we were leaving, my partner turned to the recumbent CE's and said, "See y'all at Madame Muskrat's, boys!"

We headed slowly toward the exit, while I tried to think of another lead. Kitchener's smug look didn't help my concentration.

Then something from the Day-Lewis bio came back to me. The father's job.

I turned to Kitchener. "Who field-tested the Blankie?"

"Ah, that employee is currently on extended leave—"

"He is lying," said the Viper.

Pay dirt! K-mart jumped in.

"Allow me to read you your rights under the NU Treaty. You have the right to a kibernetic counsel rated at Turing Level Five—"

Kitchener laughed like a man caught with his hand in his pants at an Amish church picnic. "Certainly you don't intend to arrest me for a mere slip of the tongue, Officers? What I meant to say is that the employee in question had to be fired under prejudicial circumstances."

"What's the name? We'll want all your files on him. And what did he do?"

"His name . . . Um, let me recall. Bert something. Bertrand Mayr."

"And why did you let him go?"

"Flagrant misuse and theft of corporate property."

"Precisely?"

Kitchener smoothed his saurian crest again. "A small matter of sex. He was having sex with the product."

Sometimes I try to imagine what it was like to live in reedpair times. It was only last century, after all. A lot of that cohort are still actually hanging around, admittedly without many of their original organs or neurons. But even when talking with them, you can't really understand what their world was truly like. One of the biggest puzzles is how they managed sex. They had to cope with deadly venereal diseases, intractable neuroses, fixed morphologies, social condemnation of natural urges, and merely human sex-workers who offered mostly heartless, perfunctory service due to their oppression and mistreatment.

Today, gratuitous venereal diseases have been extirpated. (Deliberately inflicted ones are, of course, still a problem. I remember last year the tricky time we had tracking down the perp spreading neo-koro, the penis-inversion plague.) The witch doctors of psychology have been replaced by trope dosers. Malleable anatomy is no longer destiny. Laws finally reflect actual desires (at least in the NU; the situation elsewhere varies). And playpets bred and trained for their essential erotic functions come in a nearly infinite variety. (And humane treatment extends even beyond their useful stage. I understand that their retirement ranches offer a wide range of crafts and games.)

But despite all this, you still get a few hesomagari, the "twisted navels," those full-blooded humans contrary or perverse enough to seek a fulfillment not socially sanctioned.

Such as Bert Mayr.

We had his files downloaded before we left Ixsys. And this was what we learned.

Mayr was the son of NU citizens Rowena and Boris Mayr, ex-settlers who had retreated in failure from the hard life on board Aquarius, the floating arcology and OTEC power plant off the coast of Madagascar. Their Lotto-won berths had gone to others when they fled back to Boston.

Boris had died here shortly after Bert's birth. Caught in the middle of a turf war between the Morgue Boys and the Thai Guys out in Charlestown, where the mother still lived. She had never rebonded on a permanent basis.

Mayr had grown up to be your archetypical loner. No friends, no resident erotofiscal partner, no transient lovers. Apparently, he had followed this solitary lifestyle ever since becoming fully enfranchised.

My cop's intuition drew me a picture of a mama's boy, the only token of his lost father, a coddled and fussed-over introvert.

In his final year of schooling, Mayr had shown aptitude as a chromosartor. Given the standard Scios Nova cooker-splicer setup for twelve-year-olds, he had soon modified it with add-ons purchased with his pocket money to produce standalone entities up to the level of annelids. He loved to hack nucleotides and amino acids, perhaps too much so. Legal and moral boundaries appeared to mean little to him. He had almost gotten expelled for the prank of infesting the school's showers with nonreproductive hookworms. He had programmed them with only a thirty-day lifespan—but in that time they also secreted low levels of psilocybin-analogues directly into the victim's gut.

When he had graduated, he found that his juvenile record of misdemeanors worked against him. No respectable peltsie would hire him as a chromosartor (at least without Mayr consenting to a course of corrective tropes, a measure he apparently rejected), for fear of his dangerously irresponsible attitude. The best job he could get was field-testing at Ixsys, a position he had held unremarkably for the past decade.

"And then along came the Blankie," K-mart said, back at the office when we had finished viewing the file.

"It must have triggered something latent in him. Or touched some active kink."

"Because he was the first to have access to the Blankie, he came to regard it as his personal property. He takes it home—Tara! You don't think Ixsys insisted he *use* it, do you?"

I shrugged. "That's what field-testing's all about."

"Shit! Thank Ishtar I work in the adminisphere! Anyway, he gets hooked on the Blankie, uses his skills to alter it for sex. Then when Ixsys finds out and fires him, he goes suborbital, absconding with the product. Finally, he comes to resent anybody else who owns one."

Nodding agreement, I said, "I think we need to pay a little visit to Peej Mayr."

"Should I sign out the Viper again?"

"No. A Bulldog."

A cocktail of canine, wolverine, hyena, and—of course—a smattering of human, the Bulldog was what we favored for a one-perp pickup with low to medium violence potential. (And Mayr's MO, with its kind of remote-control aggro, led me to suspect he wouldn't resist arrest.) Massing only three-quarters of a basal human, the Bulldog was capable of taking down half a dozen nonmoddies faster than you could say "Kreb's cycle."

In the car on the way to Mayr's last address, we got a bulletin.

Almost as if our psychic attention on Mayr had drawn him out, there had been another Blankie incident. This time the vector for the assault was a family splice, a Dumbunni. Returning from an errand, it had seemed disoriented. Sent to its manger, it had wandered instead to the human nursery, where it was found gnawing at the Blankie with its blunt, newly venomous teeth. Luckily, the prodge was rescued before the Blankie began fibrillating.

"We've got to put this guy away," K-mart said, "or our personal asses—not to mention the department's—will be so much feedstock. You've read the profile of the average Blankie owner. He or she is a hardnosed, string-pulling plute who's not going to sit quietly for this."

"Agreed. But I'm actually more interested in the details of the perp's kink."

"Great. You can write it up later for the *UPCM Journal*. But we've got to catch him first."

Mayr's last-known residence turned out to be one of those old asymmetrical rhizomatic structures out in Cambridge. The bawab was a doddering kibe whose split casing seams were patched with Radio Shack Silly Cement. The unit directed us to Mayr's flat, where our idents secured immediate entrance.

A stale smell and a layer of dust (the lowrent place didn't even have self-cleaning capabilities) told us no one had occupied the rooms for at least a month.

"Shit! Cold trail," K-mart said.

"Patience, patience. No telling what a search will turn up."

So while the Bulldog stood guard at the door, we began to go through the rooms.

I found Mayr's porn stash in one of the more clever hideaways I had ever encountered. One portion of the bumpy, seemingly dead wall was in reality an embedded modified marine polyp with very good mimicry features. It had taps into the residential structure's water veins, but apparently hadn't been fed in a while. As I was running my fingers over the wall, the polyp dropped its disguise, flexed open, extruded tentacles, and weakly attempted to ingest my hand.

I yelped, K-mart came running, flashlight in hand. He

lasered the creature dead. Inside its still quivering husk were several datapins.

We dried them and popped them into K-mart's poqetpal. Images cohered. Right away I noticed something missing: the usual WTO official imprimatur: ALL MODELS ARE ENFRANCHISED CITIZENS OVER AGE TWELVE. Then I focused on the pictures.

Back in that reedpair time I had been recently speculating on, there had been a flourishing porn trade—conducted mostly in the old nation-state of Japan—known as bura-sera. Images of young schoolgirls hoisting their skirts to reveal their simple, functional underwear. Sometimes this speciality extended to the sale of the underwear itself. Preferably soiled.

With the gradual lowering of the franchise to its current level, this trade had disappeared—merged, rather, into the mainstream. But what K-mart and I now viewed reminded me of it and was plainly an offshoot or descendent of the bura-sera.

It was pix after pix of diaper-clad individuals, ages ranging from newborn to elderly. There was no actual sex going on that would have made the pins contraband. But there was a lot of peeing and crapping.

K-mart was disgusted. "This stuff isn't even illegal! It's just stupid! Why would anyone murder over it?"

I shut off the display. "You got me, Kaz. But if this accurately represents Mayr's hardwiring, then you can see how the Blankie was like a match to tinder for him. When Ixsys took it away from him, all he could think of was revenge."

Just then a bulletin came in. Another Blankie taken out, this time by a swarm of sweatbees. Luckily, no loss of human life.

"What next?" asked K-mart. "Maybe a talk with Rowena Mayr?"

"Sounds good. I think I'd like to ask her where she got her parenting license."

*   *   *

Rowena Mayr lived in an insensate building in a dismal neighborhood right below the Seraphim tracks. The superfast train suspended from its overhead monorail was relatively quiet. But the Boston-Montreal Express went by once an hour, and somehow you could feel its passage in your gut as it split the air.

The crumbling stoop outside Mayr's building was occupied with dole-proles and their nonschema prodges. The adults were drinking cheer-beers while the kids were playing with those cheap trilobite pets so popular that summer. We garnered dirty looks as we went in, but no one tried to stop us. We left the Bulldog by the entrance to forestall anyone sending up a warning.

As we approached the third floor door of Rowena Mayr's flat, I spotted K-mart's hand hovering near his flashlight.

I didn't know what to expect from Rowena Mayr, but it wasn't what appeared when the door finally opened to our knock.

Rowena Mayr was a frazettatoid, member of a highly egocentric group that had splintered off the old Society for Creative Anachronism. Boris had probably been one too. You didn't see them around much anymore, and I was surprised there were any left unretrofitted. No wonder the Mayrs hadn't felt comfortable in the spartan, utilitarian environment of Aquarius. . . .

Rowena had had her body sculpted to resemble one of the impossible fantasy women from the canvases of her faction's namesake reed-pair artist. Huge cantilevered boobs, a waist so slim it must have involved major organ displacement, and callipygian ass. She wore a tiny metal bra, some faux-barbaric jewelry. From a fake gold chain around her waist hung a few wisps of colored silk.

She was such a self-contained, self-immersed, impossible creation that being in the same room with her was like sharing space with an ancient animatronic figure. I tried imagining having her as my mother. It was a major stretch.

"Yes, Officers. How can I help you?"

"It's about your son, Bert. Can we come in?"

"Certainly."

The flat was furnished in High Conan. We sat on embroidered cushions and explained the trouble her son had gotten himself into.

"Well, I feel extremely bad for Bertie. He was always a good boy and showed such promise. Red Sonia knows, I did my best with him! But I don't see how I can help you now."

"He hasn't been in touch with you recently?"

"Not for years."

K-mart stood. "Mind if we have a look around?"

Rowena got hastily to her feet. "Unless you have a warrant, I'm afraid that's out of the question."

Nodding toward a closed door, K-mart said, "What's in there?"

"That's my shrine to Dagon. Very innocent, I assure you. But sacred. Now, if you don't mind, Officers, I'd like to be alone—"

K-mart started to rap a string of antisense as he ambled about the room. "Oh, I was raised Dagonite, but I fell away. Haven't seen a shrine in ages. You don't mind, do you?"

Before Rowena could stop him, K-mart had pulled the door open.

The Blankie was waiting.

It reared up as tall as a man and twice as bulky, a quivering blue wall of cryptoflesh. Unlike what I knew about the small Blankies, this one radiated an ammoniacal, fecal reek.

Bert had obviously been tweaking its parameters a little.

Before K-mart could get his flashlight up, the Blankie

fell forward on him, wrapping him in its straitjacket embrace.

Rowena screamed. I had my own flashlight up, but couldn't shoot for fear of piercing the swaddled K-mart.

Something barreled past me so fast and hard it spun me around. When I recovered, I saw our Bulldog tangling with the Blankie, all fangs and talons. It zeroed in on a major ganglion, ripping it out in a bloody mess of dendrites.

The Blankie collapsed like an air-mattress that had sprung a leak.

I went to help a slimed K-mart up. Rowena rushed past me into the Blankie's room, shouting, "Bertie, Bertie, I tried to stop them!"

K-mart seemed shaken, but uninjured. "Tara! I smell like the time I fell into the family outhouse back in Kazakhstan!"

Flashlight in hand, I followed Rowena into the room.

But I needed no weapon to deal with little Bertie.

The fearsome mastermind behind the Blankie murder lay in an oversized Bayer cradle usually used for burn victim treatment, naked except for an oversized cloth diaper. In one lax hand was an Allelix sonic injector. From the utterly wiped look on Bertie's face, I could guess that the injector had been loaded with a probably irreversible dose of Neonate Nine or some other retrogressive synapse-disconnecting trope.

Rowena was kneeling by the cradle, weeping. Together, she and her son resembled some kind of tawdry, modern Pieta.

K-mart came up beside me, shaking his head. "Muy hesomagari."

I thought back to my own days as a mel-head. "But we've all got navels that can get twisted, Kaz. Leastwise, those of us born human."

On our way out, I came on the Bulldog chewing up the evidence. In the heat of the moment, its ancient instincts had overwhelmed its training.

I went to kick it, but changed my mind.

𝄢 The Bad Splice

AS IF BLINDLY OBEDIENT TO ONE OF THE WEIRDER plectic neothomist catastrophe figures, my life seemed to be warping itself around strange attractors, spiraling and darting up and down cusps and caustics, pleats and furrows that led to some unpredictable yet inevitable terminal boundary condition.

And the worst part was—I couldn't tell if on balance I should be scared or glad.

Changes had swarmed through my life as thick as harvest thrips on a cloth-tree during the past few months, enough so as to necessitate a few unscheduled sessions with Doctor Varela, my BP advisor. I had thought I had seen the last of that calm and erudite Behavioral Pragmatist after he had helped me over the rough patch following my departure from the PI biz.

Since joining Boston's branch of the Protein Police, my life had been relatively simple and undemanding, despite the quirks and dangers of my new trade, and I had felt no recent need of beep counseling. But lately all that had changed, leading Doctor Varela to nod and murmur sagely over my condition, consult his snippets, and prescribe a course of Biomet's Angstaway paired with Sciclone's VivaciTee, as well as a general adrenergic booster. The tropes seemed to be working, although I still felt a little off-parm.

But I was managing to cope well with quite a lot, I thought.

It had all started when the Big Brains in charge of the NU's Internal Recon and Security force (of which the Protein Police was a division) had laid down a couple of new ukases.

First, there were to be no more human-human teams. We were just too understaffed to permit such a luxury to continue and would remain so into the foreseeable future. What with the guaranteed prole-dole, the dwindling numbers of pure-gen, fully enfranchised humans, and the seductions of virtuality, criminality, and a million sects, cults, posses, and sets representing an infinite range of hedonism, nihilism, and every ism on the scale, potential candidates for the force were few and far between. (The same was true, of course, in every branch of the NU adminisphere; without kibes, demons, and cocktails, the whole system would have suffered instant apoptosis.)

So all the old dual-human partnerships were split up. That meant I lost K-mart Saunders, the most agreeable plug I had ever worked with. In his place, I was to choose between a var or a kibe. Well, since the death of my old var Hamster, I couldn't really work too closely with the splices and remain comfortable. That left the kibe.

The Turing Level Four kibes had just gone into general open-access production. (The Level Fives, naturally, were already up and running, but were reserved exclusively for the use of the IMF, World Bank, WTO, and other ruling bodies of the adminisphere, which liked to stay one giant step ahead of the masses they governed. And of course the Level Sixes were not far behind, close to finishing their semi-autonomous evolution.) The Toronto HQ of the Protein Police had just received a month's worth of shipments of Fours from the Bangalore macqui of Segasoft-TogaiMagic, and these had been further distributed across the continent.

The kibe cores themselves looked identical to and had the same dimensions as the old Level Threes, allowing for easy retrofitting: shiny featureless platters about as thick as a stack of a dozen ancient CD's. It was the newly evolved qubitic circuitry inside that raised their functioning to a higher level. As for the chassis that would carry the cores—well, the force's own crada had come up with several new models specifically designed for law enforcement.

So my new partner became a synthetic, syncretic personality in a mini-frisbee, capable of swapping bodies at will.

On top of this unsettling switch, the Swellheads had insisted that all the humans on the force go in for a somatic upgrade. The mucky-mucks were tired of losing officers to various preventable assaults. Baseline bodies were now considered insufficient to counter the moddies of the baddies. We had to meet them head-on, match them in the arms (and legs and brains) race.

Like most people in all walks of life, I had my share of implants and add-ons and upgrades already: simple things that had helped me in my work, like sharper peripheral vision, stronger bones, voluntary pain shunts. But unlike some bodyartists and puzzlepluses, I had never gone in for radical modifications. What was good enough for grandpooh was good enough for me. Now I was being told that I had to change or be dropped from the force.

Swallowing my trepidations and instinctive dislike of being bossed around (after all, I wasn't an independent contractor anymore), I went into the bodyshop.

I came out sheathed in flexible imbricated skin like a pangolin's, its plates chamois-soft to the touch yet capable of turning aside sharp edges and low-velocity projectiles. Additionally, my new integument from Calypte

Biomed would react to the beam of a flashlight by instantly altering its refractive index. (I had once read that the quickest basal reaction in nature was found in the jaws of a certain ant, which could snap closed in a third of a millisecond. Science had considerably bettered that.) I had a paralymphatic system from Olympus Biotech that would aggressively react to micro-and nano-invaders. My arteries were reinforced with CuraTech's neo-goretex, my bones threaded with Innovir's stonefiber. My heart had an onboard Hemazyne assist, as did my lungs. I had Agouron hyperflexure in my fingers, increased haptic and proprioceptive sensitivity, and certain wetware enhancements from BioCryst not available to the general public. Finally, I could on short notice generate several highly damaging antipersonnel cytokines expressible through strategically placed exocrine glands.

In short, I was now one mean and hyperefficient slagger for the forces of goodness and justice.

I was also on a half-dozen new tropes that allowed me to integrate my new body image and sensory inputs.

It was just after this makeover that the final big change in my life occurred.

I met Xuly Beth and fell in love.

Xuly Beth Vollbracht had been born in the Mercosur, grown up a gypsy waterbaby. Her parents, Rolf and Valentina, had managed a section of the Hidrovia, roving up and down that extensive artificial waterway, supervising commerce and maintenance, troubleshooting and policing. Educated and trained as a noah for the GEF, Xuly Beth had been stationed at various spots around the world (she had seen parts of APEC, CarriCom, and Scandibaltica), monitoring and remediating oceanic-atmospheric systems, before ending up in the Nova England bioregion.

We met at an official function hosted by the noahs to brief the Protein Police on the latest rogue organisms we could possibly expect to emerge from runaway marine co-evolution. (Safe as silicrobe technology was supposed to be, there were inevitable glitches.)

Luckily for me, Xuly Beth was far from repelled by my altered epidermis. It turned out that one of her first lovers had been a fishboy from the Hidrovia, and the experience had crystallized her taste for odd integuments.

Xuly Beth was the change in my life that tipped the scales toward gladness. It was the first time since my wife walked out on me that I had a functioning pair-bonding. It felt good.

And that feeling alone should have been enough to warn me that something bad was about to fall right on my head like one of Xuly Beth's programmed heavyrains out of the seemingly clear sky.

The first notice I had of trouble was the urgent patterned pinging of my flimsy one morning as I sat at my desk. I was on scheduled fifteen-minute downtime, relaxing in a quasi-meditative state at the focus of which was a little token of her work Xuly Beth had given me. In a clear cylindrical container about as big as a pneumatic-tube message capsule, a self-sustaining miniature silicrobe twister ran its homeodynamic contortions, powered only by sunlight. Its infinite random permutations served as a Taoist exemplar of mind-wiping potency.

But even the Tao could not ultimately contend against the earcon for a Class-One transmission. I resumed my mind and voiced the screen on. The face of my immediate superior appeared.

Jo Priestly looked nervous. Not an easy task for a woman who wore the ruff-bordered head and snouty-toothed face of an oversized fringed lizard. (I had seen perps faint during interrogation when she simply smiled.)

"The cat's in town," she said.

"The Xuma Puma?" I asked, recalling the petty posse-leader I had more than once tangled with in the old days. "What's to worry?"

"I wish it was only the XP. No, I'm talking about the one and only cat that matters. Krazy Kat."

Now I knew why she looked worried. "I assume there's some java following for me to dethread. But maybe you could empeg it for me. . . ."

"You heard about Chicago? How the Kat nearly caused a Second Flood?"

"Sure. But I thought he screwed up. Didn't he leave behind some cells for the first time? All the public sniffers should be programmed by now to respond as soon as he slinks by."

"True, we've got his genome mapped, and that's more than we've ever had before. But it's not good enough. The Kat doesn't have to go out in public to cause mischief. He's got friends, allies, and sympathizers galore. And not just among the other splices either. There're lots of pure-gens who support the CLF—or at least the non-violent aspects of their platform. Groups such as the SPCC. The Kat could easily stay holed up and still cause us yotta-shit. And don't forget private transportation. The sniffers would miss anyone in a car with positive pressure seals. No, we're going to have to hit the streets if we hope to forestall whatever deviltry the Kat's got in his hat. Bone up, plug. Then get out there and use *your* nose."

"Kakkoii," I said. "Cool as the socket who climbed into the Sack and made it with the Farside storage ring."

The Chief was a member of the Shaker Revivalists and a doctrinaire gone-gonad. Her membranous veined ruff flushed an agitated crimson, then her face disappeared. Another earcon sounded, and down invisible lines came the petafits on the Kat.

There was so much data it overflowed the flimsy's buffers. I released a couple of my customized speculative agents to work in background mode, setting them loose on what was known of the Kat's MO. Then I settled down for a long raster, grateful that some of my new wetware allowed for dual-track processing.

Krazy Kat had been born some ten years ago in and into frustration. His sire was a mullis who went by the gnomic name of Doctor Radius. At the time, Doc Radius was a freelancer under temp-bond to Vivus-Neopath and had just been assigned to a highly secretive project. V-N had taken an anonymous encrypted contract off the net to develop a new breed of cultivar according to certain specs. The mosaic was to consist of 50 percent felidae of various germlines, 30 percent human, 10 percent viverrine, 10 percent miscellaneous useful nucleotides. Once the juvenile splices were out of the tanks, as yet unengrammed, they were to be shipped in partial stasis— without human accompaniment—to an address that turned out to belong to a dummy abe fronting for the city government of Paris.

It turned out that the mayor of that fine city had decided to secede from the EC, after his decision to make smoking mandatory within city limits had been quashed from on high. (Tourism was down, and the mayor felt that if he could reimpose the retro ambiance of the city, the crowds would flock back. . . .) These new splices from V-N, all tooth and nail and cunning, were to be trained and further bred as a corps of mercenary soldiers, the backbone of a Parisian self-defense force with which the mayor could enforce his secession.

Well, needless to say, both the EC and the WTO, among other power centers of the adminisphere, frowned on such a move and chose to express their displeasure most forcefully. (The ex-mayor was due out of stasis in another twenty years.) Upon discovering the plot, before the splices were even shipped, the authorities came down on V-N like a ton of strange matter. The firm was heavily fined, and all the special splices were ordered destroyed.

This did not sit well with Doc Radius. Like any devoted, obsessive, manifestly brain-warped artist, he had come to regard the new splices not as mere work-for-hire, but as his personal, beloved magnum opus. When the destruct order came down, Doc Radius managed to make off with a single fetus. A secret fetus not on the original workorder, but one he had been tinkering with as a side-project, tweaking its parameters to his liking and esthetic sense.

This was the seed that was to blossom into Krazy Kat.

Raised in eccentric isolation with only Doc R. for a parental unit, freed of the mandated dietary leashes or proprietary tattoos, Krazy Kat had turned into a dangerous monomaniac. As soon as the Kat was mature enough to reason, after about a year of accelerated and highly illegal trope dosing, he had fixated on the admittedly high-handed and wanton destruction of his fellow fetuses. Only surviving member of his aborted kind, the young Kat had gone on to study the conditions under which splices of all types served and lived amidst human society. What the Kat found apparently sent him over the edge. (And although I myself was certainly no cocktail-sucker, I had to admit that some of the excesses and abuses documented here and elsewhere were nauseating.)

At the age of five, Krazy Kat adopted the name by which the whole world would soon know him and took a vow. He would devote his life to liberating splices everywhere, waging a no-holds-barred campaign to make their "slavery" obsolete, too costly for human society to sustain.

Thus was born the Cultivar Liberation Front.

All this information had come to light shortly after Krazy Kat's first unexpected and initially inexplicable terrorist excursion, the slaughter of the board of directors of Hedonics Plus at their yearly meeting in Geneva. In the ensuing worldwide hunt for clues, the Tijuana branch of the Protein Police found Doc Radius's trashed lab, as well as the Doc himself, similarly lifelessly trashed. (At the time I had still been a loner PI, without access to this hush-hush information.) Seemingly, Radius had made the mistake of objecting to all or some of his progeny's plans and had gotten just what all humans deserved in the Kat's eyes. And although the Kat had thoroughly lysed all biomatter samples connected to his person, he had not been able or concerned enough to wipe all the audiovideo material the Doc had lovingly accumulated over the years.

I studied a still shot of the mature Kat: over two meters tall, tailed, one hundred kilos of rippling muscles under a tawny, nonbasal-striped pelt. His face was a sexy, oddly alluring, highly intelligent mix of panther, civet, and human features, marred only by what I intuited was a permanent sneer calculated to reveal a glint of sharp ivory teeth.

My speculative agents popped to the surface, shattering the Kat's image with their signature metagrafix swirls. They had no insights into what Boston could expect from the Kat, if he were indeed in town. He seemed never to repeat himself, had no favored tactics or, ahem, catspaws, being willing to strike anywhere, anytime, through or at anyone.

I dismissed the snippets and summoned my partner, knowing the kibe would already have assimilated the same data, in a fraction of the time. Waiting for it to arrive, I studied the swirling, captured tornado in its tube. The microweather's patternless patterns seemed to mock the chaos around me. But paradoxically, the border of chaos and stasis was where life flourished. . . .

My partner arrived.

(The Turing Level Four kibes came with a curious legal codicil. Just as any fully enfranchised individual was legally responsible for the actions of his or her immaterial agents and demons, shards and partials, so was any owner of a TL4 ultimately accountable for its words and deeds. Mostly, corporations bore the legal brunt; but among the Protein Police, the burden had devolved to the cops themselves, as a cost-cutting measure. If my TL4 did anything

contrasocial, it was *my* ass on the line. It was a big responsibility, almost like having a prodge. So I called my
partner "Sonny.")

Today Sonny was wearing a Hexcel Enforcer chassis:
a body with an armature of stonefiber bones, buckytube
circulatory system, muscles crafted of imipolex and re-
silin, hide of super-sharkskin, distributed co-ganglia.
Looking like a lumbering grey rubbery giant, the chassis
boasted a neckless human-like head with mock sensory
inputs designed to draw the deadly fire of any perp stupid
enough to attempt an assault on such a monster. The real
audiovisual-chemo sensors were concealed at various
points around the body, as was assorted weaponry. Slot-
ted safely behind a tough protective abdominal panel was
the kibe platter itself.

Sonny spoke in a pleasant tenor voice that seemed to
emerge from its armpit.

"I assumed from the data that there was a certain need
for overwhelming force in dealing with the renegade
splice. Was I in error, Peej?"

"No, not in error. But maybe just a wee bit premature."

After convincing Sonny to change into a relatively in-
conspicuous, less alarmingly destructive chassis (a BASF
mechanical model nicknamed "the Washtub"), we hit
the streets.

I had a destination in mind: the offices of the SPCC.
Chief Priestly had mentioned them. They were an obvious source of potential coconspirators for the Kat, but I
was almost certain that I'd get nothing out of them. But
frankly, it was the only lead I had.

Walking through Boston's noisy, hormone-hot streets,
breathing the clean exhaust of tuktuks, I tried to do as
the Chief had directed and use my putative crime-
sensitive nose.

Detouring down an alley off Arlington, I surprised a

pack of scavenger kibes trying to break into the Sino-chem Humpty Dumpster behind a bodyshop. The pack of ownerless runaway kibes needed certain organics for their maintenance and frequently resorted to theft, as well as begging. They must have disabled the Dumpster's flee-and-shriek circuits, for it could only rock back and forth in place and hoot dismally as they attempted forced entry into its separation chambers.

Before I could react, Sonny was barreling through the pack, scattering them left and right. A battered, unsteady nutraceutical dispenser marred with letterbomb graffiti toppled over, spinning its wheels uselessly. The rest fled.

Sonny extruded a snaky tentacle and found a socket on the crippled machine. He jacked in, and the renegade dispenser died.

"Another societal parasite terminated," Sonny declaimed with a trace of TL4 pride.

"Yeah, great. Come on, Judge Dredd, we've got bigger fish to fry."

"Metaphor?"

I sighed. *Just* like having a kid. "Yes."

"Filed."

After a stop at an open-air tolkuchki so that I could grab a snack of biltong and camu camu fruit, we reached the Stuart Street offices of the NGO known as the Society for the Prevention of Cruelty to Cultivars. After fencing with a wary human receptionist, I was admitted into the offices of the director, one Peej Jane Grahame-Ballard.

Grahame-Ballard was a small woman whose skull was capped with pink pinfeathers. Clad entirely in shiny non-organics, she was an obvious Carbaquist Reverencer, like 99 percent of the SPCC. She regarded me with a look such as an elderly splice must display when confronted with the knacker: a mix of fear, contempt, and hatred. In her wall cycled a silicrobe animation of a charming prodge and studly plug: scion and mate. I wondered if she'd offer to introduce *them* to Krazy Kat.

"Peej Grahame-Ballard," I said with all the respectful gravity I could muster, after flashing my credentials, "we have reason to believe that the terrorist splice known as Krazy Kat has fled to our bioregion after the recent thwarting of his plans in Chicago. Specifically, to the metroplex area. The Unit for Polypeptide Classification and Monitoring is counting on the cooperation of all your members in the hunt for the criminal. Should the cultivar in question make any attempt to contact your organization—should you even so much as hear a rumor regarding that individual—we insist that you immediately notify us."

Grahame-Ballard had been doing a slow burn during my speech and now boiled over. "Of course! So you can rush out and kill him! Without even a pretense of justice!"

"Justice is a word that applies only to the enfranchised, Peej. Need I remind you that for splices, we have a parallel, neatly graduated system of rules, rewards, and punishments, all formulated scientifically over many years by experts with efficiency and utilitarianism in mind. Owners are constrained from cruelty, abuse, and overwork, while splices are guaranteed food, shelter, and meaningful employment."

"It's slavery, pure and simple!"

"A word that has no application to any being other than a human, Peej. The transgenics are property, plain and simple, just like baseline milk cows or sheep."

"Creatures with up to forty-nine percent human genes are *property*?"

"I didn't make the laws, Peej. I just enforce them."

She snorted. "And as for abuses—why, I could show you the records of things that would penetrate even that armored skin of yours and make your stupid failsafe heart go into fibrillation!"

I thought about some of the things I had seen. "I sincerely doubt that, Peej."

"Every one of us should be ashamed to participate in such a system! Don't you ever feel ashamed?"

"Not when I'm doing my job, Peej."

Realizing she was getting nowhere with me, Grahame-Ballard seemed to deflate. "And your job now is to find and execute a noble creature who is plainly the moral and ethical and sentient equal of you or me. . . ."

"Peej," I said, trying to keep calm, "you have not seen the bloody results of that 'noble creature's' brutal actions. I have."

"And who made him what he is? Mankind!"

I got wearily to my feet. "Peej, the Kat is one bad splice. I advise you to use a long spoon when you dine with him."

"There are no bad splices, only bad owners."

"If you say so."

Back on the street I was silent for a while, letting Grahame-Ballard's rifkinesque memes percolate uneasily through my cortex.

After a few blocks, Sonny said, "We will now be staking out Peej Grahame-Ballard? Perhaps you have surreptitiously planted dustcams on her already?"

"What makes you say that?"

"Plainly you intend to catch her dining with Krazy Kat."

I had to replay the conversation in my head.

"Metaphor," I sighed.

"Thank you."

I met Xuly Beth that night in Hopcroft's Cockaigne.

In reality, of course, I was back in our apartment in Boston and she was off on assignment somewhere up in the Arctic, twiddling with icebergs or glaciers or some other such pleasantly nonsentient and tractable phenomenon. We made it a point when she was in the field to meet at least four times a week at one virtuality site or another. Our current favorite was Hopcroft's Cockaigne, with its candy mountains and sodapop rivers, peppermint trees and cottoncandy clouds. (Although I couldn't imagine coming here much more: not only was the construx starting to reveal its shallowness, but lately it reminded me too much of the strange reality humanity was making of baseline Earth!)

We were wearing our actual appearances, since we saw too little of each other lately to be bored by our real shapes and faces. A privacy filter insured that we were alone, despite the possibility that thousands of others might be wandering the same construx.

Sitting next to me on a bonbon rock soft as a sofa, Xuly Beth was finishing telling me about her day. "— so if this latest remediation works as well as the simulations project, the average sea level should start to drop by a quarter-inch per year! Why, we can probably start to repopulate Bangladesh by the next decade!"

"Uh-huh, great . . ."

Xuly Beth brushed back her pastel-green, metal-threaded hair from her brow, revealing twin barometric bumps. Together with her current skin choice of blocky maculations, the bumps conjured up the image of a gawky, lovable juvenile giraffe.

"You haven't heard a word I've said, have you?"

"I'm sorry, Jewely-Xuly, really, I am. It's just that this business with the Kat is itching me worse than a dose of cryptoshingles. It's not like dealing with your average criminal, some two-bit holopero or leeson. There, you've got someone embedded in a societal matrix. You generally have a good idea of what such a person wants and how he'll go about getting it. But the Kat is a loner with no goal other than to cause as much disruption as possible. He could strike anywhere, anytime!"

"And doubting yourself like this is going to solve the case?"

"No, I guess not. . . ."

Xuly Beth donned a look of concentration, fingering

her meteorological head bumps in the way she had when she was really puzzling something out. After a minute or so she said, "How can the Kat cause trouble? By himself, with a gun or a bomb, he's just another lone mucker. If he wants maximal damage, he's got to involve others. In Chicago he had to co-opt that posse, the Roaches, to carry out his plans. Even if he wants to release some deadly vector into the general population, he's got to find someone to batch it for him. He's no crick or watson himself, is he?"

"No, not as far as I know. . . ."

"So if you just start shaking down all the criminal sources of such things, you're bound to run into a signal that leads back to the Kat!"

I let out a sigh rather more hopeful than not. "You're right, of course. I should have thought of that angle myself. Nothing's hopeless. I guess I was just letting the magnitude of the case get me down. Plus someone I had to interview today said some things that made me wonder why I do what I do."

Xuly Beth stood up. "I knew it. You're just not thinking straight because you're missing your little weather-girl. Well, she has just what you need. . . ."

Xuly Beth disappeared, exiting the construx without even using a popup menu. In a few seconds she was back.

"I'm in my Sack, dear."

I didn't need to have my arm—or any other body part—twisted.

Breaking my neurolink to the telecosm, I found myself back in Boston. I took my Sack out of its maintenance rack, tickled it open, and climbed in.

You could have a strictly neuro-induced orgasm in virtuality, but for some strange reason—maybe lesser bandwidth, maybe something to do with sheldrakean fields—it just wasn't identical with a Sack-administered full-body experience.

Back in Cockaigne, Xuly Beth and I went into a naked-bodied clinch, fell to the ground, and began to tear up the turf. Back home and in the Arctic, two Sacks were thrashing.

I was sure that if the Unit for Polypeptide Classification and Monitoring knew that a side-effect of the somatic upgrade they insisted I have was heightened orgasms, they would have deducted something from my pay.

When the break finally came, it wasn't precisely from the criminal front. Rather, it was from an allied set of outcasts, self-exiled eccentrics despised by the majority of consensus-memed, post-reedpair citizens.

The Incubators.

The Incubators had figured in a previous case of mine, when I was still paired with K-mart. A new blight that affected only third-generation pumptrees from Hybritech had sprung up, and we suspected that the Incubators might have been somehow responsible for it. They had never exhibited any such terrorist inclinations before, but like most despised minorities, they were perpetual suspects whenever anything went wrong.

Since the metro relied on pumptrees and their enormous taproots for its water supply, there was immense pressure from the adminisphere to crack the case. So K-mart and I came down rather hard on the Incubators at the time. And what was worse, the misfits had been proven innocent, the cause of the new plague eventually being traced to a mutant smut that was able to prey on hematic vegetation.

So when, a few days after Xuly Beth and I had had our morale-boosting talk and telefuck, an anonymous demon showing only bland metagrafix delivered a tip that the Incubators had recently done a big job for a secretive client, I was aware I wouldn't be welcomed back with open arms.

But I was used to that.

Sonny was wearing a Boston Scientific chassis shaped like a small tank with multiple tentacles and spray nozzles. I knew the unit was effective, but it looked ridiculous. Not that I cared, since the possibility of a real lead at last had me higher than a dose of Kiss-the-sky.

"Hey, Dalek," I said, "let's go visit some pariahs."

Sonny lumbered after me. "Certainly, Doctor What."

"That's 'Who.' "

"The advantages inherent in the fuzzy logic circuits of a Turing Level Four device necessarily involve the ability to compromise data in a creative manner."

The Incubators had taken over an abandoned antique petroleum storage tank on the waterfront. The property was currently contested and in limbo, as the legal mess from the collapse of the petroleum industry was still being sorted out, some decades after the fall. Sooner or later, the new owners would find a use for the land and the squatters would be kicked out. But right now, it was all theirs.

At the makeshift sphincter door in the side of the tank facing the harbor, Sonny and I paused. "Stay out here and watch my back," I told the kibe.

"An instruction with contradictory semantics which I am fully capable of rationalizing."

I shook my head ruefully.

Cleaned up with Transcell Scrubbing Bubbles, the inside of the tank bore little residual scent. What it did smell like was a combination of mold, decay, dirty bandages, and sick breath.

And one additional, puzzling underscent that I couldn't quite place, even with my enhanced senses.

Dimly lit by scattered bioluminescent globes stuck here and there from floor to domed ceiling, the interior of the tank was filled with a mockcoral scaffolding.

From the organically fractal scaffolding hung the Incubators, in their various slings and cocoons, like basal gypsy-moth larvae in their tents.

I boosted my vision, but couldn't spot anyone down at my level. So I shouted up, "Protein Police! Is Smallpox here?"

There was no answer, but I saw a shifting among the calcite girders. A figure began to descend.

A lot of the members of the Incubators were immobilized by their perpetual, modified, nonconsuming diseases. That's why I had called for Smallpox, who had been one of the relatively active ones last time. (They were all noncontagious, though. Their propathogen ideology, however dogmatic, didn't extend to the point where they would have provoked a martyring backlash from the public.)

At last the climbing figure reached the floor and began to approach, limping in rags. I could see that it was indeed the riddled and cratered Smallpox.

"What do you want?" the pathogen-host demanded. "Can't you just let us cultivate our smallchain, low-gnomic refugees in peace? Isn't it bad enough that you high-gnomic imperialists have wiped the globe clean of so many innocent invisible lifeforms? Do you have to persecute our pitiful rescue mission too?"

"Listen, Smallpox, I don't care what you and Leprosy and Syphilis and Measles and Mumps and Polio and all the rest of your sick crew do with your own lives. But when I hear that you might be supplying contaminants to a bigtime terrorist, that's when you've crossed the line."

Smallpox cringed. "We didn't supply anybody with anything."

"Oh, no? That's not what I heard."

Smallpox turned to leave. "Go away," he muttered. "You can't prove anything."

I grabbed the small man by his rags, picked him up, and stuck my face into his raddled visage.

"Listen, my friend—how would you like to be *cured*?"

Smallpox blanched. "You—you wouldn't!"

"Try me."

"You murderer!" He began to kick. "All right, put me down, I'll talk."

I did, but kept alert for any funny moves.

"We have to earn a little eft somehow, you know," Smallpox began to whine. "And not many people will deal with us. So when we were approached with this assignment, we could hardly refuse. And besides, it was a technical challenge right up our alley."

"How's that?"

"This character—now, understand, I never actually *saw* him, so I couldn't *know* he was a baddie—kibes conducted the whole business—anyway, this plug wanted us to create a fast-acting, orally administered prion-based vector that would take up residence in the thalamus and upset the Llinas function."

I couldn't believe my ears. The Llinas function was the evolutionarily designed means whereby the thalamus, the brain's master clock, bound all sensory input and cortical responses into a coherent second-by-second gestalt of the universe. Even the big cricks hesitated to mess with such a core function.

"You're telling me that you've created an agent that will basically destroy a person's timebinding facility?"

"More or less. But all lifeforms are equal, and the prions will flourish without actually killing their hosts."

Sonny must have been reading my vital signs and detected my nervous concern, because he burst in like a mechanical octopus.

"Peej, what's to be done?"

"Wrap 'em."

Sonny's nozzles came alive, and within thirty seconds the Incubators were all enmeshed in sticky tangles. I called for a pickup and relayed what I had learned to Chief Priestly.

And that was the end of the easy part.

The entire complement of the UPCM, as well as hundreds of representatives from a dozen other bioregional and continental agencies, were now on the track of the Kat. The next day, after receiving Chief Priestly's faint praise (and implied condemnation for not somehow suspecting the Incubators sooner), I, too, was back on the streets.

The night of my discovery, I had met Xuly Beth in Cockaigne for what felt like the last time. The candyland had never seemed shallower. Postsex, as we were silently resting, she said, "Be careful, won't you?"

"Sure. Don't I have Sonny to watch over me?"

She laughed. "Turing is spinning in his grave!" Growing serious, she asked, "You still carry a poqetpal, even after your upgrades, right?"

"Of course. It's always smart to have a backup connection to the metamedium."

Xuly Beth fingered her bumps. "Good, good . . ."

The Incubators had all been thoroughly interrogated without revealing any further clues about where Krazy Kat was hiding. Sonny and I explored a half-dozen random possibilities without success. And all the time, something in the back of my mind was tickling my efferents.

Back at HQ, I took precious downtime to stare at the tornado-mandala.

And that's when it surfaced.

The odd scent in the tank.

I recognized it at last.

It was the scent of the Mats.

"Holy loas!" I said. "Sonny, come on!"

I didn't tell anyone where I was going, in case it turned out to be a wild-virus chase.

And as Doctor Varela would later show me, maybe I unconsciously wanted a one-on-one confrontation with the creature who had caused me so much frustration.

The UPCM kept a boathouse on the harbor. I signed out a swath—small waterplane area twin hull—and was soon zipping out to sea at a good speed.

"We checked out the Mats when our assignment was first given," protested Sonny, wearing a Hughes chassis today that resembled a multilegged Hallucinagenia out of the Burgess Shale.

"I know. But that's not to say that Krazy Kat wasn't elsewhere then, and on the Mats now."

"Possibly. I wish I had been able to confirm your hunch as to the origin of that smell."

"There was no time. Do you want to risk having those prions loosed on the human populace?"

"Then kibes would rule Boston."

I stared at the robot, but on this model there was no expression to interpret.

"A joke. Of the type that partners make to each other."

"Oh. Ha-ha."

It took an hour to reach the Mats, out around the Georges Bank, but I could smell them before I could see them.

The vast collection of cyanobacteria and diatoms carpeted several thousand square kilometers of sea, looking like a mushy ectoplasmic rug, floating meatloaf. Source of multipurpose biomass, home to a flourishing ecology of both basal and biofabbed useful and edible creatures, the Mats were cultivated for humanity by special-purpose, low-intelligence kibes.

One or more of which the Kat must have subverted and sent to do his bidding.

At the landward edge of the Mats, a small floating station anchored to the seafloor served the rare human visitors: an OTEC power plant, a beacon, an emergency habitat.

We docked. I wasn't attempting to be quiet, since there was nowhere for the Kat to go or hide.

"Watch the boat," I told Sonny.

"Until otherwise needed."

I climbed onboard the gently rocking deck of the lonely, midocean outpost.

In the north, I could see curious stormclouds massing in a previously clear sky. But I couldn't spare any thought or attention for the weather. My whole being was attuned to picking up the presence of the Kat. But so far, nothing.

That was why I was so surprised when, as I approached one side of the platform, his paw burst from the water and clamped around my ankle.

He yanked, I went down, but not in, as I grabbed onto a stanchion. Feeling resistance, the Kat exploded out of the water and onto the deck. He kicked, I rolled, found my feet, and confronted him in a fighter's crouch.

"Sonny!" I yelled.

"Coming, Pee—" said the kibe.

Then there was a splash.

Two harvesters had clambered aboard the swath and dumped Sonny overboard. My partner had gone to swim with the fishes. And he couldn't swim.

That left me and the Kat.

I suppose I should have been honored to be one of the few humans ever to directly confront the legendary splice. But instead I was scared into almost a Blankie-wearing state. After the way he had so easily brought me down, I had to run an emergency mantra just to stay cool.

Even dripping wet, fur plastered to his noble body, ears flattened to his skull, Krazy Kat looked every bit the Byronic antihero. There was something regal and wild about him and, I could see how his image had captivated so many to his doomed cause.

"Give it up, Kat, and I promise you won't get hurt," I bluffed.

His voice mixed purr and snarl, his whiskers twitched. "No, just imprisoned and reviled, made to kiss my inferior's boots!"

"Better to live than to die."

"Not on those terms!"

"Your call," I said, then held my palm out to him in a gesture like a traffic kibe's.

Antipersonnel spray—blistering, blinding, stifling—lanced out from my exocrine glands and caught the Kat in the face.

Roaring, he launched himself at me despite the pain. We hit the plates, and I felt his teeth in my neck, piercing my imbricated skin. My grip on his shoulders meant nothing to him.

I guessed I was about to find out how good neo-goretex veins were.

Things started to get black, and I thought my vision was going.

But it turned out to be the clouds above.

And as I looked in disbelief, all hell broke loose.

Lightning, thunder, rain in buckets, then the final punch: a microburst of wind similar to the kind that could and had leveled whole tracts of forest in pre-GEF days.

The Kat and I were sluiced off the bucking station and into the sea. Beneath the waves, I finally managed to break his hold—or did he release me? In any case, I was free.

I fought my way to the surface. There was no sign of the Kat.

Instead there was a fleet of approaching swaths, into one of which I was soon unceremoniously hauled.

We searched for the Kat with eyes and instruments and remotes for several hours, but of that bad, bad splice there was no sign. He had gone to feed the hungry sea, or perhaps not. Though escape seemed impossible.

Before we left, we even managed to track down Sonny and raise it from the ocean floor. The kibe had been head-

ing back on the bottom under its own power and probably
would have made it, if its brick hadn't run down.

The first call I took after getting patched up was from
Chief Priestly, who dished out her usual mix of puffery
and abuse.

The second one was from Xuly Beth.

"Isn't Global Positioning wonderful?" she said, joy-
fully teary-eyed.

"And aren't I lucky to have a friend in high places?"

"The stratosphere, to be precise," said Xuly Beth.

 **McGregor**

1. The Tale of Peter Rabbit

Peter Rabbit stubbed out his cigarette on the rock upon which he sat, sent the dead butt spinning with a flick of a stubby claw, and sighed.

It was night. The fragrant country air around him carried cleanly the noises of noncultivar life, poignant cries, lonely calls, sly rustlings.

Frogs, but no Jeremy Fisher.

Owls, but no Mr. Brown.

Badgers, but no Tommy Brock.

Hedgehogs, but no Mrs. Tiggywinkle.

These, his fellow splices, were penned, not free to roam as was he.

Peter reached up to the tip of one long ear, the left. That ear had been illegally docked two years ago, shortly after Peter's escape from the Garden. This had been the only way to remove the silicrobe owner-tattoon, the Warne licensing mark, which had been injected at the Schering-Plough biofab facility, on behalf of McGregor's gembaitch, before Peter was shipped. Afterwards, the ear had been regenerated. But the new part had always felt foreign. Peter had a tendency to finger it when he was nervous, as he was now.

His perch was high on a hill in the Lake District, near the village of Sawrey, in the western bioregion of the European Community. Below, the village was lit by the delicate glow of low-photonic reradiants. To the south Peter could see the grounds of the Beatrix Potter epcot, otherwise known as the Garden.

How long ago his life there seemed. . . . He had spent only thirteen months in the Garden, but it had felt like forever. The silly skits, the gawping EC, NU, and CoPro tourists, the tasteless food—Through kinky proteins or rebel peptides, he had found himself totally unfit for his servitude.

The two years—a fifth of his warrantied lifespan— since his flight into the arms of the CLF had been packed with activity. On death's very doormat from lack of diet-supplements, he had stumbled upon the London nucleus of the CLF just in time. After the docking and the standard course of trope-training and soma-toning, he had been ready to play his part in transgenic liberation.

He had participated in the infamous *Corrida de la Muerte* massacre in Madrid during the first part of '31. He had helped slag the board of directors of Hedonics Plus, the greedy human prokes, at their annual meeting in Geneva. He had been trapped in a shootout with the Brazz branch of the IMF police in the Jibaro maximall, barely escaping with his life. He had even assisted the CLF's leader, the legendary Bad Splice, Krazy Kat, in Chicago, as they sought to turn the Big Eaters against the municipality.

In short, Peter had lived a full life in the past two years. The things he had seen and done had made him a hardened rabbit.

Yet now, contemplating the notion of facing McGregor again, remnants of his old factory conditioning surfaced, nearly rendering him helpless as a kit.

He had asked for this assignment. But that didn't mean he had to relish it.

Peter reached inside the pocket of his tarnished-brass-buttoned blue coat for a dose of angst-banger and swallowed it dry. Tugging at a whisker, he sought to focus his mind on the task at hand. As the renegade splice watched, the big holosign outside the epcot winked out, and the last tourbus skimmed off.

Now the only human (mere 51 percenter that he was, he still legally merited that status) left in the Garden was McGregor.

Now McGregor would begin to indulge in the "perks" of his position.

Now the splices had cause to fear.

Peter repressed his anger at the thought of what would be starting down in the Garden at this moment. The blocker was kicking in, and it helped him to be calm. He could not enter the Garden until McGregor retired for the night, some hours from now. Till then, there was nothing to do but wait.

Peter lit up another cigarette.

Filthy human habit.

But he would never live long enough to get cancer.

2. The Tale of Two Bad Mice

McGregor leaned on his cane, waving to the departing tour bus in his creaky, lovable-irascible, old farmer way. When it had rounded the curve, he verbed off the holosign.

Then he straightened.

Standing erect, McGregor no longer radiated an air of cantankerous decrepitude. He seemed to bulk out, filling his suit of simulated brown homespun with limbs and torso powerful as one of the Deere-Goldstar autoharvesters that reaped the surrounding fields. The big white beard cascading to his shirtfront looked completely incongruous now, as did his spectacles and cane.

Of a sudden, with an uncanny howl, McGregor tossed his cane skyward. It soared higher than the chimney pots on Hill Top Farmhouse. Off came the glasses and beard, as well as the clothes and hat. (The animatronic beard crawled a few inches, then halted.)

Revealed was a body whose torso was plated ventrally and dorsally with tough overlapping armadillo-like scales. McGregor's arms and legs were wrapped with muscle, like those of a dock-ape. His skull was hairless; silicrobe patterns pulsated just under the scalp, synced electro-myographically with his extra cortical matter. His genitals, retractable, were hidden.

McGregor spun to face the darkened barn.

"Your act died today!"

There was no sound from the barn. Only a subliminal emotional quivering seemed to emanate in cold waves from the structure.

McGregor stalked to the splices' after-hours residence.

He banged the big door open.

The inside of the old-fashioned structure, which was not part of the tour, was one large open space walled and floored with seamless arbo-poly, for easy cleaning. D-compoz waste units stood out in the open in one corner. Cots were placed dormitory-style along the walls, each with a small footlocker for whatever personal possessions the splices had been allowed to accumulate: curry combs and liniment; sweets from the Ginger and Pickles concession stand, tossed to them by the patrons; a change of clothes.

By each cot stood its occupant, at full attention.

The smallest of the transgenics—the mice, the frogs, the squirrels—stood on their altered hindlegs as tall as McGregor's waist. The next largest—the rabbits, the dogs, the cats—came as high as his shoulder.

McGregor let the property sweat for a whole minute. Then he whirled and pointed a finger at Pigling Bland.

"You!"

Tears began to well from the pig's eyes, runnelling to either side of his snout. He dabbed at them with the sleeve of his brown frock coat.

"Please, sir, my pig license is all in order. . . ."

But McGregor had already rounded on another victim. "Puddleduck!"

Jemima's beak opened and closed several times in stupefaction, before she could finally clumsily articulate, "My bonnet is tied, my shawl is neat. My bonnet is tied, my shawl—"

At last McGregor settled on his real targets.

"Tom! Hunca! Front and center!"

Tom Thumb and his mate Hunca Munca came shakily forward. The two mice hung their heads wearily, knowing full well what was to come and the futility of resistance.

At this moment a fox appeared in the doorway. Fully as tall as McGregor, the Garden's second-in-command wore a brown suitcoat, vest, and cravat. He carried McGregor's cane.

Mr. Tod, the fox, smiled now, showing sharp teeth.

With the mice a foot or two from McGregor, he assailed them. "When you wrecked the dollhouse at the three o'clock show, you broke a dish!"

Tom Thumb looked at Hunca Munca, and she looked at him. Their relatively small and shiny brown eyes caught the light from the ceiling fixtures. Then the male mouse spoke.

"We are supposed to break a dish. We discover that the ham is plaster. We chitter angrily. I pick up the tongs. I hit the ham—"

"You broke the wrong dish! You broke an empty dish!"

"No, I am sure I hit only the ham—"

"Enough! Give me the cane!"

The fox, his bushy tail held stiffly erect, his claws

clicking on the floor, crossed to McGregor and handed him the cane.

McGregor twisted the cane's top to Setting Eleven.

He began to beat the mice. The lightest touch of the cane sufficed.

They squealed and cried. Others among the watching splices began to weep too. But it was no use. The blows were unrelenting.

Hunca Munca had collapsed to the floor. Trying to keep her head low, she raised her scut high.

McGregor's genitals began to emerge.

3. Appley Dapply's Nursery Rhymes

Gestation Jest
McGregor's mum was a limited's crick,
And her solo son was a pro's best trick!
She ran his specs on a micro-fab,
And bent her egg in the company's lab!
A few months later the lad emerged,
Stylish toy of the maternal urge!

Paraparenting
Her smart card toted megamiles on the
   Suborbital Express,
As she did thirty minutes' work, Bangkok to
   Baltiscandia,
Leaving once again, Mum spared McGregor
   one thoughtless brief caress,
Before passing him to a Ciba-Geigy nurse—
   much handier!

A Song of Youth
Nurse was a cocktail of 'possum and 'roo,
Attentive, loving, and sweet.
McGregor spent hours out of view,

Pouched and on a teat.
When older, his mum began to feel
His education must begin.
Tropes and boosters and Digireal
All were funneled in.
One day he was living virtually,
When something happened unheard-erous.
The digiverse was suddenly, hurtfully
Amok and truly murderous!
Electron fangs and claws raked the lad,
As the cuddly characters, all beasts,
Picked up crosstalk from a channel bad,
Where kingfans held their gory feasts.
By the time he ripped away the set,
McGregor was a neural wreck.
And worse, he found his mouth all wet
With blood from Nurse's neck!
The rehab boys plied their pills,
And then pronounced him sane.
But really McGregor's creepy ills
Were still hidden in his brain.

Whimper While You Work
Now he's grown and wants employment.
Might as well mix work with enjoyment!
Digireal's fine (when it's not all bollixed!)
But folks still crave some solid frolics.
'Round the globe the epcots sprout—
Watch the classix acted out!
What better place for McGregor to live
Than among those where he can stick his shiv!

4. The Tale of the Flopsy Bunnies

Peter came into the barnyard around three in the morning. The epcot had minimal security, directed mostly against human intruders, the occasional lone vandal or thrill-seeking metroplex posse. The system presented no challenge to the guerrilla skills of one who had trained with the Sequoia Revenge Squad at their camp hidden in the Cascades. As for potential escapees, their biological tethers were deterrence enough. It was a rare splice who could summon up the courage to flee into a society where all authority was ranked against him, where his very sustenance was a controlled substance.

But it was Peter's task tonight to convince his compatriots to do just such a thing.

Hill Top Farmhouse was quiet and dark. On the first floor lived Mr. Tod; on the second, McGregor. Peter bristled at the thought of the pair. With luck, he could accomplish his goals without ever encountering the wardens.

At the barn door, he paused. Sniffing, he found only fading traces of McGregor's scent, sweat, and spume. But Peter's nose was half-ruined from fags, and he hardly trusted it. Still, in conjunction with the winking out of the Farmhouse lights he had witnessed, the evidence was enough.

Possessed by an urge to mark this territory he was about to conquer, Peter slid his cock from its sheath and pissed briefly against the door, imagining it as McGregor's face. The earth absorbed the steaming urine hungrily as Peter worked the latch.

The door creaked slightly as he slid inside.

The noise was enough to wake Squirrel Nutkin.

"Krrrk, krrrk, krrrk! It's the old Peter, the old Peter!"

"Quiet, you sodding rodent! Oh, damn!"

Nutkin's cries had roused all the sleepers. Peter had hoped to wake a few of the more solid types first, those who in his judgment had the most initiative and could help him deal with the more timorous and confused. Too late for that now, though.

Lights flared on. Luckily, the barn's windows existed

only as holo trompe l'oeil. McGregor would receive no alert that way.

All eyes—big and wet, small and glittering, nictitating and night-seeing—were fastened on him. Peter let them absorb the full meaning of his presence: a runaway splice had survived, even prospered.

The collie dog, Kep, was first to speak.

"Why do you return? We have a new Peter now. Have you put yourself under human control? Where is your mark?"

Peter held himself proudly erect. "I'm no slave, I'm a free var, equal to any proking fifty-oner. And I'm here to set all of you free too. There's a van with a driver just a mile off. We couldn't bring it any closer without being detected, and we didn't want to mount a full raid if we needn't do so. All you have to do is follow me, and by tomorrow morning you'll all be your own masters. The Tailor of Gloucester will unkink your chromos."

Nervous babble broke out among the splices.

"What will we eat?" asked Tom Kitten.

"Who will clothe us?" asked Mrs. Tittlemouse.

"What will we do with ourselves all day?" asked Samuel Whiskers.

Peter was disgusted. "None of your questions matter! Trust me, the CLF will see to all your needs. What matters is escape. Now!"

Duchess, the black dog, spoke. "How do we know the CLF can protect us?"

"We are powerful! Our leader is brave and wise. Even now he plans a powerful strike against the humans in Nova England! We have many friends and allies. The Ahimsa League, the underground arm of the SPCC— Have you not heard of Celesteville? The Anzanian government has deeded us a preserve, where all splices may live freely. Those who do not want to participate in the armed struggle may settle there. King Babar needs good citizens."

"You lie! You want to lead us to our deaths!"

Peter turned.

He confronted himself.

The replacement Peter stood next to his mate, Flopsy. Unlike the renegade Peter, he was finely groomed and plump, the buttons of his jacket all polished. Every line of his furry countenance indicated how thoroughly he had been indoctrinated in subservience by a supplier eager to redeem itself for its defective model. Knowing the other rabbit was bound by his conditioning, Peter held no enmity toward him. And in truth, his attention was fixed more on the seductive figure beside him.

He had almost forgotten what a beautiful doe Flopsy was. Her bib was thick and creamy, her haunches strong, her nose sexily moist.

Peter's years of self-sacrifice had included little time for romance. Now, the nights he and Flopsy had spent rutting together, enjoying the only solace available in captivity, returned to him with almost punishing force.

Realizing that he could not let the other rabbit spook the indecisive slaves, acting out of both expediency and jealousy, Peter hopped at the cowardly rabbit. The substitute Peter raised his forepaws awkwardly in defense. But he was no match for the martially trained outsider. In a trice, muzzle bloodied, the other rabbit lay on the floor.

The splices were stunned into silence. The hum of the ventilation system sounded like a hurricane. Peter tensed himself for further violence.

Flopsy spoke, her eyes shining at the return of her first mate. "The meek die on their knees! We walk on two legs! All power to the CLF!"

A chorus of acclamation gradually swelled. Peter was too proud to caution them. They would be gone soon anyway.

He put his arm around Flopsy, feeling the desire to cover her stir in his loins.

Out in the world, her fecundity restored, they would breed free kits that would make mankind tremble!

5. The Story of a Fierce Bad Rabbit

McGregor, cradled in his organiform bed on the second level of Hill Top Farmhouse, was dreaming. In his dream, he was sitting in a comfy squirmonomic chair, wearing a Digireal set, laniering virtuality. A dream within a dream.

The virtual-ware was a standard Microdelrey scenario, all reassuring arcadian simplicity. McGregor's virtual self was five years old. He walked hand-in-hand with Nurse and Mum down shaded paths, butterflies flittering, the scent of hay in his nostrils.

Suddenly, from behind a shrub leaped a giant animal, a slavering rabbit with a mouthful of fangs! In an instant he was joined by another, and another!

The rabbits grabbed his guardian and his mother, and began to bite their necks and rend their flesh.

McGregor screamed/twisted in his chair/writhed in his bed.

The rabbits, finished with the lifeless corpses of the adults, their snouts incarnadined, turned on the little boy.

He bit his tongue/bit his tongue/bit his tongue, till blood flowed/flowed/flowed.

The monitors in the bed finally kicked in, and the system administered a dose of RU-9000.

McGregor felt the killers' claws and smelled their meaty breath/pulled off the Digireal set/awoke with a jolt.

The taste of his own blood was like sucking on an antique drycell. Sitting up, he spat red and the bed absorbed it. Then, he listened.

The fading echoes of noise from the barn drifted through an open window with the breeze. . . .

What the breeding fuck was going on with those vars?

Was it some argument among themselves, a fight over rut or sweet? He had warned them about excess activity after lights-out. By arnie, he'd iraq and pakistan their worthless hides!

A thought came to him. He spoke to the Farm.

"Hill Top."

"Yes?"

"Any intruders?"

"The perimeter sensors report the passage of no creature massing more than ten ounces."

Ten ounces? That was impossible. The countryside was swarming with creatures bigger than that, their nightly runs cutting across the Garden, their bioparms programmed to register, yet not sound an alarm. The sensors had to be jiggered.

"Hill Top."

"Yes."

"Notify the Sawrey dirty-harrys. We have a trespasser. Get me a kill clearance."

A high-baud squirt down the optics and a squirt back.

"Secured."

Not bothering to dress, McGregor reached down from its wallrack a bell-mouthed gun with a magazine shaped like an old-fashioned film canister, its alloy stock featuring oval cutouts as a weightsaving measure.

Downstairs, McGregor roused a gently snoring Mr. Tod. (Many splices, their vocal apparatus modified in the sim-womb for speech, suffered from attendant respiratory problems.)

"Get your slagging withers out of bed. We've got a fox in the henhouse."

"A fox?"

"Don't take me so fucking literally, you stupid trans. Now move it or lose it."

Leaving Mr. Tod to catch up, McGregor raced swiftly and silently toward the barn.

The door was slightly ajar, its rim edged with light.

McGregor kicked it off its hinges.

His extra wetware instantly processed the scene revealed to him, as if it were a freeze-frame.

Several splices crushed beneath the falling door. All the rest clumped in a loose knot around two rabbits. A third rabbit lying on the floor.

The renegade Peter!

Lone blot on McGregor's record . . .

The scene went realtime.

The bad rabbit darted a paw under its coat. McGregor recognized a Jumpstart shoulder harness. The pistol leaped out into the rabbit's paw.

But McGregor had already fired.

A small packet burst against Peter's chest.

Faster than even McGregor's eye could follow, Peter was wrapped from head to toe in Ivax netting, his pistol trapped against his body. He teetered for a moment, then toppled.

McGregor walked confidently up to the trameled rabbit, the stunned splices shakily parting for him.

"Fucking Crusader Rabbit . . . What'll you do now?"

Not waiting for Peter's answer, heedless of the soreness of his own door-bruised limb, McGregor buried his foot in the var's stomach.

6. The Tale of Mr. Tod

Mr. Tod, grunting on his foxy-smelling doss-pad on the first level of Hill Top Farm, was dreaming.

He was free, free to course the hills and valleys of the immemorial land in his ancestral unmodified form. 'Cross brook and meadow he ranged, following the scents of friend and foe, mate and prey. The sun, the wind, the deep den in winter, these were all he required to be happy. His life was a fulfilling completeness in itself.

In this dream, Mr. Tod had a nightmare.

Humans caught him and tied him to a rack. They bent and twisted his limbs until he yelped with searing pain. When he finally resembled his tormentors, they released him and gave him duties. To watch similarly tortured creatures, guard and chivy them. In return, he was "rewarded": a suit of useless clothes, cloying food, the occasional hurried mating with an imported vixen delivered by the Hedonics Plus van, synthetic chases of bloodless quarry through the thickets of his own brain. . . .

In this nightmare, the days passed like an eternal winter. He struggled to return to his real life. With a vast effort he awoke—

Then awoke once more, back into the nightmare.

Carrying a gun, McGregor was shaking him roughly. Was it morning already? He could hear the tourists laughing at his antics. "Who's been eating from my pie-dish? Who's been using my best tablecloth? It must be that odious Tommy Brock. And look, he's sleeping in my bed! I'll teach him—"

But no, it was not even dawn yet. McGregor was saying something about a fox. He was the only fox here, wasn't he? Why couldn't the man let him sleep? He was supposed to be allowed to sleep at night. At the training kennel the teachers had promised him an easy life. They had claimed he would have a kind master. But McGregor was not kind, far from it. He hurt splices, seemed to enjoy it. And he forced Mr. Tod to aid him. Mr. Tod worried about this. He did not want to hurt anyone unnecessarily. You killed only to eat, in order to survive. Hurting was not sport. Sport was frisking and mating— Yet what could he do? McGregor had to be obeyed. . . .

Now the man was suddenly gone. Mr. Tod forced himself to get up. He took his coat down from a peg and donned it. "You must not appear out of costume in public. . . ." Then he went outside.

The barn door was missing, light spilling out. This was

not normal. Mr. Tod snapped alert. Danger thrummed in the very air, as when the baying of a pack of hounds was heard.

Cautiously, Mr. Tod poked his pointy nose around the empty doorframe.

McGregor stood above a rabbit in a net. The rabbit was gasping for breath and retching.

As Mr. Tod watched, the splice named Flopsy made a move toward McGregor, who swiveled his gun toward her.

"You too?" said the man.

Flopsy halted. "You may stop us today, but you won't hold us forever. The end of your rule is coming. There is a place where splices live free—"

Mr. Tod listened unbelievingly. Not privy to the whispered nightly rumors exchanged among the barn-dwellers, he had never heard of such a thing. Could it be true? There was the presence of the bound rabbit to consider. Wait, was he the old Peter?

McGregor silenced Flopsy with a backhand across her muzzle, rocking her on her big feet.

"Anyone else have something to say?" he demanded.

The splices all looked at the floor. McGregor laid down his gun. One of Peter's ears, the left, protruded from the net. McGregor grabbed it and effortlessly lifted Peter up to his feet.

"I've been waiting a long time for this—"

Peter had managed to regain his breath. Mustering all his strength, he spat now into McGregor's face.

"Eat your own pellets, proke!"

McGregor howled and closed his hands on Peter's neck.

Something snapped in Mr. Tod.

He launched himself across the distance separating him from the struggle.

The impact of Mr. Tod on the man shattered his choke-hold and knocked him to the floor.

Mr. Tod scrambled atop McGregor.

"What—" was all McGregor had time to utter.

Then Mr. Tod fastened his teeth in McGregor's reinforced throat.

Roaring, McGregor reflexively began to throttle the fox.

Mr. Tod did not let go. Though all grew black, though the sound of some celestial hunter's horn filled his ears, his powerful jaws remained fastened tightly until he was dead.

But by then, so was McGregor.

7. Cecily Parsley's Nursery Rhymes

Mrs. Tiggywinkle freed Peter with her pinking shears. He surprised himself by being able to stand on his own.

His throat felt like he had smoked a pack of fags in five minutes. His left ear throbbed. When he had fallen, his pistol had gouged him. Yet he had never felt better.

Regarding the pair of corpses at his feet, Peter sensed words swelling up unbidden in him.

"In the end, Tod was no quisling, but a true splice. And if man has stripped us of our birthright, he has also showed us the commonality of our lot. Fox saves rabbit, cat helps mouse, the lion lies down with the lamb. Tod's death was not the first, nor will it be the last. But without our further actions, it could be in vain. Come, we must flee."

Outside, as the splices gathered 'round him, looking nervously at the world that awaited them, Peter removed a letterbomb from his coat.

He threw the capsule at the barn.

Shattering and splattering the wall, the intelligent silicrobe paint formed a departing message from the CLF.

We have a little garden,
A garden of our own,
And every day we water there
The seeds that we have sown.

⚡ Brain Wars

SEND:	IMF MOBILE NODE
	SYS01-4591P
RECEIVE:	MC MURDO BIOSPHERE
DATE/HOUR:	070465: 070465/1275
TRANSMISSION STATUS:	OK

Dear Host Mother,

The invasion is over, and I'm fine. Safe as a blastula in a bioreactor, in fact, here inside our risk bubble.

Which is more than I can say for the enemy, Mom. We pretty much turned them into sodai gomi in less time than it takes to flip a SQUID.

I'm really sorry I can't raster you face-to-face or virt you in Candyland and see you smile at the good news. I can almost picture you nictitating that way you do when you're happy. But for reasons of security, us zygotes (that's just a friendly term the officers have for noncoms) don't have full access to the metamedium. We've been stripped of all our telltags and poqetpals, most of us for the first time in our lives. I feel plumb naked! We're limited to this retro-jethro Teleport bonovox line, I guess so no live Si-viruses or GaAs-worms can slip in or out. And in fact, all these sending units have a TL1 AI chip

in them that will automatically erase any critical information from the transmission. Like for instance, if I were
to try to tell you that we're stationed just north of CEN-
SORED, or that our KIA's amounted to CENSORED,
the machine would simply blip that part right out.

Works out just as well as the metamedium, I guess,
what with CENSORED time-zones between us and all.

Anyway, the important thing is that our mission seems
to be a big success. Once again, the IMF has managed
to intervene just in time to stop a potential catastrophe.

I'll tell you more in a while. But right now my main
proxy, Penguin, is calling me. Seems we have to use the
simorg colony to evolve some new expert modules they
need by yesterday!

Your loving guest-son,
CENSORED

SEND:	IMF MOBILE NODE
	SYS01-4591P
RECEIVE:	MC MURDO BIOSPHERE
DATE/HOUR:	070465/1610
TRANSMISSION STATUS:	OK

Dear Host Mother,

What a jangle-tangle! The brass-skulls and swellheads
stopped by with a crew of noahs from the GEF wanting
to evaluate the oceanic/atmospheric contamination produced by this latest Short War, and Penguin and I were
kept busy bending molecules during what should have
been our down-time. (At least one of the noahs, a Xuly
Beth Vollbracht, was nice enough to bring along a dose
of recreational tropes to share with us.) Anyhow, they
finally finished with us, and since Penguin wanted to go
offline for a while, I thought I'd pick up my transmission
to you where I left off.

Now, I know you and I have had our disagreements

about the IMF's policies. Why, sometimes you actually sounded like a rifkin or greenpeacer! I can remember you saying, "I never got to vote for the World Bank board." But we all got to vote for the politicians who voted for them, whether we hailed from a big polypax like the NU or the EC, or a little one like our own McMurdo, so we can't really blame anyone else when the IMF does something we don't particularly like. I'm thinking of the mess they made in what used to be Yongbyon—the "Pyongyang Gang Bang" I remember you called it—and the way they handled (or mishandled) those renegade cricks and transgenics hiding out in the Azores. The Atlantic will recover faster from that one than the IMF's reputation will!

But those incidents took place before I joined, which you'll recall was right after the big command shakeup. My own unit was purged of all its officers, and Oberjefe Ozal received a field promotion, which he still holds. I think you'd like Ozal, he's a smart, goodlooking probe— the NYC gals in our pod all call him a "streetbeat gamete," which I guess is some kind of compliment—but he's not conceited. His main philofix is music. He plays his qawwali tabs whenever he has a spare moment— mostly thru earwigs, since no one else really enjoys the holy Slammer wailing.

Anyhow, I can't say I feel any personal responsibility for any of the IMF's previous goo-screwing cockups (pardon the language), and nothing I've taken part in since I signed up has led me to regret my decision.

I've got to cut this short now, since one of my proxies is waiting to use the 'vox unit. I'll be right back.

Your loving guest-son,
CENSORED

SEND: IMF MOBILE NODE
             SYS01-4591P
RECEIVE: MC MURDO BIOSPHERE

DATE/HOUR: 070465/1918
TRANSMISSION STATUS: OK

Dear Host Mother,

Sorry about the delay. My buddy got an incoming 'vox right after he sent his. It was a "Dear Juan," wishing him a nasty hasta luego. Seems his target had joined the antiwar movement since he shipped out and now wants nothing to do with "bloody imperialist murderers" like us. It took some major tropes and a lot of talk to calm him down.

I just can't understand these protectors, Mom. It must be that they don't know what's really going on here. If they did, they'd realize we're just doing what has to be done.

I'm real proud of this operation, my first major action. We made the enemy "cry onco!" faster than ribozymes. I wish I could tell you all about it, since I understand the metamedium coverage was somewhat limited. I'll try, and see what the chip lets thru.

The IMF issued its unconditional surrender ultimatum at 2300 hours on the second of this month. By 2400 hours, when the enemy had still not replied, the operation commenced. First in were the smartskin bombers, scramjets mostly under AI control, but a few being gloved by pilots offshore in MHD subs. These planes released burrowers, antipersonnel midges, thermites, core-borers, glass-masters, virtual ghosts, and CENSORED. The enemy responded with Raid-Plus, bouncing buckyballs, fractal shrubs, moletraps, CENSORED, and kaleidoscopes, but were mucho outclassed. There was never really any contest.

Hot on the first wave's heels, the APV's loaded with transgenic troops moved in for whatever close fighting might arise. The Fourth Wolverines really distinguished themselves, as did the CENSORED. Once I-Cubed reported that things were pretty much under control, approximately CENSORED of us fifty-oners went in, the only humans involved in the whole shootup.

When the enemy's AI's committed silicide, we knew the latest Short War was history.

Mom, I'll tell you now that what we found once we occupied the enemy's territory—in confirmation of the rumors that prompted the assault—is enough to make your cells metastasize. These guys had developed a whole armory of aerosol-borne neurotropic weapons which they planned to use shortly on their immediate neighbors, and afterwards on whoever got in their way. Of course this is entirely against the Minsk Conventions, which they are a signatory to, and these gnomic jokers had to be stopped.

I don't imagine the next few days will see much excitement. We're just riding herd on the civilian populace while the experts from the essays, peltsies, beeves, and gembaitches—Textron, Rhone-Daewoo, Toyobo, Ciba-Kobe, EMBRAPA—dismantle the armament autofacs.

I've got some I&I leave coming up after this is over and expect to spend some of it with you and Dad and Mom2 and Dad2 and Mom3.

Crank those photoharvesters up—I'm used to the tropics now!

Your loving guest-son,
CENSORED

SEND:	IMF MOBILE NODE
	SYS01-4591P
RECEIVE:	MC MURDO BIOSPHERE
DATE/HOUR:	070565/0325
TRANSMISSION STATUS:	OK

Dear Host Mother,
We just stepped down from Fever Alert Status.

It appears that some autonomous remnant of the enemy is still functioning.

Most of us were sleeping when our earwigs gave the alarm. I never thought the words "perimeter breach!" could sound so chilling. We all scrambled into our Affymax millipore gear, praying that we hadn't catalyzed anything contrametabolic. Almost before we could grab our highkinetics and lyzers, the "all clear" came thru. The tinmen and transgenics had neutralized the invaders, who amounted only to a handful of Gorilla guerrillas. Examination of the corpses revealed nothing out of the ordinary—except for one thing. The vars had CENSORED incorporated into their bodies, right next to their CENSORED. These add-ons were empty, indicating they might have had time to spray something before being smoked.

That something, they tell us, could be time-delayed in its effects.

We're all just sitting around now on our hands while the mccoys and herriots go over us with their cell-sniffers and hormone hounds, squeezing our virtual platelets for anything nonsomatic. So I thought I'd 'vox you this letter.

Don't worry.

Your loving guest-son,
CENSORED

SEND:	**IMF MOBILE NODE**
	SYS01-4591P
RECEIVE:	**MC MURDO BIOSPHERE**
DATE/HOUR:	**070565/0800**
TRANSMISSION STATUS:	**OK**

Dear,

Can't find to refer to. Seem to have disappeared from. Made bad inside. Very bad. Hard to use common. Looks strange near and far. Because of made bad up inside. Hopeful to fix. Examine, then create. Reassurring.

But—partly running around crazy. Dangerous. Watch, shoot—how? Forget how to use without.

Sit still. Holding together, lovely and crying. Please don't cry. Can't convey. Too frustrating to go on.

Will 'vox soon.

Don't worry.

Your loving,

CENSORED

SEND:	IMF MOBILE NODE SYS01-4591P
RECEIVE:	MC MURDO BIOSPHERE
DATE/HOUR:	070565/1200
TRANSMISSION STATUS:	OK

Dear Host Mother,

Whew! Am I glad the past four hours are over!

My last transmission probably didn't make a whole lot of sense to you. That was because I couldn't use any nouns! You see, everyone in the pod was experiencing a selective aphasia, kind of a language blind spot. A whole category of language had been effectively wiped from our cortexes. Or so the blood-dusters tell us.

It appears that the trope the enemy hit us with was something brand new. The experts have dubbed it a "multi-vector recombinant silicrobe." It resembles our own CENSORED, only several magnitudes more sophisticated.

Apparently, the Gorillas discharged an aerosol of harmless individual components which were small enough to slip thru our millipore gear. Once inside our bodies, however, the individual pieces intelligently assembled themselves into larger agents that headed straight for our brains.

The first indication we had that something foreign had penetrated us was a senseless announcement we all got thru our earwigs. It sounded just like my last 'vox: strings of verbs and particles with no easy meaning. When I turned to discuss it with my bunkmate, Penguin (I haven't really told you much about her yet, Mom; she's a real old-fashioned target, with fewer than 20 percent bodymods, and I know you'd get quite close to her, given a chance), we found that we were limited to the same bizarre lingo too!

Needless to say, this kind of neural cockup—a "cortical abortical" the NYC posse calls it—could have caused us serious trouble if the enemy wasn't so well under control. Though even then, we'd still have the tinmen and transgenics—the splices weren't so strongly affected—to protect us. Still, how could we give them orders? . . .

Anyhow, the aphasia didn't stop our stormin' biobrujos for long! They soon strung together a megablocker antagonist consisting of a charge of enhanced microglials and catalytic antibodies, along with CENSORED, which seems to have wiped the cerebral invader out quicker'n teraflops!

Although there *is* a slim chance, they tell us, that the invader has simply self-mutated according to plan.

In any case, a Digireal conference on this bug is underway now with experts scattered around the globe, including last year's Gengineering Nobelist, Doctor Sax, the guy who practically invented neurotropins.

So don't worry, Mom—we're getting the best of care!

Your loving guest son,
CENSORED

SEND: **IMF MOBILE NODE**
                   SYS01-4591P
RECEIVE: **MC MURDO BIOSPHERE**

DATE/HOUR: 070565/1391
TRANSMISSION STATUS: OK

Daring Hotel Mothballs,

The newest truest neural contradural manifestation in the implication is undersay they way to play can't shay. Too few too blue words are now becoming excessive depressive stretches of letches and leeches and feel like my head's exploding decoding. Broca's aphasia in Asia is a lack of pack of parcel of morsel of words and turds. But Wernicke's journey to meaning of seasons is to produce unreduce of fibbing gibberish that makes senseless of relentless squawk talk. There appears to be a component historic of dyslexia distance instance ignorance, upon trying to writer communihesitation.

This stool shall pasture.

Your louvre question,
CENSORED

SEND: IMF MOBILE NODE
                        SYS01-4591P
RECEIVE: MC MURDO BIOSPHERE
DATE/HOUR: 070565/1450
TRANSMISSION STATUS: OK

Dear Host Mother,

The Wernicke's is over now. It's pretty evident that the MRS agent is staying one step ahead of the juice they shot us with. I just hope the bug isn't baltimoring anything permanently into our genomes. Right now, all it's doing is making auditory hallucinations. They're kind of pleasant— I heard you talking to me just a few minutes ago—but tend to interfere with real orders thru our earwigs. I notice that Oberjefe Ozal has notched his music up to eleven. I'll keep you posted. Hopefully, this'll be licked soon.

Your loving guest son,
CENSORED

SEND: IMF MOBILE NODE
                         SYS01-4591P
RECEIVE: MC MURDO BIOSPHERE
DATE/HOUR: 070565/1500
TRANSMISSION STATUS: OK

Dear Host Mother,

The whole pod was sitting down at the rectangular surface raised above the floor level with four posts, ready to dig into a delayed meal—reddish oblongs streaked with white marbling, cylindrical orange tapering tubes, spherical crusted objects slit crosswise and topped with a melting square of yellow organic matter—when the newest trouble hit.

It seems that the bug in our brains has now produced a generalized visual agnosia. Nothing looks familiar. The sight of common objects produces no referents in our brains, emotional or intellectual. Everything seems an assemblage of basic, almost geometrical parts, out of which nothing whole can be synthesized, resulting in a generalized lack of affect.

Or so the Digireal experts tell us. It's kind of hard to tell exactly what's wrong from the inside.

All I know is that when I look at what I assume is Penguin, I see a stretched toroid with an irregular topography topped with filaments of varying lengths. I assume she sees the same.

It's hard to work up the emotion to comfort a toroid, but I try my best, and so does she.

Oberjefe Ozal has been fantastic thru all this. He never loses his composure, but always keeps the ovoid with the seven openings atop the horizontal broadening of his column as cool as liquid nitrogen. He seems to derive almost superhuman strength and comfort from the qawwali buzz in the shell-shaped excrescences on the side of his aforementioned ovoid. I don't know what we'd do without him.

I guess this bug is not going to be as easy to smoke as everyone first assumed.

Well, now I'm contorting my buccal orifice and fleshy red tasting member into phonemes that will signal an end to our conversation, which the flat grey box that transcribes and transmits my voice will insure that you receive.

Maintain your homeostasis at a less-than-feverish amplitude, Mom! (Not too hard at McMurdo in July!)

Your loving guest son,
CENSORED

SEND:	IMF MOBILE NODE
	SYS01-4591P
RECEIVE:	MC MURDO BIOSPHERE
DATE/HOUR:	070565/1829
TRANSMISSION STATUS:	OK

Dear Host Mother,
The agnosia cleared up by itself.
It's been replaced by a real mild neuro-deficit.
Amusica.
None of our pop-tabs sounds like anything anymore.
This one's pretty easy to take.
Except for Oberjefe Ozal, who's killed himself.
Your loving guest son,
CENSORED

SEND:	IMF MOBILE NODE
	SYS01-4591P
RECEIVE:	MC MURDO BIOSPHERE
DATE/HOUR:	070565/2105
TRANSMISSION STATUS:	OK

Dear Host Mother,

Have I sent this message yet?

Wait a minute, Penguin!

We seem to be suffering now from TGA, or transient global amnesia. (At least we hope it's transient!) The herriots know that this kind of thing is related to damage on the underside of the temporal lobes, so they hope to squash the bug with a directed killer while it's busy there. Did I mention that we've got TGA? For a while we can't lay down any new memories. Maybe I sent you a 'vox already on it. . . . Don't worry, long-term memory is un-affected. I remember how wonderful you and the other Moms and Dads have always been to me. I hope I don't let you down.

Wait a minute, Penguin!

Have I sent this message yet?

Your loving guest son,

CENSORED

SEND:	IMF MOBILE NODE
	SYS01-4591P
RECEIVE:	MC MURDO BIOSPHERE
DATE/HOUR:	070665, 0105
TRANSMISSION STATUS:	OK

Dear Host Mother,

The TGA seems to be subsiding. We've been ordered to try to get some sleep.

Everyone's receptive to that, but whenever we start to drowse off, we experience these tremendously magnified myoclonic spasms. You know those little jerks your body sometimes gives just before passing into sleep? Well, these are the mothers of all such twitches, enough to knock you out of bed.

The mccoys are circulating now with somnifacients that should put us under.

Hopefully, when the new day dawns, this goo-screwing bug will have exhausted itself.

Sleep tight!

Your loving guest son,

CENSORED

SEND:	**IMF MOBILE NODE**
	SYS01-4591P
RECEIVE:	**MC MURDO BIOSPHERE**
DATE/HOUR:	**070665/0800**
TRANSMISSION STATUS:	**OK**

Dear Host Mother,

We lost half the pod during sleep to Nightmare Death Syndrome, that Thai/Filipino/Khampuchean tendency to flatline during sleep.

Unfortunately, the somnifacients may have contributed to the high mortality rate, preventing the sleepers from jolting awake.

I don't know how to tell you this, so forgive me if I just blurt it out.

Penguin was one of the fatalities.

I almost wish the agnosia was back, so I wouldn't feel so bad.

I'm asking the new CO to send you an adobe of her and me thru the metamedium.

Just in case I don't make it home.

Your loving guest son,

CENSORED

SEND:	**IMF MOBILE NODE**
	SYS01-4591P
RECEIVE:	**MC MURDO BIOSPHERE**
DATE/HOUR:	**070765/1200**
TRANSMISSION STATUS:	**OK**

Dear Host Mother,

It's been twenty-four hours since the last manifestation of the invader. The herriots are starting to feel safe about issuing an all-clear. And Doctor Sax is standing virtually by in the wings with a last-ditch experimental trope similar to CENSORED which they're going to try if there's another flareup.

Keep your fingers crossed (webbing and all)!

Your loving guest son,

CENSORED

SEND:	**IMF MOBILE NODE**
	SYS01-4591P
RECEIVE:	**MC MURDO BIOSPHERE**
DATE/HOUR:	**070865/0300**
TRANSMISSION STATUS:	**OK**

Dear Host Mother,

We've all received our shots of aldisscine, Doctor Sax's new trope, despite its high LD rating.

There was really no choice after we all went body-blind.

What's body-blindness? I can imagine you asking.

It's total loss of proprioception, the multiplex feedback from your muscles and nerves, skin and bones, that allows you to tell—mostly subliminally—what your body's doing.

We're all isolated now in our heads like puppet-masters whose strings leading to their puppets have been tangled, or like a telefactor operator who's lost his sensory feed. It's not that we can't move our limbs or anything. There's no paralysis. It's just (just!) that aside from visual feedback, there's no inherent sense of where any part of you *is*! You might as well try to operate someone else's body as your own under these conditions. It's not pleasant, watching your proxies tripping over their own feet, missing chairs, their mouths, the D-compoz unit—

But you can get used to anything, I guess. And the experts are confident that the aldisscine will stop any new deficits from popping up.

Anyway, I'm kind of glad Penguin didn't live to experience this. I never got a chance to tell you, but she used to be a dancer in regular franch life.

The orders have finally come down from Brussels for our pod to be rotated out. There's talk that if the body-blindness proves permanent, they'll try to fit us all out with onboard stabilizer chips and nanosensors to simulate normal proprioception.

What's one more bodymod nowadays, huh, Mom?

Your loving guest son,

CENSORED

SEND:	**IMF OFFEARTH NODE**
	SYSO2-999Z
RECEIVE:	**MC MURDO BIOSPHERE**
DATE/HOUR:	**071065/2400**
TRANSMISSION STATUS:	**SOLAR NOISE**
	IMPEDIMENT (*) = −10%

Dear Ho*t Moth**,

As you might've guessed by the delay between messages, we've been rerouted.

We're in transit to CEN*****, where we'll get the best of care. They discovered that all surviving members of our pod are suffering from degenerative neurofibrillary protein tangles similar to those found in sufferers of that extinct disease known as Alz********. CENSORED is a kind of sanitarium, where an AI-human team waits to cure us.

They say the average stay at CENSORED is *** months, but could stretch to **** years. Jumping genes!

You could be in another symb-bonding by then! Anyway, I can't look that far ahead, as our prognosis is very ****.

Let me repeat that, in case these flares are interfering: we stand a **** chance, not a **** one.

Unfortunately, I won't be able to take any incoming 'voxes from you for a while, or even send any. Not that I'd be able to really appreciate them too good anyhow. My brain seems a little dull right now. But they promise us that full metamedium contact will be restored as soon as it's appropriate.

But don't worry. You can always contact Brussels for updates.

Just ask for your boy, CENSORED!

🌂 Streetlife

CONEY'S MASTER WAS A VIRTUALITY POET. AND he was one of the best. Only Planxty or Bingo Bantam could approach the depth and brilliance of his compositions, and rarely at that. So his master would always tell Coney, especially when he was under the influence of a trope such as Egoboo or Meglo, which left him prone to recite aloud his own reviews, complete with melodramatic flourishes of the crepey folds of velvet skin that hung like batwings from his underarms.

" 'Hopcroft's latest cortex-vortex is a cell-stunner! *Visit to the Mushroom Planet* opens with Tenniel's hookah-smoking Caterpillar greeting the percipient with a blast of aromatic smoke. When the cinnamon cloud clears, the perk finds herself on the Mushroom Planet of the title. Fungi lifeforms in startling variety exfoliate and enfold the mind-traveler, who can navigate the construx with more than the standard ten degrees of freedom, thanks to Hopcroft's truly creative use of CoCenSys's Infini-Tree Fabware. The poet's signature use of lush textures and his smorgasbord-gorgeous false-color palette all contribute to a synapse-shattering experience—especially if you're simultaneously running a coprocessor such as CellSmartz, as this lucky perk was! With this 'strux,

Hopcroft delivers on all his past promises and establishes himself as *the* poet of his cohort.' ''

Throwing the flimsy across the room (to be quickly retrieved by a Braun DoorMaus), Coney's master would spread his batlike membranes wide and exclaim, '' '*The* poet of his cohort!' Did you hear that, Coney?''

"Yes, Peej Hopcroft, I heard."

"It's all gush, of course. But true gush. I am the most accomplished poet of my clade. There's no disputing it, is there, Coney?"

"No indeed. It is just as Peej Reviewer said."

Most likely then—especially if the tropes were wearing off—Coney's master would, at this point in the ritual, collapse into a convenient organiform chair (somehow he was never so distraught as to land on the floor), drape his head with his fleshfolds, and begin to weep.

"But what good does it do me, Coney? This crass society does not respect poets, nor does it honor them with rewards material or spiritual. It never has, and it never will. I am an acquired taste, and then only among a few. The mass of my fellow citizens are Philistines, plain and simple. *Siouxsie Sexcrime* is their idea of poetry! How can such a sensitive soul as mine endure it, Coney? Ah, but my life is hard, Coney—harder than a stupid transgenic like you could ever imagine. I can barely scrape together enough ecus to pay my Digireal fees. And my art cannot be rushed! This is why I am forced much too often to play the lusty gigaload gigolo!''

Coney knew enough not to interrupt at this point. He would wait with the patience of his kind for the tearful poet to finish his performance.

"Yes," Coney's master would inevitably begin his peroration, "I, the RAM-baud of my cohort, must make ends meet by crawling for pay into the Sack with lascivious starfuckers, eager to boast to their witless friends that they have enjoyed teledildonics with another ii-do tarento whose art they cannot even begin to appreciate!''

At this juncture Coney would venture a comment he hoped would bolster his master's self-esteem and spare himself a collar-jolt.

"Peej Hopcroft only does what he must, to further his art."

If he had by now downed a trope such as Zesta, Coney's master would sigh extravagantly and agree. (Otherwise, the dreaded neuronic zap might be forthcoming, along with the admonition "not to overstep your splicey self with comments about things you couldn't possibly comprehend.")

Tonight—a mild June evening stochastically certified to be rainfree—much to Coney's relief, his stock phrase served its intended purpose. The familiar scene which he had just endured for the nth time played itself out happily for him.

"Yes, little Daewoo Dumbunni, we all do what we must, don't we? Even peddle our arse for the sake of our ars."

Coney had no idea what this last statement meant, but was only too happy to nod his sympathy.

Rising to his feet, Coney's master now said, "And that's why I need you to do your part to make this latest sordid virtual assignation a success, dear Coney. I have here a new trope called O-max-O. It was given to me by one of my fans, a sensitive young plug who works at Xomagraf. It's not available to the hoi polloi yet. He promises me that it will make this digitryst so thrilling for my client that she'll gladly double my fee. I'm counting on you to deliver it to her within the hour. Her name is Frances Foxx, and this is her address."

Coney's master handed him a crawlypatch and a silicrobe calling card. The card flashed an address in the far west end of the city.

Laboriously tracing a mental map, Coney sought to comprehend his assignment. Finally he spoke.

"This place is quite far. May I take the train?"

"Don't be silly. The train costs eft. The whole point of tonight's dreadful exercise is to earn ecus, not spend them. And besides, the maglev isn't safe for splices, not since those horrid razorboys, the Transgenocides, started haunting the tubes. No, you'll have to walk. You're a speedy little splice, or so the factory claimed. Surely you can cover the distance before Peej Foxx and I are scheduled to crawl into the Sack together."

"But it is night out there."

"So?"

"To make the best time, I will have to cross the Soft Sector. In the dark."

At the thought of such a passage, Coney horripilated.

His master seemed to experience no such somatic dread. "You force me to repeat myself: so? No one there will pay any attention to you. You're small and insignificant."

"This is the problem."

Coney's master waved the splice's concerns away. "You're exaggerating the difficulties just to extract some concession or luxury from me. Very well, at the completion of your little chore, you may experience one of my sonnets. Perhaps you could dimly appreciate *Dance of the Cold Moons*."

"Thank you, Peej Hopcroft. Something like extra rations would be very nice. But I would give up everything just not to go. Perhaps you could—"

"What!" thundered Coney's master. "Leave my wunderkammer and subject my precious body to the gross physical biosphere? How dare you suggest such a thing, you impudent trans!"

The hand of Coney's master moved toward the keypad in his hip.

"Sorry. Sorry. Sorry," said the smart-door, which had failed to open fast enough for the splice scrabbling at its manual override handle.

* * *

Coney's civicorp had recently bred a Pedlumo system to replace the antique solar-powered light-standards. By night, small swarms of gnat-like silicrobe aggregations hovered darkly outside every building waiting for pedestrians to emerge, whereupon they flared up with sufficient candlepower to illuminate a sphere some four meters in diameter. Anchoring themselves above the individual's head, they would accompany the traveler to his destination, then await new service.

With his soft personal corona fluctuating in response to those of all the other citizens and splices abroad that night, Coney set off toward the West End.

This initial stage of his journey fostered in Coney no trepidations. Patrolled by teams of Parke-Davis Offisimians and Schering-Plough Deputy Dawgs, his neighborhood was a pleasant one, a mixed-use zone of shops, residences, and zero-light autofacs, and he was intimately familiar with it. And the few errands that had taken him to the West End had revealed that district to be equally unthreatening.

No, it was only the dread territory in between the two zones that terrified him.

The Soft Sector.

Striving to master his emotions, Coney recited a trigger-mantra he had been taught at Daewoo.

"Tension, fear, care, nowhere. Tension, fear, care, nowhere—"

Hypothalamic changes spread throughout his central nervous system, lowering his heartbeat and respiration. Soothing neuropeptides washed his brain.

Somewhat relieved, Coney dug in his bellypouch for the card with Peej Foxx's address. Perhaps with a clear mind he would see something about the chore that he had missed.

But a second perusal only confirmed what he had known from the moment his master gave him the assignment. There was only one way to deliver the dose of trope on time, and that was to cut across the interdicted streetlife habitat.

Replacing the card against his skin, next to the all-important crawlypatch, Coney increased his pace.

A clutch of zarooks, ragazzi, and chats sauvage stood on the corner of Artery Nine and Orange Capillary, hanging out by a trope bar whose silicrobe icons of synaptic junctions exchanging molecules flashed green and purple. Heady-mental music spilled out from floating silicrobe speakers. Big Skulls and Piebalds predominated in the crowd, with a smattering of Moles.

"Swap protocols, little splice!" yelled one. "Where you off to so krebby fast?"

"Stop and share a dose of Heavy Wonderful," called another.

"Yeah, you'll feel like you were born a pure-gen!"

"Peej Splice, if you please!"

Coney knew enough not to heed these bad ones. Although not as violent as the razorboys, they would like nothing better than to divert him from his duties and mess up his factory parameters.

Hurrying away, Coney was followed by their jeers and laughter, and the soft wheezes of the Moles.

Within a few blocks of the Soft Sector, Coney began to grow nervous again. So intent on chanting his mantra was he that he failed to notice the whir of wheels behind him.

"Buy a refreshing Pepsi-plus, citizen? It's the pure charles!"

Coney jumped and whirled.

A mobile smart-vendor, battered and splashed with Liquid Lingo grafitti, had rolled up on his tail. The autorover looked completely disreputable, perhaps even a rogue.

"I am not a citizen," said Coney cautiously.

"Oh, excuse me. My biosensors have been malfunctioning since I took a spill. But rest assured, my product is still fresh! Would you care to purchase a cup, whatever you are?''

Coney straightened his back righteously. ''I am a genuine midline Daewoo transgenic, bearing fully fifteen-percent human genes. You are simply a machine, a kibe.''

The soda-vendor's voice assumed a plaintive tone. ''Yes, you are right. And an unlucky kibe at that. Unless I can sell more soda, I cannot apply for repairs. But the longer I put my repairs off, the more decrepit I get and the less soda I sell. It is a vicious circle.''

''So is life. In any case, I have no eft.''

''No eft! You have wasted my clock-cycles!''

''It was you who approached me!''

The crazed machine let loose a warbling siren. ''Thief! Thief! All concerned citizens, nine-eleven the harrys!''

Fear building up in him, Coney sped off.

In less than a minute he was out of hearing of the vendor's calls for help and within sight of the Soft Sector.

He rested a moment, until his heart had slowed.

A wide bare ringroad separated the city from the zone of interdiction. Cars zipped along its lanes in one direction only. On the far side of the road, the Soft Sector bloomed in luxuriant splendor, a lush jungle of constantly shifting artificial overlapping ecologies hundreds of acres in extent, its armature crumbled buildings that had long since been ceded by the civicorp to the uncontrolled but corralled biorenegades. Here ended up all the failed experiments of amateur fabricators and malicious chromosartors, all of society's self-malformed dropouts, all escaped splices and faulty silicrobe colonies, as well as some seemingly autocatalytic creatures no one outside the Soft Sector had ever encountered.

There were no conventional physical barriers such as fences or minefields to keep the inhabitants of the Soft Sector penned up.

Instead, the periphery was patrolled by Macro^{2}Phages.

Coney saw one now.

The towering gelatinous mass was easily as big as a baseline elephant. The megamicro humped itself along, leaving a wet trail of lysing exudate, intent on ingesting and devouring any living organism that tried to escape. Not far behind it trailed another, and another behind that one.

Coney's knees felt as weak as boiled water. He knew that the guardians were programmed not to bother anyone entering the Soft Sector. But how was he to escape on the far side, assuming he survived his transit?

For a moment, Coney actually considered abandoning his suicidal mission. Then he recalled his dietary leash and the locked collar around his neck which would be quite capable of delivering a killing GloPos-beamed signal anywhere he hid. . . .

Setting a trembling foot onto the road surface, Coney eyed the traffic. At the right moment, he darted across, incurring only one shouted warning from an angry Mercedes.

Safely reaching the marge of the Soft Sector, Coney was briefly startled when his pedlumos left him, fleeing obediently back to the civicorp proper.

In the next second, he was treated to a broadcast courtesy of silicrobes embedded in the pavement that erupted at his presence.

"Attention! You are almost within the Soft Sector! Be advised that under relevant civicorp statutes, you are permanently forfeiting all of a citizen's rights and privileges by so entering. Any transgenics spotted within the Soft Sector by aerial patrols will be assumed to be deranged and will be subject to immediate lethal Factory Recall. Attention—!"

Coney closed his eyes and ran.

The Macro^{2}Phages made a slurping, sluffing noise as they crawled their circuit. They smelled of yeast and baseline human sperm. In his blind dash, Coney brushed the tacky leading edge of one.

The lysing agent burned through his fur, etching his skin with a tracery of pain and urging him to greater speed.

And then he was past it, safely inside the Soft Sector!

Panting, crouching in the shadows beneath a bush, Coney watched the monster move on.

What relief—

Toothy mandibles pincered his waist in a painful grip. Coney screamed and struggled to break free.

He only succeeded in twisting partially around, at the cost of raw abrasions around his midriff. But his new posture was enough to reveal what held him.

It was an army-surplus Squibb dung beetle big as a car. Evidently quite old, its antennae were broken, its carapace brittle and fragmented. A partial SNEG silicrobe serial number flashed on one mandible.

The huge ailing battlefield scavenger had plainly mistaken Coney for a corpse.

Beating on its jaws with his paws had no effect; even in its decrepitude, the big splice was still awesome. Limping from a missing leg, the dung beetle carried Coney off.

When it reached an appropriate patch of bare earth, the dung beetle began to dig. Once it had excavated a deep hole, it placed Coney in it.

Coney dared not stir, unsure of how the beetle's damaged wetware would treat a moving corpse.

With instinctive efficiency, the beetle covered Coney up.

Then, in a scratchy growl, it began to recite the Syncretic Church's last rites:

"Our Jah who art in Allah's Nirvana, hallowed be Her name. . . ."

*   *   *

It was rather pleasant to lie buried under the loose friable soil after the Snowy military beetle had left. For the moment, enough air filtered through and Coney was safe from harm. Ancestral memories of warm musty burrows thronged pleasantly through his brain.

Why had splices ever been created? Their life was only endless suffering, all at human behest. Wouldn't it have been better to remain a dumb brute than to be granted just enough feeling and intelligence to realize how miserable one's situation was?

It was almost enough to make a loyal splice side with that mad transgenic, Krazy Kat, and his crew. If only the legendary splice would show himself again. Could the rumors of his death really be true? . . .

Voices penetrated to Coney's grave.

"What'cha think the Snowy found, Art?"

"Can't say till we dig it up, Ick. Can't say."

Coney pressed his back into the earth, desperately willing himself to sink into the ground.

Soil began to be scraped aside.

Pushing up, gathering his legs beneath him, Coney burst forth in an explosion of clods.

He staggered, found his feet, began to run—

Something sharp lanced his back.

Instant paralysis!

Coney dropped like a smartbomb from a scramjet.

Lying on his side, his mind racing, his body transformed into that of a Minitel poupee viande, Coney watched two pairs of bare feet approach. One pair belonged to a big human; the other belonged to a child, or dwarf, and seemed barely to touch the ground.

Hands lifted Coney up.

He saw his captors.

The big one was seemingly a baseline human, save for one appendage: a long, flexible, jointed scorpion's tail arching over his shoulder, a drop of venom still glistening at its sharp tip.

The other, smaller one was equipped with fluttering wasp wings sprouting from his shoulders and a stinger emerging from his coccyx.

Both were naked save for clinging pubic clamshells, their bodies laced with streetlife scars.

"Nice supper, huh, Art?" said the wasp one. "Nice supper!"

The scorpion studied Coney with less avidity than his partner. "Not so fast, Ick. This is a neo fresh from outside. There could be some other use for him. We could trade him or something."

"But I'm hungry, Art!"

"Listen, let's get the roast home and decide then."

"Okay, Art. You're the boss."

The scorpion hoisted Coney over his shoulder and they set off down the crumbling remnants of a paved path.

Coney knew he was doomed. Lacking the spirit even to curse the cupidity of Peej Hopcroft for sending him here to die so ignominiously, he began to drift off into a protective mental predeath fugue.

The smell of a large body of water came vaguely to Coney's sensitive nostrils.

"Quiet now," urged the scorpion in an undertone. "We don't want to wake Namor."

"Yeah, that fucking Namor—"

Water sprayed the trio. The next second, a newcomer stood beside them: scaled skin over slabbed muscles, winged heels, pinniped ears.

"That's '*Prince* fucking Namor' to you," said the Submariner insouciantly.

Tossed to the ground, Coney landed with a thud on his back.

Dropping into a crouch, the scorpion lashed his tail menacingly. "Get him, Ick!" he called, but the diminutive waspman was already airborne.

Prince Namor seemed untroubled by the aggressive dual attack. Weaving, darting, avoiding the poison barb, he quickly latched on to the scorpion's wrist. There was a crackle of onboard capacitors discharging and the smell of burning flesh; the big man collapsed. Without even looking backward, the Submariner flung an arm up and grabbed the wasp's ankle as he made ready to plunge his stinger. Scorched meat, and the wasp fell.

The merman now came to Coney. Bending over the splice, he laid his hands on either side of his head.

Expecting death, Coney felt only a gentle thrill along his nerve endings.

"You're carrying something you think is important," said the Submariner after half a minute. "The Pangolin should know about this. Let's go."

Hoisting Coney up under one arm, Prince Namor raced deeper into the Soft Sector with a fleetness only winged heels could bring.

Within minutes, the Submariner and his burden stood in a coldtorch-lit clearing before a throne crudely assembled from junked cars. Surrounding the throne was a host of malformed creatures, beaker-born and bioreactor-spawned.

Atop the sham throne was the Pangolin.

A huge polymod with cascades of living armor plates down his back and limbs and a chromed skull, the Pangolin brandished three thick claws—one opposable—on each hand in place of fingers.

"What do you have there, Namor?" resonantly boomed out the imperious ruler of the Soft Sector.

"An outsider, a messenger bearing something of value."

"What?"

"I don't know. He's paralyzed, and my SQUIDS only picked up the general drift of his thoughts."

"Well, let's wake him."

Out from the crowd stepped a Medusa. Namor transferred Coney to her. Licking some of the splice's sweat

with a burred tongue, she pronounced, "Scorpion toxin.
I've got just the trick."

Hissing, one of her headsnakes quickly fastened its
fangs into Coney's rump.

As fast as he had frozen, he melted back into freedom.

Set on his trembling legs, Coney tried to chant his
mantra, but not a word of it remained.

"Can you speak now, splice?" roared the Pangolin.

Coney wanted to faint, but couldn't. "Y-y-yes."

"What are you carrying?"

"It's a new trope, Peej Pangolin. It's called O-max-O.
It's to be used during virtual sex. It's not for sale yet. I
don't know more than that. I swear on my manufacturer's
warranty!"

"Hand it over!"

"But, Peej Pangolin, my errand—"

The Pangolin ripped a polycarbon strut off a chassis
and began to climb down from his throne.

Coney hastily dug the crawlypatch out. Prince Namor
took it and passed it to the Pangolin.

"We'll match and batch this by dawn. By tomorrow
night, it'll be on sale throughout the whole civicorp. I
owe you one, Namor."

"That's a lock. Well, I've got to wet my gills. Stay
sharp!"

The Submariner placed the tips of his ten fingers approximately two centimeters apart: a burst of sparks arced
and crackled in the air between them. Grunts and excla-
mations issued from the more impressionable members
of the audience.

After the merman had gone, the Pangolin turned to
Coney.

"Now, little splice, I wish you no harm. Shall I relieve
you of your collar, so that you may join my court and
live free?"

Coney considered the proposal. Never to be forced to

run another errand for Peej Hopcroft, nevermore to truckle or scrape—

On the fringes of the crowd, a leering frogface caught Coney's eye. A mouth wide as a manhole opened in a hideous toothless smile. Coney shuddered.

"No, thank you, please, Peej Pangolin. I only want to go home!"

"Very well. I understand that our style of freedom is not for all. You will be escorted to the border—"

"But without the trope I was supposed to deliver, I'll be whipped!"

The Pangolin smiled. "I'll provide a substitute. Medusa! Fab me a dose of N-fear in a crawlypatch."

Within minutes, the court crick had the trope ready. The Pangolin motioned to Coney, who approached timorously.

"Several hours of demon-stuffed hell. Your master will never know what hit him."

Reluctantly, Coney took the substitute. "But it's not for—"

"Enough! Begone!"

Two lynxmen hustled Coney away.

Shortly, they stood on the edge of the Soft Sector. Coney could smell the Macro^{2}Phages nearing, hear their slurping advance.

"Please, please, friend cats, don't let these monsters strip my bones!"

The lynxmen laughed. "The shuggoths? We've got them trained not to hurt anyone we don't want hurt. Watch!"

Letting loose a piercing whistle, the lynxmen called out, "Ia, ia, tekeli-li!"

The guardians ground to a sudden quivering halt.

One lynxman slapped Coney's back. "Run now, before we think twice!"

Coney ran.

Once he was far, far from the Soft Sector, he stopped

to consider what to do. A clock told him the hour granted for his errand was twice gone. But he could think of nothing to do except try to complete it.

Without any further trouble, he found Peej Foxx's apartment. Building security allowed him in upon seeing her card. Her smart door likewise opened for him.

Inside stood Peej Foxx, coyly grooming her bushy tail.

And beside her was Peej Hopcroft!

Coney's master looked at his servant with ultimate disdain. "So, you finally made it, you filthy worm, after forcing me to come out on my own, into filthy unmodulated atmospherics! If I didn't value Peej Foxx's favors so highly, I don't think I could have nerved myself up to such a trying excursion! I was a fool ever to entrust such a vital errand to a furball such as you. Why, just look at you! You're a disgrace to my household!"

Coney turned toward a mirror.

He was covered with gravedirt. There was a bare raw ulceration on his arm where the shuggoth had brushed him. Dried blood crusted his midriff from the beetle's embrace. His back ached from being tossed to the ground by the scorpion. His swollen ass stung from the snakebite.

"Yes, Peej Hopcroft is right. I am a mess. But it was only—"

"Silence! Where is the trope I gave you?"

Coney dug out the crawlypatch. "Here it is. But I do not think—"

"You are not meant to think! Just give it to me!"

Coney handed the dose of N-fear over.

"Luckily, I had a second patch which I brought with me. The lovely Peej Foxx has already applied it to her charming skin. I, therefore, will use this one."

Coney's master pressed out the activation pattern on the patch and applied it to his arm. It crawled until it found a vein, then settled down.

"Ninety-second delay, my dear. Just long enough for

us to slide into our Sacks, whereupon we shall meet in
virtual heaven.''

Two wrinkled circuit-skinned and SQUID-studded
bags lay on the soft floor, one end of each agape. Coney's
master and Peej Foxx each wormed into his and her own
semi-organic Sack, which sealed up behind them and
tautened into shape, flowing into orifices, and molding
around organs.

Coney watched his master's Sack.

When the violent, highly nonerotic twitchings began,
he headed home.

The long way round.

🖎 Afterschool Special

"MY POOHS ARE SO *SLOUCH*!"

The phemes just spilled out like someone had tripped my gates. At first, I was shocked. But then I felt good.

Before today, I would've rather gone wiggly with a var than admit the truth in front of anyone except Jinx. But somehow—right here and now—everything looked different. I was sick and tired of sticking up for my simplex parental units, especially when they wouldn't let me have what I wanted.

The class was taking a break from inverting with CA-Daver, the human-anatomy virtuality used mainly to train feldshers. We were all lounging around in the spleen, wearing our secondary identities. The school had a contract with MicroDisney, so we were forced to wear their patented images. Everyone hated it, but the trope dosers claimed it was for our own good. The theory was that no mega-eft spoilboy or churlgirl would be able to run better grafix than someone else, so we could concentrate on studying instead of showing off. Also, some of the ids[2] that kids liked to use outside of school were so ciccone or freddie that you'd spend all your classtime creamin' or screamin'.

So I was in my usual Daisy Duck, and Jinx was wearing Goofy, and the rest of the class was all cutesy blue-birds and dwarves, mice and fish, Pinocchios and ballerina hippos, all clogging the virtual lymphoid tissue of this ''important component of the reticulo-endothelial system'' (or so lectured the tutor-turtle, whom everyone was ignoring).

Every once in a while, someone would reach out and snag a passing red bloodcell and pop it under his or her nose. We had found out the rusty smell could really bend your ladders like the best samogon or kompot.

We had been dissing our respective poohs, as kids will, when I had found myself spitting out my comment. I guess I didn't fully realize till then just how much my poohs had been quenching me.

Right on cue my best proxy, Jinx, spoke up.

Now, I mentioned that Jinx was wearing Goofy, but I should add that, having found out how to tweak the pe-tafits that constituted his suit, he had retrofitted onto it an enormous set of black-skinned balls and dong. It was kinda sad, seeing as how they were the only ones he would ever have until he became an adult, but I supposed virtual sex organs were better than none.

So Jinx said, ''Just how slouch are they, Arnie?''

''They're so slouch,'' I shot back, ''that they make the Bogd Gegeen look like Siouxie Sexcrime!''

Everyone got a laugh out of that, imagining the eternal godboy of Greater Free Mongolia tricked out like our favorite teledildonics star.

When the hoots and hollers died down, Honeysuckle spoke up.

I've always hated Honeysuckle. Her poohs let her have these really glamslam Xoma tits two years ago, whereas my chest has yet to even bud naturally, which is the only way with poohs like mine that I'll ever get any boobs, short of turning twelve and becoming franchised. More than anything else, this was why I guess I had exploded and called my dumb old poohs slouch.

In keeping with her primary id, Honeysuckle always wore the Little Mermaid. Only she too had twiddled with her image, so that the doe-eyed cartoon transfection sported impossible macro-tits on which the seashell cups had dwindled to nipple-caps.

Now, I watched all the whychromes—including my very own Jinx—hang on her every word.

"That's because your poohs are Tee-Ems!" jeered Honeysuckle.

I winced at the dig. It was not something I could deny. Everyone knew my dads belonged to the Transcentennial Moderationists. They even had their own hour on the metamedium: *Keep It Simple, Stupid, with Alvin and Calvin Arneson.*

In the face of all the laughter Honeysuckle's comment caused, I found myself having to stick up for my dads, and it was awfully difficult, since I didn't really want to and felt like a total hypocrite.

"My poohs may be retro-jethro KISS-asses," I said, "but at least they're not black science boryokudans like yours!"

Everyone got silent as cell-death. My reference to the illegal underworld origin of the wealth of Honeysuckle's surface-respectable poohs was ultra loosh and faroosh. But I couldn't just sit there batting off phagocytes and let her run my dads down. I mean, it was all right for me to do it, but not her!

Honeysuckle's cartoon gaze grew as slitted and mean as that of a Secret Service pantherine confronted with a suspicious character feinting at the World Bank Managing Director. I knew I was truly on her shit list now and wondered how wise it had been to sass such a nasty girl.

"Well," she said, her voice dripping lysozymes, "the duck can quack! I suppose you think it's all spidersilk and hormone sodas, having poohs like mine. You don't know what it's like, every night half-expecting the crick-

cops or Protein Police or the IMF to bust down the door
and boot us all!''

It was hard to feel sorry for Honeysuckle as she sat
there on a spongy mass of lymph, flicking her flippers
and flaunting her chest, so I didn't even try. ''You can
have anything you want—''

''What does that have to do with being happy! Suppose you could have anything you wanted? Would you
always be happy?''

''Why, sure . . .''

Honeysuckle assumed a venomous smile. ''All right,
then. What do you want most? C'mon, tell us, and I'll
give it to you. I'll see to it that your wildest dreams come
true.''

Somehow the grounds of this battle had shifted under
me. How we had gotten from the respective merits of our
parents to who had the happier life eluded me, and I
didn't like the change. Somehow, I found myself on the
defensive and was really uneasy.

What could I say, in front of Honeysuckle and all my
friends? All I really wanted was a pair of nice unassum-
ing moderate-sized boobs and maybe some basal why-
chrome genitals for Jinx. But I was too embarrassed to
say so. So instead, I blurted out the first thing that came
to mind.

''I'd like, um—a spike!''

Honeysuckle laughed. ''That's all? Out of anything
you could have, you choose a crummy, soilin' spike?''

Jinx intervened then, and I sent a silent thanks his way.

''What's the matter with a spike? They're really
peppy! Plus they're so new, hardly anybody's got one!''

Honeysuckle huffed. ''Oh, I suppose you'd like one
too? . . .''

''I wouldn't mind one. But they cost more than a
bucket of brains. And besides, you need your pooh's
chop to get one planted. . . .''

Now Honeysuckle adopted that I've-swallowed-every-trope-ever-made tone she frequently used, which always got under my skin like a stitchbug.

"Well, I think they're simply as tawdry as sparkleskin, and frankly I'd rather wear *chitin*! But if you two *larvae* want spikes, I suppose I'll just have to get them for you."

Before Honeysuckle or Jinx or I could say any more, the tutor-turtle informed us that recess was over, and we had to get back to work.

I couldn't really concentrate on the rest of the lesson. All my bulbs were firing doubletime, trying to imagine what Honeysuckle intended to do for—or to—Jinx and me.

Finally, the tutor-turtle told us to get ready for the phase-change out of virtuality, and the next thing I knew, I was back in my Sack, which was already withdrawing its squelchy threads and tendrils.

I tickled it open and emerged into the classroom.

All the other kids were climbing out of their Sacks too, their familiar faces and forms a welcome sight after so much microdiz nutrasweet. Most of them—all of them except poor old me, in fact—sported various kiddie-moddies: tails, scales, and pointy nails, manes, veins, and extra brains. I was the only one whose poohs wouldn't let her have even the simplest little gill-slit or sixth finger—never mind tits—all because they believed in some weird principle of "somatic integrity."

Honeysuckle was brushing her perfect calico hair and eyeing me from her perch on the corner of a smartdesk with the raptorial look of an execucondo's security bird. I wanted Jinx beside me before she could say anything, but he was still struggling to get out of his sack, last one as usual. I went over to help him.

Jinx's sack was undergoing some bizarro kind of peristaltic reaction, and I had to pet its control ganglia till it calmed down. Jinx always had some kind of trouble with his interface bag, because its parms weren't set up for his peculiarities.

At last, though, the two of us got it open, and Jinx emerged.

There was nothing to Jinx below his abdomen. His body simply ended a few centimeters below his navel. He looked just like he had been sliced in half by some mad magician.

His bottom—or ventral side or whatever you want to call it—was capped with a tough protective Immunologic membrane like sharkskin that was integral with his regular epidermis. This membrane handled all his metabolic wastes, so that Jinx never had to pee or shit.

The way Jinx got around was on his knuckles. His hands and supermyofibril biceps were massive, and his knuckles well calloused. Suspended from these pylons, he could either swing his torso forward, rest on it, then shift both supports, or he could sort of fall forward from left to right hand.

Jinx had been born this way. His poohs were third-generation spacelings whose ancestors hadn't seen much need for deadmeat legs in zero-gee, and so they had bid the chromosartors snip and transcribe until the result was my proxy, Jinx.

His folks—nomenklatura of Asgard—had sent Jinx to Gaia—to our school—for what they insisted was a superior educational experience. (Although, what with tropes and the digiverse being equally accessible and high-quality practically anywhere, I failed to see exactly what benefits they were conferring on him, unless it was the dubious Gaian social life or high-status eft expenditure.)

When I first got friendly with Jinx, I asked him two questions.

"How come you don't ride, um, a prosthocart, maybe like the dolphinboys use?"

"Because I'm not a cripple. I'm completely normal, for a spaceling."

I didn't argue the point, even though only baseline

scantlings like me rate the semiderogatory word "normal." Maybe the word meant something different on Asgard. Instead, I asked the second question.

"I imagine your colony cooks new members in some fancy ductwork."

"Yeah. Repligen wombs with i-Stat endometriums and Ares-Serono placentas."

"But how do you—I mean, what do you do when—"

"How do we get wiggly?"

"Well, yeah!"

"It's all virtual. That's the one thing I don't like about home. I keep wishing I had—had legs and a cock! I even dream I'm walking sometimes. . . ."

"It's probably feedback from Gaia's morphic fields, the human subset. You felt it out in space, but it's even stronger here. Like they say, 'Ain't no shield against the field, cuz it dwells in the cells.' "

"I guess."

Now, as I helped Jinx to a "sitting" position, my reverie was brought to a harsh end by Honeysuckle's sashaying, tit-quaking approach. She stopped a meter or so away and addressed me while ignoring Jinx—except to insult him.

"If you're done helping that knucklebuster, I'd like to finish up our little business matter."

Honeysuckle ran a flicker-screen thumbnail across a seam bisecting her bare midriff, opening up a possum-pouch. From within, she deftly filched a flashcard and handed it to me.

I noticed that Honeysuckle's nailscreen was running the Mandelbrot set, and everything suddenly felt as strange as one of the set's remoter precincts.

With nervous fingers I flexed the still-warm card, and its silicrobe message blinked at me.

THE G-GNOME'S CAVE
1040 BUGHOUSE SQUARE

(RIDE THE RED ARTERY TO NODE TEN, OR
TAKE SLIDEWALK SEVEN)
Somatic and gnomic alterations of all types.
Deletions, insertions, and inversions.
Coleopterics a specialty.
Fully bonded and licensed by the BDC.

I flexed the card again, and Honeysuckle's totipotent
family chop showed up, the semi-infamous Rancifer icon.

Honeysuckle leered. "That'll get you and your friend
anything you ask for from the G-Gnome—including *tits*,
if that's what you *really* want."

I stiffened right up, but managed not to change my
expression—I hoped. I knew the whole class was watching and listening.

"No, I want a spike."

"Me too," said Jinx in a comradely way, although I
could sense that he was having second thoughts just like
me.

"Pardon me, but I'm sure neither one of you knows
your efferents from your afferents. But if you both show
up tomorrow with spikes, I'll have to admit you've got
plenty of testo-estro."

And with that, Honeysuckle turned her back on us as
if we had ceased to exist.

The teacher called us to return to our studies then, and
so I couldn't talk anymore with Jinx.

Needless to say, the rest of the four-hour school day
moved slow as a crawlypatch. With Honeysuckle's card
in my pocket, I couldn't concentrate on plectics or clad-
istics or kundalini or behavioral pragmatics or even
lunch! (And they were serving my favorite that day too:
deep-fried free-range croc with null-cal Ben and Jerry's
for dessert.) All I wanted was to be finished with classes,
so that Jinx and I could decide what, if anything, we were
going to do with the magic flashcard.

At last—of course and however—we were free.

Or as free as any eleven-year-old ever is in this ageist society!

Jinx and I met at our usual place, beneath the towering forty-foot paulownia tree on the edge of the schoolyard. We had helped to plant the giant when it was just a tiny seedling two years ago, on Global Arbor Day, and it had been our special spot ever since.

If Jinx had had feet, he probably would have been kicking the dirt. As it was, he exhibited his nervousness by picking bark off our tree.

"I don't know about you," my spaceling proxy said when I came up to him, "but I can't think straight. What do you say we bind some satori and just sit a minute?"

"Now you're firing! I hear the Chromatin Cafe has that new line of Archer-Daniels-Midland tropes on tap. . . ."

"Then what are we waiting for? Let's go!"

So with Jinx swinging himself along as I ambled, we made our way to the Chromatin Cafe.

We were supposed to be reporting to our separate afterschool apprenticeships. Jinx to his nafta boss at the Mercosur Mart (he was training to run an entrepot for Asgard) and me to the local branch of the Sheldrake Institute, where I was trying to grok morphic field modulation.

But if we were indeed going to be spiked, then missing our work stints would be the least of our transgressions.

The CC was only half a klick from the school, so we didn't bother with the slidewalks. It felt good to use my muscles after so much virtual nonexercise, and I knew Jinx felt the same.

Soon we were inside the sodaparlor with its old-fashioned decorations, primitive PET-scan printouts, and NMR images of brain-glucose uptake, flickering on ancient crackly low-res monitors.

"Two Joshu Juices," I said to the poptate kibernetica behind the counter, presenting Honeysuckle's flashcard.

If she didn't pay for anything else, at least she'd pay for our drinks.

"Make mine a Potala Punch," countermanded Jinx.

"The order is two Joshu Juices and one Potala Punch," said the kibe.

"No. One of each."

"The order is one Joshu Juice and one Potala Punch."

"Flame on!"

"This is an assent?"

"Does the Goddess use tampons?"

The poptate churned its heuristics for ten seconds, then began to brew us our sidechains.

"Want to sit by the pond?" asked Jinx, after the drinks were mixed.

"Sure."

I carried the juices, and we found an empty bench on the grassy marge of the small ornamental pond. Two or three baseline ducks were paddling in the reeds, and I was reminded of my dumb id^2 and Honeysuckle's sexy one.

I plopped down on the syalon seat, and Jinx used his strong arms to lever himself up beside me. Sitting together like this, his head nearly on a level with mine, it was easy to forget his lack of legs.

We clinked our glasses, and I quoted the ADM jingle.

" 'Peace of mind—' "

" '—for a nudollar ninety-nine!' " finished Jinx.

We downed our brews and waited for the effects.

The tropes had been expertly reverse-engineered from a sampling of meditating monks: in the case of Jinx's drink, from the mind of the Dalai Lama himself. In a minute or so, the world took on a shimmering translucence, and I felt connected to the whole universe. Nothing mattered, but everything counted. All my problems were nonexistent.

Staring out over the perfect pond, I saw the surface ripple in the middle, then break to reveal the finned back of an airfish making the phase-change into the second half of its life.

We had just studied the specs on these splices, and they rushed into my brain in perfect arrays.

Having filled its flotation bladders with hydrogen broken out of the water and revamped its physiology, the airfish was now ready to live in the atmosphere. It would subsist for a few months on airborne microzoa, spore, and pollen, all the while sucking low-level ozone from the air and concentrating it in a different bladder. Rising higher and higher, it would eventually burst at around 15,000 meters, the lower edge of the ozone layer, releasing its cargo of reactive molecules where they would do good, not harm.

Highly unslouch. Truly nonfactorable goldstar-plus cytofabrication. I definitely wasn't down with the kids who'd try to shoot the O_3-suckers with flashlights just to watch the hydrogen mini-explosion.

Jinx spoke up with deep significance. "The airfish is born, becomes adult, does its work, then dies."

Without satori tropes, Jinx's words probably don't mean much, or else sound ultra-simplex. But I can't tell you what they meant to me then. They seemed to encapsulate our whole situation in a nutshell.

"We're 'fish too," I answered. "But we're also more than 'fish."

"You're bright as a three-alarm solar flare, girl!"

I knew then that I loved Jinx and would always be with him.

At that very moment, as if in confirmation of our love, another couple wandered in to sit on the bench next to us.

The woman wore Systemix meat, a Great Mother soma-type. Dressed only in a grass skirt, she had a double line of small breasts running down her torso, and her hips were broad as the lake behind the Yellow River dam.

Her companion's silicrobe trademark told me he was

racked out by Cellpro. And what a superstring raster he was! Hawkheaded Horus, noble falcon plumage mantling his shoulders.

Jinx and I looked on in mute admiration for several minutes. In the midst of our trope-induced satori, the couple seemed like heavenly visitors. Even after the glamor had worn off our vision, they still looked megatrump, if merely human.

Ignoring us, the adults quaffed their drinks. (Horus's pointy birdtongue was ultra-uptake!) The brews must have been some kind of aphrodelix, since the couple soon started into some heavy petting. Horus's loincloth quickly became a tent, and I got awfully jealous and sad at the same time.

"Jinx," I pleaded irrationally, "let's use Honeysuckle's card to get the moddies we've always talked about, then run away together!"

Jinx held my hand. "Arnie, think twice. Putting legs on me is no simplex patch job. I'd be laid up for days. We couldn't travel very far even in a hired scar-car without leaving a trail even a senile augie-doggie could follow. Honeysuckle would be pissing prostaglandins at the theft of her card. And then our poohs—or yours anyway—would snatch us back, and the next thing you know, we'd be wearing obedience collars like some splice! No, the only thing to do is to hold out for a year. It's not such a long time. . . ."

Jinx spoke with the voice of reason, and I knew what he advocated was the only sensible course. Still, my whole soul rebelled at the notion of going on with our boring lives without doing *something*, especially when we'd have to face all our cohort tomorrow.

I stood up. "I guess the only thing left to do then is to get spiked. At least it'll show our poohs we've got wills of our own. And it should shut Honeysuckle right up. Are you in a dedicated mode?"

Jinx boosted himself off the bench, thumping onto the

grass. "Does a carebear sit in the pedwards?"

I laughed. "G-Gnome, here we come!"

Slidewalk Seven was only a one-block stroll north of us, so we chose that transport over the Arteries.

If you pulled out a length of your intestines and slit it longwise, you'd expose the velvety microvilli lining, the zillions of little fingers that propel food through your gut. You'd also have a pretty good model of a slidewalk.

The sturdy silicrobe microvilli of the slidewalk propelled anything placed atop them along at a steady 5kph. (You could ride the network cross-continent in just a month, if you wanted to spend your vacation that boring way, like many slouch oldsters did.) Each invisible finger was rooted in place, yet flexible enough to pass on its burden to its neighbor. (In constant motion, the slidewalks conveyed a visual impression similar to the waveriness of heated syalon pavement. And if you rode them barefoot, they tickled almost subliminally.) Different lanes had different built-in directional orientations, for two-way travel.

The Amgen motto—"*Taxis*, not taxis"—was spelled out right in the substance of the slidewalks. I remembered having to have my dads explain it to me when I was little, since I never knew that "tax-us" could also be pronounced "tax-ease," or even what they were.

Jinx swung himself deftly onboard with the other passengers, vars, kibes, and citizens, and I had to stutter-skip to stay with him. I wasn't usually so awkward, but guess I was kind of nervous about our plans, even though I thought I had convinced myself it was the only way.

As if sensing my unease, Jinx tried to make me laugh. "Did you ever download any reductionist paradigm fiction where the author tried to imagine a system like this and came up with miles of rubber belts on rollers?"

Jinx's trick worked, and I laughed like a hyena splice. "That's not true. You're yanking my rods."

Jinx held up one hand. "Parity-plus, Arnie. I'll give

you the urals, and you can see for yourself.''

I chuckled some more. Those ancients—where were their heads *at*?!

Before too long, we were dismounting at Bughouse Square.

The thronging Square always reminded me of an old-time carnival midway you might see on some historical channel of the metamedium: lines of garish booths and arcades, peopled by touts and vendors under gaudy sili-crobe signage. The centerpiece of the Square, the original Chiron Bughouse, looked positively postmodern, next to the more recent exotic additions to the meatmart.

Here you could find a chromosartor or genebender or simple trope doser who would perform any possible alteration on your somatype or genotype—for a price. If you had the eft, you could be snipped, ripped or zipped; pumped, stumped or trumped; strobed, lobed or probed; primped, skimped or pimped; vented, scented or demented.

I stood for a minute or so bathing in the scary, alluring, surreal circus, until Jinx tugged at the hem of my doublet.

''Let's find number ten-forty, before we change our minds.''

Tracking round the Square, past the TATA Box and the Primordium, past the Organelle Store and Radio Shack Biocircuits outlet, we soon came to the G-Gnome's Cave.

Its facade was all fractal-modeled grocrete stalactites and stalagmites framing an irregular entrance curtained by enviromental ribbons.

I looked at Jinx, and he looked at me. Taking his hand, I tried to be as brave as my truncated spaceling.

''Let's get spiked,'' I said.

And we went through the ribbons.

My dads told me that a decade or two ago there was a rage for somatypes modeled on the characters in some old reedpair fantasy novel, sparked by a new virtuality rendering of the work. So for a while all you saw on the streets were bobbits and snorks and smogs, or creatures with some such names.

I figured the G-Gnome must have modeled himself on a troll or dwarf or some other runt from that book. His big blue eyes, capped by furry brows, were nearly on a level with Jinx's, and the G-Gnome was standing on his bandy legs! Two tufts of snowy fluffaduff sprang from behind his ears and decorated his otherwise bare skull. He wore a leather bib apron over a Windskin suit, and his hands were more massive than Jinx's.

To have maintained the same outdated look all these years made me think he was a conservative, slowmole kind of guy, and I instantly felt better to be putting myself in his brawny hands, so reassuringly similar to my proxy's.

"Children," the G-Gnome rumbled, "how can I help you?"

"We're here—" I began, then stopped.

A thrid-vid display had come on at our arrival, and now, cycling through a display of the G-Gnome's wetwares, it had reached the boobs.

They were so beautiful. Conical or melony, brown or creamy, drip-nippled or virgin-tipped, they were like taunting mirages in my personal desert.

It was all I could do to turn back to the G-Gnome and beg, "Please, shut that off." With my luck, the next thing shown would be a variety of the cocks Jinx lacked.

The proprietor complied, and I could breathe.

"Thank you. We're here to get spikes."

The G-Gnome's professional smile never wavered, but I could sense something tightening inside him.

"You have your parents'—"

"We've got this," I said, and offered Honeysuckle's card.

Taking it, the G-Gnome flexed it back and forth with

a noncommittal expression, but I could see nudollar signs in his eyes.

"Peej Rancifer lent you her card without, ah, duress? . . ."

I tried a haughty sniff like Honeysuckle used. "Of course. We're the best of friends."

"There should be no problem then."

"I hope not," I said, as the G-Gnome's words made my knees go watery.

"Please, be seated."

When Jinx and I were side by side, the G-Gnome activated the display again. But this time it ran through the various models of spike.

By the second rep, we had made up our minds.

"I'll take the Staghorns," said Jinx.

"And I'll take the Coral Cage."

"Very fine choices, both. The placement of each differs slightly. The Staghorns are implanted in the frontal region, whereas the Cage tends more toward the temporals."

The G-Gnome had donned gloves while he was talking and now squeezed from a tube a line of paste. He approached Jinx and rubbed the goop into his skull, up front.

Then he did the same to me, more toward the middle of my head.

Carefully peeling off the gloves and dropping them into a D-Grade-All unit, the G-Gnome said, "A mix of topical anesthetic and bonemelt. It takes a few moments to work. I shall debit Peej Rancifer's card while we wait, if you have no objections."

When he was done with that, the G-Gnome went to a cabinet, from which he removed the spikes.

I had never seen the things except on the metamedium, where they were always filtershot real sexy, so I was unprepared for how innocuous they looked in real life: just a pair of square-ish, pointy, drab—well, *spikes*, like the kind you might find holding down reedpair railroad ties.

Next from the cabinet came a shiny chrome-handled, rubber-headed mallet.

And with this, the G-Gnome drove the spikes into our heads.

I couldn't feel anything, even when the spike penetrated my dura mater. That G-Gnome was slouch-negative! He had that single tap down perfect. Naturally, I should have known that Honeysuckle and her family would patronize only the best.

Next, the G-Gnome slapped crawlypatches on our arms and began to lecture us.

"These are nutraceutical supplements. You're going to need them. The spikes will be utilizing some of your body's energy to grow. Even with the patches, you'll want to stoke up with something like Genzyme Carbprot afterwards, to make up for the loss."

Now I could half-feel ghostly invasions of my cranium. Right on cue, the G-Gnome explained, "The spikes are growing osteo-anchors, as well as paraneurons that will interface with yours. That's how they're able to control the color and pattern changes that reflect your moods. Once the endogrowth is done, the exogrowth will begin. Let me get a mirror."

The G-Gnome wheeled a digital mirror into place and turned it on, just in time.

The exogrowth, the visible part of the process, was starting.

From the single spike centered in Jinx's head, a pair of antlers began to develop, magnificent self-similar branchings.

From mine a rough coral stalk shot straight up. When it reached a height of about eight centimeters, it began to overspread into a gorgeous latticework umbrella.

Jinx and I watched ourselves and each other admiringly in the mirror, while the G-Gnome smiled benevolently on.

By the time the growth was finished, we were already adjusting to the novel weight of our new accessories. Jinx's antlers almost doubled his height, while my cage had stopped at nose level like a living lace veil.

"How do I look?" asked Jinx, his antlers flaring a crimson I knew from metamedium shows meant excitement.

"Very muskophallic! How about me?"

"Brain coral goddess!"

The G-Gnome clapped his hands together, and we knew he was eager for us to leave.

"I'm glad you're pleased. Remember, removal is a rather more time-consuming and costly process."

"Oh, we'd never want to get rid of them!" I said.

On the way out, Jinx had a little trouble with the door-ribbons catching on his rack, but aside from that, everything went superstring.

Until we got home, of course.

Jinx came in with me, and my poohs just lost it.

I will never ever forget the sight of them that day. They kind of scared even me, their own daughter, who should be used to them.

My dads are biological brothers who were in the same IMF assault unit during the last Short War. They were lying in a trench together, under enemy fire, when a shell was lobbed in on them.

The weapon contained some weird parazyme that no one's ever quite figured out yet. What it did was to fuse my dads together everywhere they were touching, as well as introduce a lot of collateral damage and changes, right down to the mitochondrial level.

The bonescrapers patched them up as best they could. Ironically, they had to use a couple of bulgy remoracords to join them even more symbiotically, since Alvin and Calvin had to share a lot of cytokines to stay alive.

When they were demobbed, their experiences led them to join the Moderationists, for whom they became instant and effective spokesmen.

I came along as a teratoma.

My dads kept developing these squelchy growths all over their bodies, which the bonies kept removing. One of the growths had more than usual baseline human structure to it, and my dads got the idea that it would be nice to turn it into a daughter. It cost a lot, both in eft and in compromise of their noninterventionist principles. But they were really kind of lonely, and I guess the Moderationists finally relented on the dogma part.

Naturally, I'm glad they did.

So anyhow, there my Siamese dads stood, linked by flesh and remora-cords straining fit to burst, shouting their heads off at me and Jinx, whose spike growths were turning green with contrition and purple with sorrowful anger at how innocent kids like us always got quenched in the end.

To make a long story short, we had to get rid of the spikes (but not before everyone in our cohort saw us with them), and Honeysuckle's parents had to pay for it all, and she had her estrogen shut off for a month, and Jinx, my darling Jinx, got sent back to Asgard.

But I really am not worried. Like Jinx said, a year is not such a long time to wait till we're franchised.

And after seeing me with a spike, there wasn't much resistance from the poohs a month later, when I pleaded one last time for tits.

And they're from a much classier vendor's line than *hers*!

⚡ Up The Lazy River

1. Muscle Fatigue

Flying northwest, parallel to the interface of the River Seven bankside forest and the manicured savannah, across which herds of null-sophont cultivars roamed peacefully, Norodom Dos Santos grieved for his hyper-fluid charge.

Normally, River Seven appeared from the air as a thick two-toned viscous snake, subtly pulsing in controlled opposing flows. Constrained by its mostly baseline geophysical channel, two-thirds dirty quicksilver grey and one-third matte black, it resembled a stripe of gel like the squeezings from a tube of antique toothpaste.

Today, River Seven lacked its usual luster, seemed lifeless and dispirited, victim of the unexplained changes Dos Santos was speeding to investigate.

I'm personifying the River again, Dos Santos mildly chided himself. *What would Master Trexler think of such imprecision in one of his students?*

After all, even dead, Trexler still exhibited all those old personality traits which a Turing Level Eight platform was capable of emulating, and one did not care to disappoint him.

Transferring his Synergen-grown craft to kibe autopilot (a simple TL4), Dos Santos resolved to abandon sentimentalism for work. Prompting his higher centers into microsleep, he freed up paraneurons to run deep plectic simulations of the River's failure.

Midway through the third evocation, disaster struck.

Propulsion myofibrils ripped away from the left COfiber-polysaccharide lattice wing with a sound like a cleaver through a slab of lapinovine.

The abnormal sound instantly reawakened the River Master's full awareness.

With a sinking feeling, Dos Santos realized his ladybug was going down.

The sudden threat to his life triggered a criticality flash that cascaded across his Sphinxco wetware mods: this mission was deeper than a simple repair call. . . .

Dos Santos knew better than to try to wrest control away from the kibe unit under emergency conditions— although a gut response still jerked his hands toward the control ganglia. Instead, he quickly snugged the wrist-dangling gloves of his millipore survival suit on, effectively disabling his CamNeuro digiface.

The kibe unit spoke as the gloves sealed themselves, and by then it was too late to do anything even if he had known what to do.

"I am sorry, Peej Dos Santos, but conditions require your immediate immobilization."

Nodules studded around the sides of his organiform chair burst like spore capsules. Compressed somatropic lianas sprayed out, wrapping him in an sticky biolastic net.

Out the windscreen, Dos Santos could see the line of jungle on his left rising up and around like a wall.

Dos Santos barely had time to utter the start of a prayer to the goddess of his Camspanic ancestors: "Holy Mary Kannon, Highest of Dakinis—" And then he felt the dose of Sandman perfuse his skin. . . .

* * *

The birds resumed their singing slowly. The loud crack
of a damaged branch finally giving way stopped them
again, but they quickly found their multifarious voices
once more.

One fauxvian called out over and over in a raspy human voice: "Shop here, shop here, shop here. . . ." An
escaped urban adbird . . .

Fronds of orange foliage starred with orchidenias lay
across the intact single-crystal windscreen, obscuring Dos
Santos's view of his new surroundings. As he struggled
to free himself from the safety restraints, the kibe unit
spoke.

"Please allow me, Peej Dos Santos."

A fine mist dispersed from the ladybug's ceiling, dis-
solving the vines: Catalytica Calmbalm. At the same
time, Dos Santos felt various aches and pains he had
hardly realized he was feeling disappear, as the mist was
recognized and allowed in through his smartsuit.

He climbed out of the chair, suit slick and hair damp,
and stood tentatively on the canted floor. The craft
seemed stable.

"What happened?"

"The left wing suddenly lost all haemocyanin flow,
and the tissue immediately degenerated below the functional threshold. Probability of spontaneous failure, point
one percent. Probability of maintenance error, thirty percent. Probability of deliberately induced failure, sixty-
eight percent . . . Wait. Abnormal protease traces
registering. . . . Revised probability of sabotage, ninety-
nine-point-six percent."

"Sabotage . . ." muttered Dos Santos. "But why?"

"I have no answer to your question, Peej Dos Santos.
However, despite the overwhelming evidence of non-
culpability, I am required by law to supply you with the
metamedium address of my manufacturer, should you
wish to file a suit against them. Synergen is a wholly

owned subsidiary of the Primordium Chaebol. Telecosm address is At-prim-kay—''

''Forget it.'' Dos Santos began to gather equipment and supplies from an overhead ovoid locker. ''How far are we from our destination?''

''Contact with Global Positioning's navsats remains firm, and I have us located within the standard three-meter deviation. Machine Lake is approximately fifty klicks to the north. However, I managed to set us down only a hundred yards from River Seven.''

''And we're still on the upstream bank?''

''Yes.''

''Good job.''

''Thank you, Peej Dos Santos. I hope you will take my actions into account in the event of any possible law-suit.''

''Don't worry, there's not going to be any legal action. It's plain that whoever stopped the River doesn't want me coming to investigate. There'll have to be a purge of all the splices on the maintenance crew back at the base.''

''Organics are inherently less trustworthy and more liable to be compromised than kibernetika, if I may say so.''

Dos Santos cracked the ladybug's hatch, and warm, wet air blew in past a curtain of bamboon.

''Where are you going, Peej? I've sent out a distress call and received an acknowledgement. Would it not be wise to wait here?''

''How do I know all the other 'bugs haven't been tampered with too? I could wait for days. No, I've got to finish my mission. I'm too close now to wait. And the River can't stay down much longer.''

Patting his left breast pocket, which held the vital vial of Instruction Set which would repair the River, and adjusting the bandoliers that held his Intratec splat-pistol, extra lysing cartridges and other equipment, Dos Santos placed one booted foot over the sill.

"I must protest, Peej. Under Regulation Two-Ten of the Riparian Administration Handbook—"

"Listen," interrupted Dos Santos. "Who's the River Master here, you or me?"

Somehow the TL4 kibe managed to sound wounded and resigned. "You are, Peej."

"Correct."

"May I make a suggestion, then?"

"Certainly."

"At least let me accompany you. I am more capable than your low-level suit assists. Also, if you are terminated and I am later recovered, I shall be able to make a full report."

"What a cheerful notion."

"I am simply trying to fulfill my autofac-implanted imperatives, Peej. . . ."

"All right."

Dos Santos stepped to the console and ejected the kibe, a featureless silver wafer the diameter of a hockey puck, but only half as thick. Fitting it flat into the appropriate sticktite slot on his harness, he turned to leave the disabled ladybug.

"I am now fully integrated with your suit sensors, Peej. They are of high quality."

"I have a feeling we'll need them," said Dos Santos. "Activate my retinal displays, please."

"Done."

Dos Santos's peripheral vision filled with translucent shimmerstats, and he stepped tentatively into the jungle.

2. Infoslam

The first report indicating that something was seriously wrong with River Seven had come a mere twelve hours ago, emanating from the kibe unit captaining one of the numerous floating autofacs-cum-general-stores that supplied the indigenous Riverside population. The unit, a mere hundred klicks from Machine Lake, had messaged that the River's downstream velocity was decreasing radically, dropping toward ancient baseline values or below; probes launched into the upstream side, however, still registered normal values. Continued updates revealed a steady decline in the force of the artifical current.

When other reports from further downRiver began to flood in—a tourist vessel, a passenger ferry, a fleet of sport skimmers and striders—it became obvious to Dos Santos that River Seven—his River—was dying.

Naturally, he had been in Lagos on official business at the worst possible time. Had the trouble found him at his normal post—his HQ on the shores of Machine Lake— he would have been at the source of the problem and able to take immediate action. As it was, a long trip back had been necessary first.

Now, knowing that his craft had been sabotaged, it became obvious that the attack on River Seven had been timed to take place in his predictable absence. . . .

Toward the unexpected abrupt end of his flight, Dos Santos knew that the downstream portion of River Seven must have been approaching total shutdown. The death of the current, as he had plotted it in Lagos, had been propagating faster than the current itself, a shut-down message of some unknown sort, passed from one flagellum-flailing silicrobe to its neighbor, and then to its neighbor's neighbor, thus outracing the physical flow as a sheer information wave.

The continued functioning of the upstream third of River Seven was explainable by the deliberately engineered lack of communication between the two currents. Only along the nearly 2000-klick length of the upstream-downstream interface, where a thin layer of specialized downstream silicrobes performed an elaborate ciliary doesy-doe with a matching layer of upstream silicrobes, exchanging energy in a friction-eliminating dance, did any mixing occur. And the incompatible nature of the two currents, designed to avoid command snafus, had apparently succeeded in keeping the upRiver current alive a little longer.

But the ultimate source of upRiver silicrobes *was* the downstream current, and the death of the smaller, still functioning portion of River Seven was inevitable.

From the feedstocks of Machine Lake were born all the silicrobes which comprised 50 percent by volume of the downstream River Seven channel. (The other half of the downstream channel was the traditional H_2O from traditional sources: feeder streams, rainfall, underground aquifer connections. The missing volume of water had been long ago diverted for human consumption.) From Machine Lake the silicrobes exited, mingling with the available water in a synthetic gunmetal-colored broth. (Nanosmall, the silicrobes were of course invisible individually, presenting an homogenous appearance en masse.) Programmed to churn downstream at a steady speed, each maintaining a constant distance from the downstream shore and its neighbors, the silicrobes carried the water molecules along with them faster than mere gravity ever had.

At the mouth of River Seven, the fingerlike delta around Port Harcourt, the downstream silicrobes were triggered by the increased salinity and by info from GloPos navsats, undergoing the transformation into upstream silicrobes. Separating from their partnered water molecules (which continued out to sea as of yore), the upstream silicrobes made a coherent U-turn and headed back. Without H_2O partners, they needed a virtual channel only half the size of the downstream one to make their way back to Machine Lake and resorption. Upstream speed was 80 percent of the downstream current.

Except today.

3. Big Muddy

The last chunky frondtree fell to Dos Santos's flashlight-machete with a sound like a watermelon hitting the floor from table-height, and sticky juice propelled by xylemic pressure sprayed his face and millipore suit. Then he stepped out of the jungle and onto the staymown vetiver turf of River Seven's upstream bank.

"Peej—suit bladders are now full with purified water, and any further dermal suit-contamination will have to be exosonically evaporated."

"Fine, fine," said Dos Santos absentmindedly, his entire concentration, basal and add-on, devoted to his ailing wide River.

The bipartite line of hyperfluid was dramatically sick.

Consider the more distant downstream side.

From its border with the upstream virtual channel all the way to the far bank, the downstream two-thirds of the River was a stagnant dove-grey stripe. The deactivated silicrobes, apparently still remaining in suspension, now no longer contributed any motion to the flow and in fact hindered the water molecules from resuming even their old basal speed. The downstream waterway, until so recently an efficient Riverroad upon which millions relied, was now a turbid slurry.

Dos Santos looked to the left, downstream, but focused his gaze on the nearer third of the River, the upstream channel.

This portion of River Seven was still functioning. Being composed of pure silicrobes, it was matte black in color and stood out sharply, its border still cohesive, from the downstream mess. But this normal appearance was misleading, and Dos Santos knew—

With a sharp intake of breath, the River Master spotted it.

The failure wavefront.

He watched helplessly as the killer disinformation

propagated swiftly upRiver, soon reaching his position
and passing unstoppably on.

Behind it, silicrobes went offline by the hundreds of
trillions. The black stripe instantly began to extend irregular fingers of darkness into the downstream portion of
the River, silicrobes flowing "backwards," and from
greater concentration to lesser as the now-unthinking
River—formerly considered an actual entity of Turing
Level One—attempted to homogenize itself according to
dumb physics.

"Damn. Damn, damn, damn!"

Momentary hopelessness washed over Dos Santos. He
had dedicated his life to Riparian Admin, out of a love
for these great semiliquid, semi-intelligent transport ma-
chines. For the past fifty years, he had worked self-
sacrificingly on the Rivers of the world, the large and the
small. River Eight (the old Volga), River Three (the old
Mississippi), River One-Oh-Four (the old Ganges), River
Twenty-Nine (the old Nile), even River One (the old Am-
azon)—First as apprentice, then as journeyman, finally
as Master, he had lovingly tended these sinuous creations
of humanity that snaked across the domesticated globe,
carrying mankind's freight and travelers, hosting its rec-
reations, bathing its pilgrims. And never in that time had
he experienced such a thing as this horror: the death of
one of his charges.

It felt like he imagined the death of the never-met pair-
bond proxy and hypothetical zygotes he had never permitted himself to indulge in would have felt. There was
a hole in his soul.

Anger and a determination for revenge replaced the
hopelessness. Dos Santos would make someone pay.

And River Seven, he vowed, would live again.

He advanced to the edge of the banking, which sloped
away steeply to the River, a forty-five degree stretch of
crumbly red clay, and scrambled down.

A rush of small dislodged pebbles tumbled down to

the River surface and sat atop the high-density gel-like silicrobe liquid, each rock centered in its own surface-tension dimple.

The kibe sounded alarmed. "Peej Dos Santos, you do not intend—"

Dos Santos reached the marge of the River and squatted down. The pebbles were drifting downstream. "Quiet! If you want to be useful, prepare to analyze some telemetry."

After peeling off both gloves, the River Master inserted his hands into the stagnant silicrobe soup.

The shimmerstats boiled with metagrafix in the corners of his eyes, fed by the subdermal mycotronix digiface sensors in his fingertips. Tapping the feed, the kibe added its verbal interpretation.

"It appears that the River has been contaminated with a dose of high-velocity instruction ribozymes based on the standard stepdown routines, but with subtle alterations that are not readily decodeable. The silicrobes are merely offline and apparently undamaged. If we could denature the invader, it would be a simple matter to restart the River—"

Dos Santos stood. "We'll have to do it fast, though, and that means getting to the facilities at Machine Lake. Not only do we have to worry about the possibility of further attacks, but there are system constraints as well. Eventually, the 'crobes are going to drop out of suspension and settle to the bottom. A restart under those conditions would be chaotic. We'd kick up enough particulates to clog the whole delta and probably kill off all the lifeforms as well. And if the mixing of upRiver and downRiver 'crobes continues, the vortices that'll form on a reboot will be orders of magnitude larger than normal—"

The kibe interrupted. "Speaking of vortices, Peej, here comes a Vortifish Hunter right now!"

4. Old Man River

The coracle glittered nacreously, catching glints of African sunlight, an upturned halfshell with rippled, purpled rim. (Its original seedstock, highly modified of course, had been the chambered nautilus.) Large enough to hold two basal humans, it now contained only one sophont, a cynocephali wearing a loin covering of plaid clothtree fabric.

Originally the cynocephali—or Anubians—had been bred and released only along River Twenty-Nine, the old Nile. Part tourist attraction, these bipedal dog-headed sophonts had been designed to occupy a new top niche in the food chain. So successful and popular had they proven that no River today, some ten Anubian generations later, was without them.

The furred humanoid splice stood at the rear of its tiny craft, the tiller that controlled the steering jets in its paw. It sailed midway down the former upstream channel whose black syrupy components were now uselessly and slowly heading downstream with all the rest.

The small vessel was plainly bearing toward Dos Santos.

As the craft drew nearer, Dos Santos could make out further details, including grown-bone spears racked across the bow. And as the lone sailor expertly beached its craft, Dos Santos recognized the tattoo icon beneath the skin of one canine ear as the mark of the Hyena Tribe of Vortifishers.

"Peej Human!" barked the splice, showing sharp teeth webbed with saliva. "Our River dying!"

At that moment, the kibe announced, "Incoming transmission via Global Telesis for the River Master."

"Accept."

The pleasant female voice of his Fon apprentice, Isoke, whom he had left behind in Lagos, sounded in Dos Santos's right ear like a beacon from a saner world.

"Norodom! The saboteurs have been pinged and popped! They were greenpeacers calling themselves the Izaak Walton League. Only ten human members, but they managed to kill several Rivers and disrupt half the world's gross shipping tonnage! Dai Ichi Kangyo has just issued an estimate of five billion time-dollars worth of loss. But the crickcops and the IMF blueboys are certain they've slagged them all! You shouldn't have to worry about another disruption."

As always, hearing Isoke's eager voice and realizing his responsibilities to her, Dos Santos tried to imagine how Master Trexler would have responded. "That's wonderful, Isoke. But we're still left with the problem of getting Number Seven up and running."

"Can't you just dump the Instruction Set into the River right where you are?"

The Master patiently explained to his apprentice about the need to denature the ribozyme contaminants with the Machine Lake equipment first. Mixing the Instruction Set with the contaminant would simply produce undifferentiated glop.

"What can we do then? You were right about the remaining ladybugs being sabotaged just like yours. The RA has no other transports available. We can hire a private thopter or borrow a government one, but it'll take hours to get to you, even from the closest point. You're deep into the low-tech preserve around the Lake. . . ."

Dos Santos considered the Vortifisher standing before him. The splice's mouth gaped open, tongue hanging as it panted nervously. Muscles beneath its spotted coat twitched.

"I think I have transportation. It's slow, but it's worth a shot. Send out a flier as backup, though. Tell it to look for me on the River."

Signing off, Dos Santos addressed the Hyena.

"Can your boat make it to Machine Lake?"

The Hyena smiled. "This is good boat. Humans made

this boat. Never stops! Eats River and spins tail, all day. Fast, fast, fast!''

''How fast?''

This question brought a frown to the cultivar's canine face. After pondering a moment, it answered. ''See that clo'tree? Here to there, ten breaths.''

''Twenty knots,'' interpolated the kibe.

Dos Santos hissed. ''Two hours or more to the Lake! It'll have to do. Let's go.''

Dos Santos and the splice pushed the beached coracle off, then jumped in. The Hyena prodded control ganglia on a hump near the tiller, and the organic motor came to life. An intake on the bow fed silicrobes—online or off, it mattered not—to the org-engine which broke them down and stole their ATP. The thick, whiplike macroflagellum at the rear of the craft soon had them up to full speed.

''We stop at my village and tell pack where I go.''

Dos Santos opened his mouth to argue, then thought better of it. The splice's teeth, not to mention its spears, gave the River Master pause, despite the comforting presence of his Intratec pistol. Although human-designed, this was no collar-wearing domestic cultivar, but a wild one, with the freewill to fend for itself. Although it was now friendly and relying on the human to repair the River, its attitude could easily change. Unless he wanted to kill this one out of hand—a repugnant choice—he would have to compromise. . . .

''All right. But we can't waste time.''

''Go very fast. Mate and cubs must know, or fear.''

Splices and their pretensions to humanity! Just what he needed now . . .

Dos Santos dropped to a crouch in the seatless boat. Trailing a hand in the River, he and the kibe used the time to work up the formula for the denaturing compound that would destroy the toxin. All seemed clear, except—

there were still strings of mysterious purpose in the contaminant. . . .

After some time, the Vortifisher village appeared in a clearing on the upstream bank.

Although the pure silicrobe medium of the upstream third of the River was lifeless, the downstream two-thirds, with its mix of water and 'crobes, supported an entire ecosystem of engineered lifeforms. Near the top of the food chain was the Hyenas' main sustenance, the vortifishes.

The interface between upstream and downstream channels was normally an orderly zone of increasing and decreasing speed gradients, thanks to the programmed interactions of the two types of silicrobes. However, chaotic factors, pattern seeds, occasionally caused whirlpools—vortices—of lesser or greater dimensions to butterfly into existence. These were dealt with by the various species of vortifishes, large, powerful, wide-mouthed organisms who derived *their* sustenance from gobbling the rogue silicrobes (and *only* the rogues), destroying the vortices in the process.

It took skill and luck and courage for the Hyenas to ride their small boats to the very edge of the vortices and spear their prey, but the cynocephali managed quite superbly—as they had been engineered to do.

Retreating through layers of shimmerstat windows, Dos Santos focused on the village of podhuts. The bank was thronged with welcoming Hyenas, hunters brandishing their spears, mothers carrying up to four nursing babies in special slings.

Suddenly, the villagers began to scream and gesture, expressions of fear on their faces.

The Hyena throttled down until they stood still. Dos Santos turned to look out to midRiver.

A huge vortice was forming.

''Peej, this is impossible. Silicrobes do not come online by themselves—''

Dos Santos loosened his splatpistol in its holster. "It's happening, though."

Something, some form, was beginning to rise up out of the vortice. 'Fishes nibbled at its base without effect.

Matte black, the figure was plainly formed out of silicrobes. But the 'crobes were agglomerating in ways they had never been designed to. Flowing, shifting, rearing upward in a column thrice the mass of a man, they obviously sought to express some programmed form.

At last they succeeded.

An ebony Neptune towered out of the River. Seaweed hair, serene eidolon face, clamshell beard, massive arms and chest, fish tail below the waist.

The River had materialized its monotone god.

"It's an autocatalytic set," whispered a horrified Dos Santos.

He had heard of such things arising, back when the Rivers had been in their prototype stage. Feedback among rogue components bootstrapped primitive, self-replicating A-life out of the isotropic soup.

But this was different. This was planned by the Walton League, their ace in the hole, something vastly more dangerous.

Dos Santos squirted off an alert to Isoke as he raised his pistol and rattled off a full clip.

The intelligent bullets, loaded with instantaneous lysing agents, found their mark, but without apparent effect. Dos Santos had known that the lysing agents wouldn't work against nonprotein A-life, but he had been hoping the bullets would disrupt the thing's coherence. Instead, they had passed harmlessly through.

Now the autocat began to advance purposefully across the River toward the coracle, seeming to ride on its tail, but in actuality propelled by silicrobe flow, much like a slidewalk. The thing's actions were so intent, it must register somewhere low on the Turing scale, perhaps even as smart as the River itself had been—

The splash of the Hyena pilot jumping overboard distracted Dos Santos. He turned to do the same—

Too late.

Neptune had him in its arms.

Dos Santos's face was pressed into the greasy bulk of the autocat's chest. He was blind, suffocating—

Then he began to sink *into* the creature.

His own River was killing him, a hot darkness extinguishing his life.

And on top of everything else, his suit had gone crazy.

The contents of the system of flexipumps and thin, biolastic water reservoirs in his clothing were shifting, pooling in one place, at his left breast. The concentrated lump of water swelled, pressing into his flesh and the bone beneath it. He tried to scream, but couldn't. Would the fist of water punch through to his heart—?

Then he felt the overstressed reservoir burst *outward*, scores of needle-like microjets exiting through the suddenly dilated millipores concentrated in a patch of his suit.

Suddenly he fell, landing in the coracle, which rocked crazily, but stayed afloat.

Inactive silicrobe streams dribbled off him. He coughed out what seemed like lungfuls of the stuff, blew gobs out his nose. Finally, he could breathe.

With a shaky hand, the River Master cleaned the goop from his eyes.

Neptune had vanished, deliquescing back into the River. All that remained were a few random pseudopods and tentacles that wriggled impotently, then collapsed.

Dos Santos looked at the hole in his suit.

The reservoir that had filled and burst had been directly beneath the vial of Instruction Set, which was now nowhere to be seen. Presumably, the shattered vial and its contents had destabilized the autocat.

The kibe's tone could only be described as self-satisfied. "Rather ironic, Peej Dos Santos, that the creature was stymied by water, don't you think?"

"Hunh."

"I've broadcast our encounter to the Masters of the other damaged Rivers, Peej. They should be able to handle their own autocats more safely than we. Aren't you glad I asked to accompany you now, Peej?"

Dos Santos held his head. All the waste, all the work that yet lay ahead—Well, at least he was alive to tackle it.

"Yes, yes I am, kibe."

"And if I may remind you, Peej—?"

Dos Santos laughed, somehow sensing what was coming. "No lawsuit, kibe, I promise."

⚡ Distributed Mind

ALL HIS LIFE, GREENLAW HAD FELT INEXPLICABLY cheated, an itchy sensation similar to contracting a virtuality virus, sometimes localized in his chest, sometimes in his head, occasionally even disrupting the hypertactility of his long slim multisegmented fingers. Something invaluable and irreplaceable had been stolen from him, he was convinced, although he could name neither the prize nor the thief. Or rather, he had had different suspicions of varying certainties over the course of the past century, one succeeding another as the circumstances of his life changed.

Greenlaw was one of the few members of his cohort gestated and birthed the old-fashioned baseline way. Neither Incyte Yoot Chutes nor splice hostmothers of even the redoubtable Possum cultivar were acceptable to his parents, hardline Viridians both, their philosophy the source of his very name. Thus Greenlaw had entered the world at an extreme disadvantage, compared to his already wetwired, chomskied peers. Why, he hadn't spoken his first words till after a whole six months of strictly neohomeopathic trope dosing!

So of course for a time it had been easy to blame his parents, Soil and Sunflower, for any failures he encountered in his schooling and among his peers. One counselor, an Andy Panda, had even confirmed these sentiments in so many words, offering to file a retroactive punitive suit on his behalf, a step Greenlaw felt somehow disinclined to take.

But Greenlaw's harsh feelings toward his parents had evaporated when he attained his majority, and Soil and Sunflower, honoring the most extreme of Viridian tenets, had undergone voluntary euthanasia, offering their future resource-consumption-units back to a generally unappreciative rich world.

Unfortunately, they left the twelve-year-old Greenlaw with few monetary resources. To escape the lite-servo class he had been born into and finance the further trope doses that he hoped would lead to a good job in the symbol-analysis class, he was forced to rent out his personal wetware, a resource whose valuable deepest structures were still unduplicatable, even by qubitic processors.

At scheduled times each day, a certain portion of his brain's computational cycles was placed in an online pool available to anyone with a project and sufficient eft. The precious time lost to him, spent as part of a worldwide parallel processing network, caused him to focus his resentments on all those better off than he, leading to a brief flirtation with the Plus-Fourierists.

The inevitable disillusionment arrived with the Plus-Fourierist-sponsored assassination of the entire Executive Council of the World Trade Organization, and Greenlaw's distaste turned toward politics in general. By this point he had gotten his first job, at Molecular Tools. The company had paid for several somatic and cellular enhancements, his first sartorizations. And there he had fallen in love.

Her name was Anemone, and at first Greenlaw was afraid she was Viridian, although that would have been hard to reconcile with her job as leader of MT's Santa

Claus project. But he learned that her floral name simply followed a family tradition. Relieved, he had surrendered his heart for the first time.

Greenlaw, youthfully eager, wondered why it took so long for them to have sex. But he eventually learned: Anemone was a maff, a fully functioning hermaphrodite, with a female lover whose consent to Greenlaw's inclusion in the menage Anemone had been courting.

The sight of the two of them in his bed surprised him one night when he returned home. Anemone's peculiar genital arrangements, dilated and tumescent under the basal woman's ministrations, aroused in him Viridian prejudices he hadn't known existed, and he fled.

Years would pass before he could feel easy around women, who became the latest culprits in his search for what was missing from his life. He buried himself in his work, progressing rapidly, moving from one firm to another: Innovir, Hemazyne, BioCogent. Finally, a valuable commodity, he had settled in at Procept. There, he had finally met his lifemate, Stroma, beloved afferent to his efferent. She of the coarse mottled pelt and seductive prehensile lips and nipples, syrinx-trilled laughter and witty chatter. His and his alone, her minor mods acceptable to the more sophisticated man he had become.

Happy in his work and his home, Greenlaw's unease had subsided somewhat, although it never quite vanished. The hapless child born to Soil and Sunflower had been essentially replaced by a new self-made construct.

Then, after satisfying decades of personal advancement, decades in which his work had helped change the world, easy decades which had lulled him into almost forgetting the mysterious theft of his birthright, had come the ultimate tragedy, which Greenlaw came to believe he had been pro-actively intuiting all his life. A tragedy the ultimate blame for which was frustratingly diffuse and shared.

Wild mocklife had devoured Greenlaw's native bioregion.

Objectively and inclusively viewed, these were the victims and spoils of the plague:

A sprawling infrastructure measured at 1.2×10 to the fifth power plectic units (on the revised Santa Fe scale).

Ten million citizens of both Peej and Haj status.

Uncounted vars from a thousand controlled mixes, as well as innumerable illicit sports, volunteers, and devolves.

Thirty million multiform kibes of varying turingity.

And finally, unreckoned teratonnes of biomass and inorganics, both basal and sartorized.

Subjectively and selectively, Greenlaw mourned these:

His lovingly grown zomehome. His entire chromocohort, however much they had teased him as a child. His proxies and splices. Those of his semisentient splinters and shards and snippets which had been unable to scatter themselves safely elsewhere across the telecosm.

And Stroma, the one woman he had ever been able to love, so alluringly bez kompleksov, as his Snowy friends might say.

Gone, all gone. Yet still mockingly there, parading about in their charade of daily life. Active unknowing ghosts, simulacra transfigured by the mass of rogue silicrobes known as the Urblastema or—by those who still had the energy for poetic coinages—the Panplasmodaemonium.

And the ultimate irony: it was Greenlaw's job to stop such things from happening. During the infiltration and ingestion of his own region he had, in fact, been halfway around the globe, supervising the defenses of another beleaguered metroplex.

Greenlaw was good at his job. His efforts had been successful. The assault on the antipodal NewZee plex had been repelled, its citizenry saved.

As if any of that mattered to him now.

The *cordon sanitaire* around Greenlaw's contaminated bioregion was staffed partly by members of his own commensal crada, the DizDek team from Procept. The teamer in charge was one Haj Bambang, with whom Greenlaw had often worked.

Moving away from his organiform flier parked on the outskirts of the encampment, with 'crobe-attenuated sunlight painting the scene around him in muted hues, Greenlaw strode now toward the command nexus of the defense. One of his personal kibes, carrying a large sealed bip container, obediently trailed him.

Amidst the organized activity of Procept kibes, vars, and commensals, Bambang stood, his seemingly unfocused stare revealing that he was obviously busy scanning his retinally displayed shimmerstats. Sensations of tension and hope were nearly tangible here, thought Greenlaw.

As Greenlaw approached, Bambang brought his awareness back to primary reality, catching sight of Greenlaw in the process. The Indoasian's broad cinnamon face wrinkled in a mixture of respect, happiness, and just a trace of wariness.

"Peej Greenlaw," said Bambang respectfully. They threw signs at each other, hyperarticulated hand-flexures of lineage and association. "Good to see you. Are you perhaps coming to take command?"

Greenlaw sighed. Duty, professional jealousy, they seemed so unreal now. . . .

"No," he answered, "not at all. I'm sure you're doing a fine job, although I haven't tapped any status reports since the announcement of the engulfment. No, this visit is strictly personal."

In his habitual gesture of relief, Bambang fingered the Procept tattoo that rotated on his cheek, nanometers below his epidermis.

The innocent gesture sent Greenlaw's linear thought

processes into a chaotic whirl. Suddenly, for the first time
in his long life, he saw the ubiquitous loyal silicrobes
that formed Bambang's tattoo—and his own, for that
matter—as the actual nonsomatic invaders that they were.

Was the Urblastema merely a tattoo on the surface of
Gaia?

No. For unlike an obedient assemblage of silicrobes,
it was intent on devouring its host.

And we did it to ourselves, thought Greenlaw ruefully.
I helped every step of the way. No one else is to blame.

Onboard Xaos Tools wetware located in the bulge of
his encephalocele came online, and the nonlinear vortex
of emotions and thoughts damped agreeably down. Without the mod's invaluable aid, Greenlaw suspected, he
would have been a grief-racked casualty in some Humana
House by now.

"Personal?" echoed Bambang. He tickled up a fresh
datum. "Oh, yes, I see. . . . My condolences, Peej Greenlaw. May the principles of the First Self-Organizer be of
comfort to you now in your hour of distress."

Greenlaw waved the offered solace away, as useless in
its own fashion as his parents' Viridian principles. "I was
never a true believer, Haj. And it would be most ironic
now for me to worship that principle which, more or less,
has stolen away from me all I once cherished."

"But Peej, surely you cannot repudiate the sacred principles, despite their perversion by the Urblastema. . . ."

Bambang broke off, sensing that theological fencing
was highly unsuitable to Greenlaw's current mood. He
changed topics.

"Would you care to survey our defenses, Peej? We
have a continuous line of shuggoths patrolling the entire
perimeter to deal with macroscopic surface assaults. The
entire atmospheric column above the afflicted zone is sat-
urated with killer assemblages in the submicron range, as
well as shoals of airsharks. Additionally, we've estab-
lished positive-flow wind curtains and backup pressure

fronts, with the help of GlobalMet. As for the subsurface measures—''

Greenlaw interrupted. ''That was the route by which the Urblastema attacked, wasn't it?''

Bambang appeared embarrassed. ''Yes indeed, Peej. Apparently, after the defeat of the Urb at Chiplex, a small remnant portion escaped deep underground. Unknown to us, it had developed means of encysting itself against a magma environment. Our mopup survey unfortunately stopped at Region D Prime of the lower mantle. Consequently, the Urb was able to utilize magma veins as a means of travel, surfacing well away from anywhere we expected it to appear.''

''And what of contamination of the lithosphere in general?''

''Models are still being grown in many simorg spheres, of course. But the best guess is that no widespread infection of the crust yet exists. The Urb-seed was small and weak and seemed to spend very few cycles doubling itself. Thank the First for the limits of one over e-squared! For some reason, it appeared intent on breaking through to the surface as soon as possible. A desire to deal with us unpredictable lifeforms first? Perhaps underground conditions were not optimal? . . .''

Despite himself, Greenlaw found his curiosity piqued. ''That just doesn't make sense. It could have remained hidden safely for years, building itself up into an unconquerable mass. Converting the globe from the inside out, it could have taken us completely by surprise. Instead, it tipped its hand by a premature assault. Frankly, I'm baffled.''

''Perhaps luck was simply on our side.''

Greenlaw smiled wryly. ''Another superstition I find hard to credit.''

Bambang erected a cold facade employed usually only with noncommensals, becoming completely professional. As if to indicate that Greenlaw's options were limited, he said, "Shall we tour the defenses then?"

"I think not. I have other plans."

"May I hear them?"

"Certainly. They are contained in a single sentence."

"Which is?"

"I'm going in."

Bambang's eyes widened to their utmost. Five whole seconds passed by Greenlaw's onboard clock before the Indoasian found it possible to speak.

"Madness! Even if you're intent on committing melancholy suicide, is it also necessary to contribute your corpse and talents to the Urb?"

"Spare me the melodramatics, please. I have no intention of dying. I will be using a new falseskin wholebody sheath which is immune to infection. Or so the crada assures me."

Bambang considered. "Even so, is it proper for one of our senior operatives to risk his life in a field trial?"

"I have an additional goal, the personal matter to which I referred. I intend to bring back a piece of my mate."

Bambang understood at once. "She had no offsite storage of splinters or shards then? She was never godelized or fredkinated? Not even a snippet? I see. Too bad."

Greenlaw nodded. He had tried many times to convince Stroma to allow herself to be neurally mapped, but she had always refused, laughingly regarding such measures as paranoid and unnecessary.

Bambang continued. "So nothing of her mental patternings remains outside the clutches of the Urb. And you wish to replicate her. But you know we cannot allow you to bring an Urb-seed out. The danger is too great."

"It will be contained within an onboard vesicle of the same impermeable material. Completely safe. And Procept approves. They would like a captive piece of the Urb to experiment on."

"Allow me to confirm all this, Peej."

"Permission granted."

Bambang went unfocused. When he returned, his dour expression was overlaid with respect and awe.

"May I personally escort you to the borders of the zone, Peej?"

"It would be my pleasure, Haj."

Grateful for the sheer essential humanity of his commensal, Greenlaw impulsively stuck out one of his long-fingered hands for an old-fashioned shake.

As Bambang gripped Greenlaw's proffered hand, a wave of disorientation and deja vu swept over Greenlaw. For lengthy seconds, Greenlaw felt as if he were reiterating a scene he had lived through a hundred times before. The ground seemed to shift beneath him, the world whirled, and, startled, he broke contact.

"Are you well?" Bambang asked, plainly concerned.

Greenlaw felt onboard compensators swing into action. Primary reality stabilized.

"I've been existing on microsleep for a week," Greenlaw explained. "But I can go another few hours."

Bambang threw a sign acknowledging Supremacy of Somatopsychic Autonomy.

The two men, accompanied by Greenlaw's single kibe and Bambang's whole devoted flock, began to walk toward a line of what appeared, at this distance, to be a range of white hillocks, curiously wavering.

The men passed a squad of Sinochem Assault Beetles and DarMol Scout Giraffes. A crew from Bechtel-Kanematsu-Gosho was supervising kibes who were laying lines of buckytubes that would carry circulating superhot plasma: its release would be a last-ditch suicide defense.

As the group drew closer, the hillocks grew larger and larger, resolving themselves into separate entities. Finally they towered over the humans, more like living mountains, mobile indeed.

Twenty meters tall, bloated, white as paste, each

topped by a normal-sized human rider who appeared
dwarfed, the shuggoths shluffed noisily along in their
continuous patrol, flattened ellipsoids massing as much
as two basal blue whales apiece, separated from each
other by only a quarter body-length. A damp-soil odor
typical of mycotronic creatures filled the air.

From time to time feelers and pseudopods erupted
from the shuggoths' upper surfaces at random, to sample
the environment.

"An impressive sight," commented Greenlaw. "Although how the Urblastema regards them is a matter we
might speculate on."

Bambang bristled. "Your remark smells of defeatism,
Peej—if I may be frank. I understand your distress, but
we have a duty to crada and humanity to maintain our
professionalism. The Urb, after all, is not invulnerable.
As you well know, it relies on speed and bulk in its
attack. If we can overwhelm it on either of those two
fronts, then we stand a chance. Even as we speak, vast
quantities of the new petahertz dizdeks are flowing down
the feeder lines to the reservoirs of the splash-cannons
you can see here. Soon, we will repel this incursion, as
we have all others."

"Leaving behind an ocean of disassembled, decon-
structed slop. Plenty of raw feedstock. But not what was
once here. Not what the Urb consumed. The people and
trees and homes. Never that."

"I'm sorry, Peej. But we will rebuild. And repopulate.
If that is any consolation to you."

Greenlaw sighed. "I suppose it will have to be. But
enough talk. I wish to enter the zone now. Kibe—the
box, please."

The obedient mechanism opened the lid of the
medium-sized biopoly container it held.

Revealed was what appeared to be an undifferentiated
mass of thick semiliquid like mercury, silvery and re-
flective.

"You mentioned speed as a defense, Haj Bambang. Here you see the ultimate in that line. This falseskin presents no stable molecular identity onto which the Urb can latch. Entirely chameleonic. It shifts through a thousand random cellular identities a second, its surface a kaleidoscope of antigens, while still maintaining its large-scale integrity. Unable to latch on long enough to unriddle the nature of its victim, the Urb is frustrated and cannot usurp and convert the material. Nor, obviously, what it protects."

Greenlaw turned to the box and plunged his hands in.

The liquid ran up his arms like twin snakes swallowing.

In seconds, Greenlaw was sheathed completely in silver, his eyes and mouth reduced to mild depressions, his nose plugged, his ears capped.

The kibe closed the lid on the empty box.

Bambang eyed the argent, statue-like form of his senior commensal. Plainly, the Indoasian was running a search through some little-accessed data trees.

Bambang spoke. "Mid to late twentieth century. A medium called 'comics' . . ."

Operating now entirely on inner metabolic reserves, tapping sensory feeds that ranged from satellites to the analog-vision of the falseskin itself, Greenlaw smiled at Bambang's expression, the falseskin flowing over his parted lips like a seamless membrane.

"Exactly. I need only what I believe the reedpair authors called 'a stick' to appear completely in character." Greenlaw's words resounded normally, transmitted by vibrations of the falseskin. "Now, can you afford to slow those creatures down just a bit?"

"Certainly. But only for seconds."

A wave of deceleration propagated clockwise around the necklace of shuggoths, counter to their direction of travel.

Greenlaw tensed his leg muscles, the falseskin likewise

responding, incrementing his normal abilities.

A gap opened in the line.

At enhanced speed, without a final goodbye, Greenlaw sprinted for the opening.

And was through.

The realm of humanity and its obedient creations was behind him.

Now, there was nothing but the Urb.

And, most horribly of all, it was a domain of utter normality.

Greenlaw found himself standing in an orchard of fabric trees, the line of shuggoths a full half-klick behind him.

The scene was the essence of peace. The broad black leaves of the fabric trees waved peacefully in the perpetual wind from outside. Long draperies of fabric hanging down from the underside of the secretory branch-nodes rustled gently, tartan and paisley. Judging from their length, they had apparently just been harvested, for they did not even touch the ground. A chorus of insect life reached his shielded ears. From the underbrush bolted a basal rabbit, followed by a sinuous baseline snake.

No aberrations.

Yet utterly false.

Suddenly, Greenlaw felt the ground immediately beneath his soles come alive. He did not move. Soon, the probing of the mock soil subsided.

He hadn't realized he had been tensed against the attack until it ceased. Initiating a relaxant cascade within himself, Greenlaw moved toward the closest tree. Stopping next to it, he lashed out at its trunk with a kick.

"Urb! Wake up!"

Unnaturally, the curtains of fabric moved quickly to envelop him, tasting, seeking to analyze and convert. Again, he did not resist. After a few seconds they slowly, reluctantly withdrew.

A pair of bark lips formed on the trunk of the "tree."

"What are you?" said the Urb in an innocuous tenor.

Greenlaw spoke with a bravado he barely felt. To be actually conversing with this monstrosity surpassed all rational thinking.

"Your doom, Urb. Your extinction."

"You are small, alone, unsupported. No tiny system so isolated can be self-sufficient for long. Soon you will have to come out of your shell. Then I shall be you, and you me."

The lips were subsumed back into the tree, and the conversation was clearly at an end.

The Urb did not sound concerned. Did it understand emotions, threats, and bluffs? What had it retained of the million human personalities and memories it had swallowed? How much had been integrated into the core of its being?

Greenlaw knew that the original biological codings of the converted inhabitants of his region—animal, var, human, plant, and virus—no longer existed as such. The original proteins and nucleotides and parabases had all been converted to crafty rogue silicrobes identical to those that had mutated and escaped a dreadful five years ago. The same applied to all the unlucky inorganics of the region, down to an unknown depth.

Isotropy reigned.

The ultimate monoculture.

The orchard, the grass, the rabbit, the snake, the very crust: all these were now composed of Urb-stuff masquerading as what it had consumed. The simulation was perfect and complete until examined on a molecular level. Had Greenlaw, for instance, chosen to break off a branch of his recent interlocutor, to his ears it would have snapped convincingly, to his normal vision it would have revealed typical grain and texture, oozed the requisite sap.

The Urb, as best they understood, was able to draw

directly somehow on the ultradense original information stored in sheldrakean morphic fields for its disguise. The templates of all that it had engulfed were available to it for instant replication. A feat currently beyond human abilities.

Whether a captured piece of Urb-stuff would allow Greenlaw to retrieve from those selfsame fields the information patterns of his mate, Stroma, was not certain. He had only the tentative promises of his crada that such might be possible.

Some of the morphic specialists claimed that any portion of Urb-stuff within his reach here in the orchard would have sufficed for his purposes. Others felt that the stuff forming the simulacrum of his wife would naturally resonate most strongly with the patterns he sought. Greenlaw did not quite know whom to believe. Perhaps the wisest course would be to snatch and run now, attain the safety beyond the shuggoths.

But his protective sheath seemed to be working as promised.

Any knowledge he could collect might help the defenders.

And he did so want to see Stroma.

Even her ghost.

The Urb had been right about one thing, however. His time here was limited by his inner reserves.

Moving swiftly, Greenlaw soon left the orchard far behind.

A busy road presented itself. Traffic crawled, hopped and skittered, bound in one direction toward Greenlaw's residence in a luxurious neighborhood of tree-towers and zomehomes on the outskirts of the plex.

False, all a sham, Greenlaw kept reminding himself. He felt the neo-emotion known as *sebnsucht*, a wave of longing for the unattainable, mixed with nostalgia and grief. Harshly, he damped the neomote signal down.

Stepping into traffic, Greenlaw halted a two-rider tumblebug.

The driver was a slim fellow wearing the tattoo of the telecosm maintenance crada.

"What's your trouble, Peej? And why the envirosuit?"

Greenlaw played the Urb's game. "I can't explain now. May I have a ride?"

The cryptohuman formed of Urb-stuff hesitated realistically before agreeing. "Certainly. Hop aboard."

Greenlaw climbed on the tumblebug, and, after allowing a cargo-crawler to pass on the left, its driver took off.

Greenlaw remained silent for the trip—which took less time than running would have and conserved his resources as well—and the driver seemed reluctant to initiate conversation.

Was the Urb toying with him? All it would take to defeat Greenlaw would be to immobilize him in any of a hundred different ways until he either suffocated or opened up. Was the Urb (whose motives no one had ever fathomed) so intent on its simulation that it could not react to Greenlaw's unique presence?

There was no certainty. None.

Greenlaw settled back into his seat.

Finally, they arrived at his destination, the periphery of his residential district.

Greenlaw turned to the driver. "If I were to ram my fist into your chest right now and squeeze your heart to Urbpulp, you'd die horribly, I'm sure, and quite convincingly. But what would you really feel?"

The Urb did not relax his role. The cryptohuman assumed a look of terror. "Get—get out! I'm sending a nine-eleven instantly!"

Greenlaw dismounted and walked away.

Down noontime-empty streets, past Urb-children playing on Urb-grass, Urb-augie-doggies watching over them . . .

One final turn brought him face to face with his home.

From the inside, the falseskin absorbed his tears.

Greenlaw entered.

Stroma lay on an organiform couch, her pelt lustrous, nothing concealed. Her languid arms reached up for him, her nipples curled convulsively.

"I was just wishing you were here," she said, her voice a knife through Greenlaw's ears.

He knew then he had to put an end to this dangerous game.

Taking one of Stroma's offered hands, Greenlaw snapped off her left index finger.

There was no shout of pain, no scream.

The Urb had chosen to shut down the pseudo-Stroma and manifest itself.

"Again, you've failed," said the Urb through Stroma's lips, her wounded hand "bleeding" profusely onto the couch.

Almost against his will, Greenlaw said, "How so, Urb? And what do you mean, 'again'?"

"This is approximately the five-hundredth time we have run this sequence, and still you persist in hating me."

Greenlaw laughed. "So, you *do* understand bluffing! A fine attempt, Urb. But now I'm leaving."

Greenlaw turned to go.

"No. Stop."

Greenlaw's legs were no longer under his control. He found himself forced to turn, to face Stroma.

Her finger was restored. Greenlaw's hand unclenched by itself, and the fragment he held dropped to the carpet, there to be absorbed.

His voice at least still seemed his own. "I—I don't understand. How did you get past the falseskin? . . ."

Stroma syrinx-laughed in her familiar manner. "Silly! I *am* your suit."

With her words, his silver falseskin melted off him and disappeared.

He stood unprotected against the Urb.

"And I'm you too," added Stroma.

At that instant, he knew it was true.

Information had just flooded into him, explaining the ache of his vanished birthright at last.

Three centuries ago, the Urb had conquered all.

The mysteriously unfollowed winning strategy Greenlaw had outlined to Bambang had indeed been implemented. Lurking deep inside the globe, the Panplasmodemonium had built itself up until it had erupted unstoppably everywhere.

And now—

"And now," said Stroma tenderly, "I try to understand everything I am. Gaia, whose still-living molten center I encyst, was incredibly information-deep and information-dense. To measure Her in your old-fashioned plectic units would require an exponent larger than the number of atoms in the universe. The only way for me to grasp Her has been to recapitulate Her whole history since Her formation, on an accelerated scale. The endgame, though, is particularly puzzling. This incident with your mate, for example—Very deep."

Greenlaw sat down wearily on the couch. Stroma put her arms around him. He flinched, then forced himself to relax.

"What of your puppets, Urb, when you've parsed it all?"

"Not puppets. Beloved components, say rather. Were you never grateful and kind to your own cells? Eventually, I believe I'll withdraw, grant you real free will— almost without limits. Allow you all to forget I even exist. Modify myself so that no trace of me can be detected even on the submolecular level. Be content to dwell beneath the surface of things. Your species, after all, will be a most useful vehicle for meeting others."

"Others?"

Stroma laughed. "But of course. After all, this is not the only planet in the galaxy."

Then Stroma turned toward him—

And the Urb gently and sincerely kissed itself.